The Mobius Vector:
The Long Road Home

by

Richard Thieme

Exurban Press

Minneapolis MN

2022

Cover Design by Noel Smith.

Author photograph by Eli Omen. Copyright Eli Omen 2020, Creative Commons BY-NC-ND

Published by Exurban Press

Printed by The Workshop, Arcadia CA. Jeff Smith, Proprietor. Noel Smith, Layout/Production

978-1-7362663-3-5

Also by Richard Thieme:

Mobius: A Memoir (Book One of the Mobius Trilogy) – Exurban Press. Minneapolis MN. 2020

"The Road to Resilience: Strategies for Playing Through the Pain" – *ICS2*. Nov-Dec 2018

A review of "UFOs: Reframing the Debate" - *Journal of Scientific Exploration*. Fall 2018

A Richard Thieme Reader - a 5-volume e-book anthology of fiction and non-fiction on Kindle. Spring 2016

FOAM (a novel) - Exurban Press. September 2015

Mind Games, A Collection of Nineteen Stories of Brave New Worlds and Alternate Realities - Duncan Long Publications. April 2010

Richard Thieme's Islands in the Clickstream - Syngress Publishing (a division of Elsevier). July 2004

UFOs and Government: A Historical Inquiry - Michael Swords and Robert Powell, with Richard Thieme, Clas Svahn, Vicente-Juan Ballester Olmos, Bill Chalker, Barry Greenwood, Jan Aldrich, and Steve Purcell – a work of historical scholarship on government responses to the UFO phenomenon from WWII to the present. *Anomalist Books:* San Antonio, TX: 2012

"Silent Emergent, Doubly Dark" in *Subtle Edens,* editor Allen Ashley, Elastic Press: Norwich UK: 2008

"I Remember Mama" in *New Writing, Volume One: An Anthology of Poetry, Fiction, Nonfiction, and Drama.* Press Americana. 2013

"Entering Sacred Digital Space" published in *New Paradigms for Bible Study: The Bible in the Third Millennium* from T. & T. Clark, Ltd. June 2004

"Identity/Destiny" published in *Prophecy Anthology, Volume 1* - a full-color book featuring sequential art by artists such as Shannon Wheeler, Scott McCloud, Sho Murase, Yuko Shimizu, Nathan Fox and Bernie Mireault by Sequent Media. 2004

"The Changing Context of Intelligence and Ethics: Enabling Technologies as Transformational Engines" in *Defense Intelligence Journal*. Published in an adapted version in the proceedings of the *New Paradigms for Security Workshop (NPSW 2008)* and as "Changing Contexts of Security and Ethics: You Can't Have One Without the Other" in *Ethical Spectacle*. January 2009

"Computer Applications for Spirituality: The Transformation of Religious Experience" - Anglican Theological Review, Vol. LXXV, No. 3. Summer 1993

The short stories *Gibby the Sit-down King*, published in the *Timber Creek Review,* and *The Man Who Hadn't Disappeared*, published in *Karamu*, were nominated for a Pushcart Prize.

Speeches available at **www.thiemeworks.com**, You Tube, and via Google

What Readers Say About *Mobius: A Memoir*

Pick this book up and you won't put it down.

An incredible story, pick it up and you won't put it down. Richard Thieme's level of consciousness and storytelling is spellbinding. A hall of mirrors, instead of hiding what's true, the mirrored kaleidoscope becomes the truth. An old Jewish proverb has it that 'story is truer than truth', here the turning and twisting story becomes the truth. Here lies our unseen contemporary history, told from the inside about the people who make history

Thieme writes Mobius with all the tragic beauty of a fallen Angel.

Richard Thieme, a legendary guru of young hackers everywhere and a guy excruciatingly well-versed in life in the bowels of governmental secrecy, manages a raw and at times even tender, deep dive into a world of secrecy and nigh capricious bureaucracy that extracts a great human price. Read it at your peril, but in doing so emerge ready to better treasure your simple and honest pleasures. Thieme writes Mobius with all the tragic beauty of a fallen Angel

A George Smiley for our Times

This is Richard Thieme's best work to date. Mobius is a trip through a surreal hall of mirrors known as the Intelligence Community, at times gripping or depressing, but always dazzling. Knowing something of that world, I feel Thieme nailed it. The only unrealistic thing in Mobius was the happy ending - unlike Nick, most IC officers never pay the terrible price required to save their souls. What made the difference for Nick was his love for Penny, for at its heart, Mobius is a love story. Nick's love for Penny (regardless of whether she loves him back) gives him clarity and strength to fight the darkness threatening to engulf him. Penny's patients also move Nick (and the reader), especially Paul, an Iraq vet with PTSD who Thieme brings to life in quick, deft strokes. As for the main character Nick, he's a George Smiley for our times, world weary, cynical, yet retaining enough idealism for us to root for him despite the terrible things he does. Highly recommended.

Riveting - Can't Put Down Book

Richard Thieme's brilliance as a writer shines through in this remarkable book. Thieme delves into the harsh realities that exist in the life of a spy to the point where I couldn't put it down - even though it kept me up at night! His writing made things happen in my mind — vividly, forcefully — espionage - romance, and suspense - things we don't always want to think about or know about! A glittering gem of a book. I can't wait for his next Mobius book.

An absolute must read

Richard Thieme's latest book 'Mobius' truly is a beautiful compilation of all the occupational mental warps one develops by spending a professional career inside that house of mirrors commonly referred to as the 'intelligence community'. He brilliantly captures what it does to a person when you spend your entire life compartmentalizing both the information in your head, as well as the people in your professional and social life. It's full of these odd little quirks and mental pathways you'll recognize all too well, and you can't help but wonder how he got into your head like that. In fact, he captures all of this so well, that I spent the entire last quarter of the book wondering.... "Who is Richard Thieme really?". At the same time, it's a strong and damning social critique of the ever-present surveillance society we live in, and the tragic plight of the modern whistleblower. An absolute must-read!

What Its like to be recruited, trained and serve a lifetime in the shadows to protect their country

Thieme has created a fictitious character (Mobius) that is an amalgamation of experiences of many who have served at great personal costs in the intelligence community. Through Mobius, the reader is taken on a vibrant ride of what it is to be recruited, trained and serve a lifetime in the shadows to protect their country. Thieme delivers to the reader a deep understanding of the intoxicating excitement and often times complex moral dilemmas experienced by those who serve. Thieme is an insatiably curious, well-read, and life-long student of literature, history, theology, psychology, science and technology. Thieme's character and book "Mobius" reflects his earned sage role as a modern-day fiction author, philosopher and sometimes poet who weaves a tale of "reality" that can only be told through the lens of "fiction". WARNING – this is a book with complex adult content and therefore is most appropriate for a discriminating reader who is willing to question... everything!

At an arms reach, I know this person.

Really great. It seemed so parallel to my experience. I lived on Fort Mead for 4 years and know my way around FANX, and the main building at Fort Meade, though I was over in the S building. I also had visited Langley, Navy Offices at the Pentagon, and at the Security Group Headquarters, so as the various descriptions came by I could imagine the actual places Thieme was describing. This all made the book so very real for me, as if it were all true and part of my life. I cannot recommend it highly enough.

the gritty truth

Wow. On the scale of spy stories, we have James Bond up the fairly tale end, down past Tom Clancy and John Le Carre to Thieme's Mobius. Thieme paints a very vivid image (call it gritty) of what it is like to be in that role from the inside of the head of the person in the role. I like the naked realism of the account. But I'm definitely not signing up to become a spy anytime soon

What a Ride!!!

Möbius is an intriguing hero's journey with the pitfalls that so often plague the hero. The tale is told as an impressionistic painting of the broad narrative with the honed in story of the narrator and Penny, and the story is peppered with enough real people and events to cause one to puzzle over the extent to which this is fact hidden in fiction. And I sat there musing about who Richard Thieme really was. This book is engaging on several levels, and though a terrific read, it paints a concerning reality.

IT WILL CHANGE YOUR LIFE if you let it
- at least three levels of rhetoric
- very enjoyable, instructive spy-like novel
- a wise book
- thoughtful challenge to Intelligence-aware insiders
- what is really is going on
- encourages us to reflect on where we have been
- I loved it!

Engrossing and profound

Beautifully written. Mobius is the everyman of the intelligence world, cavalierly sidestepping ethical quandaries and hanging onto his humanity with the help of his sole (soul) friend, Penny. But every man has his limits. This adventure to the underworld is well worth taking.

The story of Mobius

This book is an intense look at the life of a spy and his search for what is real in the midst of the unreal in his life. There are poignant intermittent moments in his search because of his relationship to Penny, who is crucial in his ultimate discovery. Thieme's own journey brings rich meaning to the story of Nick. This is an excellent read, masterfully crafted.

A work like no other

This novel/memoir/performance piece which at every level of its being—genre, character, situation, history, culture—gives away its method while giving away nothing, thus raising unreliable narration to clear-eyed ontology, deconstruction to lyricism, spycraft to a level of surveillance beyond the satellite to un-firm (pun meant) firmament.

By the end of this book we know nothing about this character, which is not surprising because the book invites us to realize we know we know nothing of anything. (I love that the clearest instances are food, films, books, quotes, the ephemeral as "realism.)

I am reminded of Dostoevsky, and especially the famous quote about confession from House of the Dead (which I think now may be a predecessor to Mobius) in its fullest context:

Ordinary executioners are shunned by polite society, but gentleman executioners are far from being so...
To confess one's guilt and one's original sin is little, very little; one must wean oneself away from them completely. And that takes more than a little time.

But then time is all that the memoir's hero, Cerk— that any of us, really— has, and we watch helplessly as that sifts through our fingers.

vec·tor

/ˈvektər/

a quantity having direction as well as magnitude,
especially as determining the position of
one point in space relative to another.

an organism that transmits disease or
a parasite from one animal to another.

direct (an aircraft in flight) to a desired point.

the Mobius Vector

a narrative arc having direction as well as magnitude

a biting narrative that magically transmits
a POV from one animal to another

a means of directing a reader to a desired point

Dedication

We all have personal saints. I could not have written this book or lived a full life had they not appeared at the right time and provided wisdom, guidance, and love.

They include:

Ted Besser

Richard Ellmann

Eliseo Vivas

Edward Hungerford

Jerome Taylor

Don Morano

Tony Carter

O. C. Edwards

Otis Charles

John Updike

Brian Snow

Kenneth Olthoff

Clint Brooks

Michael Swords

and many others

Table of Contents

Chapter 1
Learning to Live Without You

T he joy, the exhilaration, the sheer relief of deciding to tell the truth, to become a whistle blower, to become what my former colleagues call a snitch, a rat, a traitor, a betrayer of relationships, a betrayer of my solemn word, a violator of the law and Constitution, a besmircher of all things sacred—that joy, that excitement, that feeling of freedom, vanished like the morning mist.

For months after leaving the agency I endured a long rope-a-dope, taking blows as consequences piled up. I held up rather well, I think. I welcomed slings and arrows with dignity and grace. They didn't think it sufficient to destroy my way of life; they simply debased me in every conceivable way. Their vengeance was creative. With access to nodes in networks in dozens of countries, they assailed me through multiple personas, false stories on diverse media (owned or controlled by the agency), former colleagues, former friends. They called me every name in the book, as if we were back in sixth grade. The worst? They said I was a Snowden. They called *me* a Snowden.

They called *me* a Snowden. Do you hear that? They tortured innocent people, destroyed evidence, denied the truth, broke old laws and invented new ones—and *they* called *me* a Snowden.

As if they didn't know the difference. As if heroes and traitors were the same. As if a "hero of the revolution," as I was called on whistle blower web sites (a meme retweeted many times) and a dumpster fire like Snowden who didn't know what to pick and choose, as if we were the same, as if he had not gone to Moscow while I stayed in-country to take the heat and disclose how we went off the rails and trashed our ideals and became like the people we fought. (Do you know, not a single head was cut off until Abu Ghraib? Call it blow back. Call it karma.We turned interrogation into torture and pretended that fictional plots—Scalia cited Jack Bauer and *24* as precedent—happen in the real world. They don't. Anyone can stand pain for fifteen minutes if their reward is a nuclear explosion.)

There was no need to kill me. We're Americans, after all, and don't want our killings known. That's a political decision. Israelis use targeted kills and want their enemies to know it. Russians want traitors to know they'll be poisoned. For both, killing is communication. We prefer to take away a person's desire to live; then they kill themselves on our behalf and down the memory hole they go.

The pressure, the attacks, the threats, made me more resolute. I wasn't alone in responding that way. Most of the blowers (as we call ourselves) say the same. When we're stripped of everything that made us who we were, what is there to lose? We were like martyrs tortured until that point of no return when we slip from agony to bliss. Ecstasy explodes in a purifying flame and our pain goes up in smoke. The light of gratitude shines from our eyes.

That light, sanctified in victimhood, shines not only in our eyes but in our words. We are witnesses, we are the ones who make a brighter day (sing it to the Coke tune playing in your head). So keep assailing us, assaulting us, destroying our reputations. Drive us into bliss. Every time you smear us you are convicted in the court that counts. There is a watchful eye—look at a dollar bill if you doubt it—from whom no secrets are hid. We know we can't win on your terms. You have a near-monopoly on weaponry; we know how it works. But we can make it difficult, we can mess you up, we can increase the cost of your so-called "lawful" behavior. We can expose the heart of darkness. Time is on our side; all we have to do is wait for opportunities. We only need to be patient.

You use hammers. We use jabs and stabs. Poke poke. I studied tapes of Ali, stinging like a bee until he had his opponents dazed, their eyes shut, their faces like puffy marshmallows.

Ali was more than a boxer. He thought a million dead in Nam was more than enough. He wanted neither to kill nor be killed by people fighting for independence. He was tried and convicted in the press, before he became a hero again—which will be my fate as well, I am sure, although it will likely happen after I'm dead. Now we use an image of Ali as churches use Jesus, as an icon to admire.

A dead martyr is more useful than a living pain in the ass. I recall a disciple of Gandhi confessing what a relief it was when Gandhi was shot. Living with a constant upward call is exhausting, whether from Gandhi, Jesus, MLK, even our posse of blowers, Ellsberg, Colleen Rowley, Russ Tice, Tom Drake, Cathy Harris, all my newfound friends. Our mere existence makes our persecutors feel the sting of guilt. That's why formal confession is built into religious programs. It erases everything from lying on a resume to mass murder. OK, says the hidden guy on the other side of the screen, do you feel sad for doing that? Do you hope you won't do it again? Yes I feel sad and I certainly hope I won't do it again. OK, then. Say a Hail Mary, drop some money in the plate, and I'll see you next week.

Even after the persecution by the establishment abates, we have to be careful. Double agents move through our networks like slithergadees. They intercept everything. They trump up charges and make our lives miserable. If we signed agreements as part of our deal, as I did, they can say we broke our word and throw us into jail. We have to avoid giving them a reason to bang down our doors without a warrant. No knock, just a crash and a flash bang and back to the cell you go.

We all use encryption. We exercise tradecraft as we can. Proton mail, Signal, work to a degree, but only to a degree. We built back doors, didn't we, Jack? Good ones, too. We broke our encryption before we made it a standard.

I am an example of the power of telling the truth. I was a living reproach to my former colleagues simply by virtue of being alive. Succeeding in my new life, frustrating their hopes to see me destroy myself, was the only way to win. They knew what they had done and the choices they made. They knew what I had done, too, and the choices I made. They had to attack me to justify their egregious moral flaws. They circled the wagons and shunned us—except for my friend Nat Herman. Nat balanced our friendship with loyalty to the Man. He did not want to give up his career so he picked his spots carefully and stayed in touch. He let me know he gave a damn.

I defended myself as best I could. I took more punches than I threw because I was outnumbered. I don't know what their punches did to my head. Neither did Gronkowski, who played until his brain was like a souffle. Listen to him, for God's sake. Is anybody home? I played a different game, but I took plenty of hits. Am I as good as I was before? I have no benchmarks for measuring that. I know I was traumatized. I had to live with the impact of the blows. I ask you to understand that, is all I can do. My emotions get a little wobbly. They are too close to the surface for someone proud of hiding and controlling the personas he presented. I am not crazy, as some claim, I am simply a human being who was beaten to a pulp by his former friends, and even before they got their chance, my work had drained me of my humanity. It is that humanity I am trying to recover.

The "mental health experts" who define trauma remind me of the prisoner in *One Day in the Life of Ivan Denisovich*. Their academic treatises suck all the juice out of the steak. How can a man who is warm understand a man who is cold, asked the shivering protagonist, trying to prolong his time in a warm office. How can smug sons-of-bitches inside the safe harbor of consensus reality (which they define in the first place) know what it's like to be an outcast, an exile, damned and despised? What they call paranoia, we call recon. What they call anxiety, we call vigilance. What they call apathy, we call detachment. What they call aggression, we call "rising up and killing first when someone comes to shoot you." What they call impairment, we call adaptation. What they call psychosis, we call visionary thinking (a la Philip K. Dick). What they call bugs, we call features.

They are prisoners of their paradigms. If they're wrong about a diagnosis, they revise definitions and issue a new manual. If we're wrong, we die. We pay attention to every noise in the night. We sleep with one eye and both ears open. If we underestimate our enemies, we pay a heavy price. I *was* the enemy once upon a time so I ought to know.

If you haven't been there, you don't know. You simply don't know.

I function well enough, limping through the blasted landscape of my life. I talked to people who had been tortured to learn how they found a way to live. I read Elie Wiesel and Victor Frankl and Dostoevsky. I looked at *Drawings From the Gulag*. I learned that human beings can endure anything. We have an intrinsic capacity for elasticity, resilience, and in our case, genuine heroism.

I know I am not as smart as I thought I was. I am trying to say what I think I know but I question my own analysis. I doubt the truth of what I say. My words are like a rope I uncoil as I crawl into a dark cave but which runs out before I come to the end of the cave.

I hold one end of the rope in my hand and peer into the darkness. I fear a sudden drop. (These are metaphors, you understand.) I am trying to replace an old paradigm with a new one as it evolves. I have to climb back through the darkness to the light at the cave entrance and return to the world I left behind, but with a difference. My habitual way of thinking went away as I felt my way through the cave. I hope reemergence in the daylight is a symbol of rebirth. I hope I am the same man, but different. I hope I am teachable.

In another way, of course, I am talking about what spies do all the time. We gather data and try to connect enough dots to create a useful if imperfect image. Then we devise a strategy. We strive to be flexible and zig or zag as new variables come at us at point black range. We know our vision is distorted. Good spies understand their limitations. Bad spies believe in their beliefs. They want to have their yellow cake and eat it too.

"A whistle blower is a spy, but a spy for God," one of the whistle blowers said in the back room of the Barbican. "Our vocation is to see clearly, say what we see, and kick against the pricks," or maybe he said, "kick the pricks." That insight spurred a lot of discussion. We spend a lot of time reflecting on our fate. In a way, we have nothing but time to reflect on our fates.

In the immediate aftermath, however, such philosophical concerns were not on my mind. I had more practical worries. Living without a steady salary or benefits wasn't easy. They tried to deny me even the pitiful living I could make. Prospective employers heard whispers, and whispers were usually enough. They wanted my head on the city gate, and how they got it there didn't matter. One example is Julian Assange. Another is Chelsea Manning. Drive them crazy with prison time, isolation and threats. Because I avoided a jail term, they had to create a simulation of solitary confinement by isolating me with calumny. I lived inside the cage they created out of words, looking out through the bars. But I found a way. I found companions and support. Our whistle blower posse rides with purpose. We reinforce one another, keep ourselves accountable to why we had to speak out. From deep within ourselves, within different vaults of consciousness, we discovered that what we do to another human being, we do to ourselves, Once we knew that, the world turned inside out. We were obligated to live out of that lesson. But living like that in a broken world is not trivial.

Finding rent money was a monthly challenge. That was new to me. When you have enough money, you never give it a thought, and when you don't, it's all you think about. The apartment building in which I had to live had been built in the 1920s; it looked out on parked cars on a narrow side street. The view across the street through the branches of honey locust trees was a wall of walk-ups like mine. Rectangular patches of grass had fences around them that were decorative but useless. Dog walkers and smokers left butts and turds on the grass, snow-covered in winter, reeking in the spring. I lived on the second floor and heard noise from above and below. The ceilings and walls and floors were thin. I believe the couple above me had a secret cat, contrary to the rules, that ran back and forth at night. They were both obese and went to the bathroom a lot, sounding like hippopotami as they trundled down the hall. I imagined floorboards breaking and their legs breaking through. I imagined myself beating their legs with a stick. Living in dreary lower middle class confinement was a real adjustment. Sometimes on assignments, because I had to play the role of an executive or money-laundering middle-man, accommodations were quite plush, while other times they were seedy, but playing a role made it fun. Pretending to be poor was a game; being poor was not. Now I had no role to play, or if I did, it was like improv, saying yes to whatever life brought. A one-bedroom flat with a kitchenette and a dingy bath was all I could afford. I had no false identity with which to build a more pleasant front. I had no false documents or pretense I was someone else.

Snowden, I learned from his videos, had a money problem too but his was easier to solve. The Russians weren't footing the bill, he claimed, they just let him stay in Moscow and do propaganda for them every time he opened his mouth. He was only in Russia, he said, because the Yanks yanked his passport before he could board a flight out. So he charged for speeches, interviews, consulting on the dark web, because, he said, with the voice of a man for whom rationalization had become habitual, a man's got to do what a man's got to do. (He had benefactors too, sponsors and contributors and fanboys here and there and "offshore accounts" in Sioux Falls.) He made more than a million last year giving speeches, telling the world how righteous he was, so he's doing pretty good. I am not in that league. Hackers like Mitnick, once they're out of jail, make up for lost time—and wages—pretty fast. Revealing that torture had become common practice was Class B ball. Everybody knew it pretty soon, and everybody yawned and said, so what?

Sometimes, however, Snowden made sense. A man does have to do what a man's got to do. I had to make a living. The landlord wanted rent every month. I couldn't get consulting jobs in competitive intelligence, not at that time, maybe, I hoped, when things simmered down. But I had a mouth. So that was my motto: Have mouth, will travel. I gave speeches for non-profits and religious groups which paid next to nothing, not the insane fees they gave to retired pols and athletes, fifty thousand bucks for giving the same speech over and over. That was Snowden's minimum too, in case you want to hire him. Former criminals clean up. Abnagale comes to mind (once a con men, always a con man.) The sheep bleat with glee as he fleeces them again and again, making up stories and saying he reformed. He still brings a tear to the eye of the gullible.

I didn't care who wanted a speech. What do you talk about? I was asked. Give me a topic and ten minutes, I would say. I spoke for as few as four at a breakfast in a diner, driving for an hour to get there, and as many as forty-two in a school gym, forty-three if you counted the janitor who came in toward the end and sat in the back row, his mop beside him in his metal bucket. He told me after the speech, having listened closely to my stories, that he was the invisible man I described. "I go everywhere and hear everything. No one sees me. I'm in the background. Hire me sometime, you want to know what really goes on in this crazy school." He was right: we were comrades in the dark arts, and if I wanted to know who the principal was fucking, he was the one to ask. (It was Mr. B and Ms. C as it happens.)

Speeches paid the rent but barely and I made, I hope, some little difference in the thinking, the lives, the decisions made by the scanty crowds that nodded along and laughed at punch lines and clapped in the right places. It was easy to hit the buttons that made them bounce and whoop—I learned the right triggers from their tweets. Like children at bedtime, they found it comforting to hear the same stories again and again. It reinforced the way they thought, and that's all most people want, like church goers seeking consolation and reassurance rather than a challenge. My speeches fed the anger and resentment at imaginary slights that seemed to have built up like toxins in the body politic. In the short term, it worked: a few what-I-called clients called. In the long term, God help us, everyone.

I did get sick of it, though. Talking to, talking at, talking talking talking. I wanted a real job again. I stopped doing speeches and waited for the universe to give me a reward.

My advice? Don't count on the universe to give you a reward. It's busy with other things. It's just not that into us.

But as I was saying, the euphoria, the high felt in those first weeks after we settled my case and I became a hero to the dispossessed, didn't last.

It took a while to realize it, though. I knew my high spirits had waned when one day I noticed my sad face in the mirror as I shaved. I had not seen how dejected I looked. I had not dared to feel how down I felt until that moment of clarity, but once I saw how I looked, I couldn't deny what my woeful countenance woefully said.

I saw despair. I saw anxiety and fear. I saw grief. I saw how much I had lost—my colleagues, my work, and last but not least, Penny, my stabilizing mate. I had to live without her after thirty-seven years.

I crashed to the floor of my soul and lay there, panting like a shipwrecked sailor thinking he was going down for a final time when his toes touched sand and a wave propelled him onto the beach. I lay as it were on the wet sand until I could stand and walk again. I was too exhausted to feel relief or elation at surviving. I could barely bring myself to leave my bed. It occurred to me when I had barely moved by noon that I was depressed. I had never been depressed before, not really. It wasn't like my breakdown, as some called it. I prefer to think of it as a transition to a new way of being because it compelled me to reassemble the pieces of my life in a new pattern, rebuild myself from the inside out. After the breakdown, the fragments of my psyche were like broken pieces of colored glass in a kaleidoscope that I had to rebuild. I made it sort of a stained glass window, and when the sun was at the right angle—when life had become livable again—angels and demons danced in a harmonious colloquy. But that hadn't happened yet. I needed a Marshall Plan but the government wasn't up for that.

I lay in bed a lot, thinking. The "intelligence community," I saw, was an oxymoron. There was no community. We were loyal to one another like soldiers in a bunker, bound by Platonic love, or gay love, one. It had limits. If we had to sacrifice someone, better him or her or they than me. Bill Webb, a clergyman I got to know (the Rev. William Charles Webb, Father Bill to some but just plain Bill to me) said calling his congregation a "church family" was the same kind of sham. For one, he said, it's not a family, although it may be as dysfunctional as one, and for two, he laughed, so many people grow up in unhappy families, the word "family" evokes pain. A lot of people asked him not to use the word. So his job, he said, was to generate a myth that made the congregation seem to cohere as if it were a family. The myths we created and believed in the IC worked the same way. We defined ourselves as the few, the happy few, and we needed to believe it, lest cynicism weaken our resolve and open us to a dangle.

Stripped of my specialness, there was no one in bed but me, the real me, and that me was depressed. Over my days there crawled a mantle of despair. The autumn daylight grew less and the nights grew longer. I lay in the dim bedroom, covering my ears with a pillow to dampen the noise of neighbors and traffic. I hated who I had been, what I had done. And what had I done? I had lived a life of moral insanity and justified it with patriotic puffery.

And what had I accomplished by disclosing our crimes? People in basements continued to be beaten. We delegated torture to partners in the worst prisons in the world. People were tortured to death by the tens of thousands. People were bombed by their own leaders by the hundreds of thousands. People fled their countries by the millions and lived in shit-hole camps without sanitation or decent food. Death indeed had dominion. The eyes of that woman that we—I mean I, not we, the woman I had tortured—who turned out to be innocent—haunted me, mutely accusing. They were as indelible as the grin of the Cheshire cat. She was my Medusa, turning me to stone. I couldn't forget how she screamed as we applied our dark arts to her flesh—me and my former colleagues, now called patriots and heroes.

My only consolation was, I was no longer on their side. The challenge was to find a new side. I sensed correctly that I couldn't do that alone. I had to find a way ahead and I needed a new posse.

When morning became afternoon and I was still in bed, the sheets pulled over my head in a futile attempt to block the light, I discovered that depression was not sadness but an inability to move, a refusal of my body to get out of bed. The momentum of my life ceased. Mornings were no longer invitations, as they had been, to which I responded by bounding out of bed, rested and ready, with gusto and anticipation. All I could see were the bars of my cage.

For years I had swallowed one blue pill after another. The bottle refilled automatically and the prescription never ran out. The red pill I had taken had been my undoing. The agency had been my fantasy home where we told one another we were different. We were socialized to a way of defining ourselves that elevated us above others. When I got to know Bill Webb, the clergyman at St. Sisyphus, he said his training for the ministry accomplished the same goal. He said with a laugh that it took three years of practice—called a seminary education—to accept that wearing a dress, a garment from the middle ages, in fact, was an emblem of sanctity. We called it a chasuble, he said, instead of a dress. Then we could come down the aisle singing a hymn with gusto because the costume we wore was a symbol that others accepted of our piety, our elevated status, and the great gulf between.

We intelligence professionals mastered pretense as well as that priest. A mask was the first thing we learned to wear. It hid us from the masses and from ourselves as well. I heard from those who retired that they could only relate to other intelligence veterans. They hung out only with one another, went on trips with one another, shared one another's triumphs and griefs. They were like mafiosi. Didn't Karen Hill say something similar, in fact? Those who had lacked meaningful clearances were not worth our time, except to use or abuse or confuse. Our levels of clearance, too, our compartmented two-letter codes, had to slot into one another's hidey-holes seamlessly, lest an item from my box drop by mistake into one of theirs. Then you had to be read in or read out. Layered classifications defined the space we created to bamboozle the enemy, but with communication moving at the speed of light through borderless portals, we had to deceive the people we say we protect as well. We had to treat "the people" as if they were the enemy. We had to define knowing what we knew as a crime, not a privilege. If someone outside knew anything we had stamped "secret," they were liable to prosecution. We had to deceive "the people" for their own good. We were keepers of the light and had to keep others in the dark. A culture of classification and secrecy strangled the so-called sunshine laws.

Then, bam! I wasn't special any more. So who or what was I? I had to find a different way to be special, My ego demanded that I be special and my whole life had been based on that. My second kind of "special" was the whistle blower kind, fed by unequivocal assertions of righteousness. That's the public face we wear. In agency work, morality was gray, but in the whistle blowing world, it was black and white.

But something else had happened as well, something unexpected. Now, this is important, and I want you to understand: I experienced a phase change in how I held myself. I oriented myself to life in a new way. I felt rooted differently. Does that make sense? The self I thought I was had emerged from, was embedded in, a deeper Self. That Self included and transcended the little self which was all I thought I was. It was as if a cell in a body became aware of being part of a body. There was no independent cell, no"self" at all, except in relationship to everything else. I suspected, I didn't know, but I had hints, that the universe might be a single conscious Self. The universe itself—itSelf?— was the larger Self.

Language breaks. I want to be clear but I can't say what I mean. The precise words I try to use falsify reality.

I had to live with a new imperative, congruent with that awareness, but I didn't know how to do that, how to change my behavior without sliding back, or if I slid back, how to find my footing again. I couldn't bootstrap a new way of being. That's why I needed a posse, I needed mentors. I needed a community to help me learn to exist in a new way.

I told Bill Webb about that challenge. He wanted to fit my experience into his religious narrative. Religious people do that. They want to tame your experience by using their terms. They want their story to become your story. They want you to graft your branch onto their tree. All I could say when he made his pitch was, that's just your opinion, man. Self-transcendence isn't yours alone. It's built in.

Bill, I said, I think psyches are hardwired for a hierarchical restructuring when the right triggers set it off. That's what happened to me. It transcends language. I get that lots of people want a narrative because it helps make sense of what happened. They want a structure that provides some stability. But that doesn't mean you're right, and besides, you all tell different stories. Those who speak don't know and those who know don't speak, is more to my liking. Don't you agree?

He changed the subject.

The first thing I had to do was practice telling the truth. I know that sounds dumb, but I had lied so long and so much, it was difficult to do. I was surprised to learn that telling the truth took so little energy. Lying is exhausting. You have to remember everything, You have to layer everything in a single coherent narrative. When you tell the truth, it's always right there when you need it. You just say it. That was a new experience.

My work had included violating laws and manipulating beliefs. Our agents had to give up every bond and loyalty and turn over the reins of their lives to us. We needed empathy, but just enough to control them. When the hood came off that woman, the boundaries dissolved. I realized that what we were doing to her, we were doing to ourselves. Did I say that already? I did, I know I did, but I can't say it enough. That was a moment of clarity, an undeniable fact, and my life made a pivot to a new axis. We are unified in a single skein of consciousness and individual selves are emergent properties. As one self goes, so goes the universe. Everything we do trails clouds of glory in our wake.

Our mission had been the primary task, collateral damage be damned. Once I woke up, I saw that collateral damage was all there was. What I did wasn't justified, torture wasn't justified, lying wasn't justified, acting as if the self-interest of a country or "us" against "them" was the highest moral good—that was all blue pill bullshit. I couldn't live like that any more. I didn't know what I needed, really, but I knew I needed something. I needed realignment. I needed feedback and people to true me up when I went astray. I can tell you now, I needed love, but I didn't know that yet. Finding the right partners was a zigzag trip that began with a burst of energy that gave me the grace to throw off the blankets and face the day and get the hell out of bed.

Chapter 2
Boats Against the Current

"Who's Penny?" Valerie said. Then she waited a moment and said again, "Nick? Who's Penny?"

I didn't ignore her, as she often thought. I just didn't hear her. I was reading an obit in the newspaper we still had delivered in paper form for nostalgia's sake, and I was immersed in the story. I began each day with a bowl of oatmeal sitting on the *NY Times*, trying not to drip the mix of grains and berries and nuts and milk onto print she hadn't yet read. She starts with the local section, keeping up with neighborhood gossip. Working at the Barbican, she knows a lot of locals and likes to see what they're doing. She likes to feel plugged in. Her world can seem a little small; I try to keep my focus on the wider world where I plied my trade, not our little neighborhood. Val says I often miss what's right in front of my nose, the rich lives of normal people—she refuses to call them humplings—in our little corner of the world, and she's probably right. She's right a lot of the time.

The piece I was reading was about an accidental death when a medical device attached to someone's heart malfunctioned. It begin with a story about the deceased. I usually skim that "personal interest" padding to get to the data, but the guy who died sounded vaguely familiar, and I read it all from the beginning. His name was unfamiliar, but I recognized some of the locations where he had worked.

The article said the deceased had "a prominent career at DOD." That was how we often referred to our place of employ. That perked me up. The bio, though, had too many gaps, and it didn't add up. The name they used—Joseph Marsh—sounded like an alias. Details had obviously been redacted because of the noticeable holes. They couldn't black out words in an obit but they could edit as they liked. I wondered vaguely who it was. I was well into the piece before I looked at the small grainy picture at the bottom of the page and realized it was Nat. Holy shit! Holy motherfucking shit! Nat Herman was dead.

He never used that alias, Joe Marsh, that I was aware of. I am pretty sure it wasn't his "real" name. I knew him as Nat, Nat Herman. I stared at the face and my heart sank into its own blackness. Memories rose: places we worked, long conversations, huddling in the darkness on a chilly night waiting for someone to show up. I remembered some of the names he used—Victor Samsara, Gabe Pearl, George-I-forget-the-last-name—but back home or over an arak in Tel Aviv or in a coffee shop in Amsterdam or an East End pub, he was always Nat Herman. I think Nat Herman might have been his real name. Had I not realized who had died, had I turned those pages quickly as I usually did, his passing would have been one more meaningless death that I ignored; obituaries filled the pages every day, people dying from illness, old age, shot when a drug deal went bad, t-boned by drunks, thousands of people who don't really matter and never will, not for us, names that slide through our minds as if we were driving past a cemetary in a small town where we never knew a soul. If we stop to wander among the graves, we often can't make out the names or dates, scoured from the stone, the wind and the rain winning the battle we wage in vain for a permanent marker. We are indifferent to the fates of the nameless. You'll be indifferent to mine. The pages turn and we fade into the darkness, unknown, unacknowledged, and unloved.

Death surrounds us, everywhere. It is the mist that prevents us from seeing clearly.

Once I knew it was Nat, vivid memories rose out of deep storage, a magic lantern show in my mind. Nat was more present to me than Val, sitting across, who I didn't see at all. Maybe my brain registered the view, but the "I" that I like to think is me was focused on Nat. The world of breakfast in Valerie's apartment disappeared. She had been sitting across the table, her hair catching the morning light, her bathrobe open at the throat, her chest framed in a vee by the deep blue terry robe. Behind her, plants in clay pots lined the sills. Through the open kitchen door, the rear windows of apartments on the next street and wooden steps to the back porches. Valerie did her best to break through what must have seemed like a fugue state. I heard her voice, muted by shock at Nat's death, and I tried to align with what she was saying. It felt like trying to tune an analog radio late at night. The shock of my loss created too much static.

Valerie's voice grew louder.

"Nick, you're out of the room again." Her voice was faint as if very far away, as if I were wearing ear plugs. "Nick! Come back!" She paused for a beat. The universe ticked off a second or two. The world turned, and we all moved inches closer to death. "Hey! Nick! Be here now!"

She was getting pretty good at reclaiming my attention, but I wanted to stay with Nat. I wanted to know how he died.

"I'm sorry," I said. "I'm in shock, One of my best friends is dead."

"Who was he?"

Where would I begin? Nat was one of the few who was kind to me after I left, as much as he could be, given his need to be careful.

He called now and then on a burner phone to see how I was. We spoke of real things, we discussed facts, we remembered events that were never written down. That made him like family, defined by shared memories that no one else knew. He must have told Miriam, his wife, what I had done; she texted to see if she could help. Miriam Lloyd was wealthy but the agency's vendetta wasn't a problem money could fix, the kind of fix she preferred. Still, it was nice of her to ask.

Nat was younger than me by ten years. I remembered him as healthy and reasonably fit. I had heard some gossip about his heart but we never discussed it. That was right before I left. He ate a lot of nonfat Greek yogurt and kale salads and worked out. He drank too much, by his own admission, but his liver was still good. Drinking too much came with the job. The agency was loaded with alcoholics but it was never discussed aloud. Nat said drinking helped him eat less, keeping him trim. I once caught him in front of his reflection in the glass window of a Sunglass Hut in Knightsbridge, admiring his appearance, deeply engrossed. He pretended to be looking at glasses on display but I knew what he was doing. He had turned to stand sideways to see if his stomach was still flat.

Nat loved the life of a spy. I asked him once, what did he love about it? He turned his chair around like Russell Hammond in *Almost Famous* and said, "Everything," just like Hammond.

Hammond, however, was lanky and tall. Nat like a lot of Jewish men was maybe five six, five seven. That was perfect for our work. Big men stand out. Medium-height guys disappear in the crowd. Nat did not attract attention. (There has never been to my knowledge a single illegal over six feet tall.) In Israel he passed for a tourist, a businessman, or someone who had made aliyah, whatever fit best. He wasn't a sabra, that was apparent. Sabras have a way of holding themselves, they belong to the desert as much as the sand and rock. Their sun-burned country has baked them hard from birth. Their antennae are always extended, looking for danger. They're ready to spring when they hear a snake's rattle. Nat wasn't wound that tight; he held himself in check. He often looked like he was pausing to say something next. He had reached a kind of equilibrium, I thought, with his work, his environment, his life. He fit into his life as if he belonged there. That helped him fit into roles he played. He moved between personas like a top-notch actor.

His Jewishness was a major factor in his life. He tried to remain objective but he pinged at the word "Jew" as if a tuning fork was hit. "Can you blame them?" he said, after an obvious targeted killing—an Iranian nuclear scientist, a leader for Hamas, a mastermind who planned attacks or built bombs. "Their enemies are everywhere, disguised as nobodies. They look like anybody walking past until they explode."

We sometimes worked together in an embassy with official cover in different vectors. I called mine the "Mobius vector," by which I meant the way I framed my strategy. Once I had a target, I liked to think I defined options so they felt as if they had choices but really had only one way to go. All I had to do, once the route was determined, was vector them onto the path they thought they had chosen. The angle of inclination, the momentum, the foregone conclusion of where they would wind up, the illusion of choices— all part of the Mobius vector. All part of an interactive game on a computer. It was like leading a reader through a narrative so they came to the only possible end and, if they had paid attention, said, "Well, of course. What else did I expect?"

As if they knew it all along.

Nat had no cute name like "the Mobius vector" for how he worked. He didn't intend to write a book. He didn't try to be clever. He just did the job.

Nat and I felt like a team. We didn't require an "authoritative voice" from some high place on the bureaucratic pyramid to give us permission to partner. We both needed a friend to endure the pressures of the work. Nat was my person. I was his. We angled to work together when we could.

Penny was my person, too, once upon a time, based on a different framework. There was no one in my life like Penny. Val was a different deal, better in almost every way, but Penny had a special niche—naturally, after thirty-seven years—until I told her who I was and she vanished into the snow, her rage like a blinding explosion.

Forgive my digressions. Let me get back to Nat.

One time I was doing TAD in London working with the Brits. The Brits were working with the Dutch who had penetrated the Saudis and shared what they got with the Brits who shared it with us. That is, we think they shared it all, but one never knows. The Saudis tried to hide their work because they partnered with Iran who pretended to be Egyptians—we all layered nested levels of false attestation that made attribution a guessing game. Half the time Arabs disguised themselves as agents from a shit-hole African country going rogue. It was hard to tell the players even with a program, but in fact, there wasn't any program, or if there was, it was likely fake as well. There were only pieces you put together for yourself. You had to hold it lightly, knowing it was incomplete. If there was a real program, it was hidden in someone else's vault. Unknown unknowns haunted our world like a cloud of unknowing. We lived in the in-between like people who believed in conspiracies and were shocked to learn there was no there there, only a chaotic system. Our chaotic system was like a bush with hundreds of buds any one of which could bloom without warning. Believing in conspiracies gives people a false sense of security, as if someone's in control. The simple truth? No one's in control.

Anyway, we were in London working with the Brits and Nat got in trouble thanks to an Israeli he trusted too much named Sol, Sol

Leventhal, the guy said, but who knows. Nat had permission from the station chief to funnel material and cash to Sol in exchange for material Sol received from a Syrian named Midhat. Midhat turned out to be a double agent, working with Iran but against Hezbollah, his loyalties divided. That was unusual, but family ties sometimes trumped sworn oaths. Tribal loyalty, you know. Midhat did what Iran requested, but in his bifurcated mind, Hezbollah was not the same as Iran, although they really were. He talked himself into working with and against both sides, deceiving himself more than others, creating too many trails, too much complexity to manage— the mullahs, the muftis, the assembly of experts, Hezbollah, and on top of that, his day job, his cover, his "real" work. He was not a very clear thinker. Someone exposed his duplicity which he should have known would leak. Next thing he knew, he was dead. Nat thought an Israeli sniper. It could have been anyone, though. Midhat was sitting outside at a cafe sipping tea when his head exploded like a pumpkin. They might have traced the killer with a shot detector but let it slide. Nobody cared. Learning who killed him wouldn't teach us anything. Good snipers are never detected anyway. Like Kennedy, you know. They disappear like the wisps of smoke on the grassy knoll.

So it goes. Thweeet.

So Midhat was dead, and Sol would have been considered of incidental interest, a middle man of sorts, except that Sol was also a double agent and had passed material in the other direction too, from Nat to Midhat and also to a fellow Israeli, also named Sol, but no relation, a woman, in fact, whose parents were musicians and named her after the note. This second Sol reported to Barak and gave him what she had. Nat did not know that he was being played. What Nat gave to Sol and Sol passed to Midhat (and the second Sol) was not worth much; it was sensitive but unclassified, restamped "secret" before it was handed over to enhance its value, so who cares? Nat didn't care. But Midhat tried to use it in non-standard ways, to show his control he could pull out plums from reliable sources. The content was irrelevant, the fact that he had it, not. Or so he hoped. It might suggest he'd get better stuff later. Raise his pay grade up a notch. Oh what a web we self-deceivers weave! On top of all that, the Syrians used it carelessly, even referring to some of it in a cell phone call (!). That made it traceable first to Sol, then back to Nat because no one else could have been Sol's—or, ultimately, Midhat's—originating source. It gets confusing, I understand. Even I get confused by all these ins and outs. The point is, Sol was careless, very unprofessional, blinded by greed; he used the money to finance his addiction to expensive wines and a prostitute named Sephora who did exactly what he scripted in exactly the right way in exactly the right-height heels. The cash flow ought to have been a red flag; he was living above his pay grade, but apparently no one noticed. Or if they did, they let it play out, better to watch him than grab him, so they could track his links and loops. Always better to see where the antelope goes after it drinks than dry up the watering hole.

You may want to map out these relationships for yourself to see the dye move through the arteries. But use a pencil, you may have to erase.

I met Sol once. He swung by to fetch Nat for one of his dinners. Like a lot of agents, he was extroverted, friendly, engaging, and a good liar. Sol and Nat often walked around Soho chatting like old friends and drinking too much wine. Nat's weakness for drink did not help. He got to like those expensive wines that Sol always paid for. He sometimes shared too much, we learned after everything blew up. Some of what he shared wound up in reports from Sol to the Syrians who shared it with the Saudis who, as I said, had been penetrated by the Dutch who passed it to the Brits so our station chief read it and went nuts. He *seemed* to go nuts, at any rate. He knew Nat's misjudgments were based on the fact that he not only didn't know what he didn't know (which is true of most of us, most of the time) but he didn't know *that* he didn't know, so his motives were as clean as they can get in our corner of the world. The station chief knew of another program we were running which conflicted with Nat's imperfect understanding, so the chief's anger was an act. He had to seem like he didn't know. Sol's name stood out when the links and loops were examined for serious threats. I believe the Israelis were tracking everything from the beginning. The world looks to the Israelis like a satellite view, comprehensive and detailed. So they settled on Sol as the biggest threat. I say it was Israelis, but it might have been one of their friends, or even one of their enemies. The Israelis play multi-dimensional chess and work with everyone, including people who say they want them all dead, because they don't really. They want the game to continue, they don't want to blow up the board. But my gut says it had to be Israelis when I look at what happened to Sol. He had just returned from Majorca where a player from the Emirates, devout and observant by the book at home, had brought him for a weekend of prostitutes and coke on his private jet. Sol may have still been drunk on his unrestrained indulgence. In any case, someone snatched Sol and took him to a safe house in Kensington, 24 Wetherby Gardens, where they questioned him at length. Wetherby Gardens was a pretty street with plane trees and, as the name suggested, nice well-tended gardens. Nannies pushed prams and toddlers played behind iron fences. Some flats had been turned into B-n-Bs. Number 24 was sound-proofed so responses to "questioning" stayed inside. The sounds of construction, sirens and traffic also muffled the noises made by the man shackled to the chair with a rag in his mouth. Sol's interrogation was not gentle. He was connected to a lot of agents, another violation of good tradecraft, and when his interrogators had drained their names and his many antics from his brain and traced payouts to South Dakota Trust in Sioux Falls and banks in the Caribbean, he was worthless to everyone, himself included, the interrogation having left him somewhat impaired. It was best to simply dispose of him lest— well, lest anything, just get rid of the guy. The Israelis did not as a rule dispose of people this way, which does make me think it might have been the Syrians. My private Jordanian source said he thought it was. In any case, the evening after they finished, Sol fell from the twelfth floor of the Knightsbridge Apartments. Suicide, they said, and in a long drawn-out way, it was. He should never have thought he was smarter than everyone else.

Nobody is. Nobody.

Sol worked too many sides at once. His besetting sin was arrogance, as it often is. The Israelis gave us only one name out of all that tangle, my friend Nat. Otherwise the whole mess was just another convoluted story with too many players to quite make sense and an "intelligence product" that wasn't worth much to anyone.

Nat had been indiscreet and, Othello-like, too trusting. His role was minor and the material he gave his friend was worthless. But that had to be confirmed. The Israelis try to proceed methodically and objectively but sometimes they do kill an innocent waiter mistaken for a terrorist. Until they finished their post-mortem, Nat was at risk. Although ... my Jordanian source said later, he wasn't really at risk at all, or so my source was told. But it was Israelis who told him, so it might have been true or merely what they wanted my source to believe so Nat would stay around. The station chief preferred to consider it all a wash and not worth pursuing. He remained impassive when I told him what I thought and puffed on his pipe. Thank you for sharing, he said. I told some of this, not all of it of course, to Nat much later, and all he said was, "Yeah, I know."

A pitfall of the business is, we always think we know.

Nat had thought the Israelis were his friends. That's what his Jewishness did, make him think that Jews had each others' backs.

Sometimes, yes, but not always.

"Nat," I said. "What the fuck were you were thinking?"

"I made a mistake," he said. "The station chief should have told me sooner what they knew about Sol. He okayed the transaction, the money, everything. The Chief had his own agenda, which I didn't know, naturally, linked to a different loop. Above my pay grade, Nick. I wasn't read into anything. But that didn't stop them from trying to put it all on me."

"Of course. When did anyone in charge of anything ever accept responsibility for a fuck-up? Anyway, the Station Chief was cool and knew you were a tool, is all."

If it turned out that Nat had compromised an operation of which he knew nothing, leaving bread crumbs on the path before the birds ate them all, one more thread in a tangled skein of who-knows-what, he would have been in danger, just from that alone. Ignorance was no excuse. If someone thought he knew what he didn't know and couldn't possibly know and therefore if he posed a threat which he couldn't possibly pose ... someone might think he too should take a dive from a high window. My private source, the Jordanian I trusted because I had him by the balls, had told me Nat night be at risk. The relevant parties were all knotted up trying to understand what everyone else had been doing, might have been doing, or didn't do, and what they knew or didn't know. When I told the Station Chief what I heard, he had to pretend he believed me and told Nat to get out of Dodge until it was smoothed over. It did go away but took a bit of time. The upshot of all this was, Nat thought I saved his life by telling the chief to send him home. Maybe yes, maybe no. In retrospect, probably not. A strong emotional bond is best based on something real but a shared illusion will do as well. He chose to believe I had done him a solid and so we became ever better buds. We whisked him home and "engaged in diplomacy," that is, convinced everyone in the mix that Sol had betrayed everyone and Nat had betrayed no one, that Nat had been doing only what he was told, which was almost true. With no evidence to the contrary, that narrative was accepted as either fact or a useful illusion which amounted to the same thing since no one cared which. The case was closed and Nat got out of jail free and passed go and lived to play another day.

"Jesus, Nat," I said, next time we were together, "I know that a Jew is a Jew and all that, but Aman and Mossad and Shin Bet play their own games. They don't share everything with us, any more than we do with them. Don't be sentimental. Think of them the way you think of everyone else."

Nat looked sheepish. He knew the seriousness of his lapse. He had rationalized his violation of tradecraft norms. His Jewish identity, which he pooh-poohed as a childhood phase he had left behind, went deeper than he thought. He learned that Israelis count on American Jews to feel guilty when they don't make aliyah. They help the cause to atone for that. They send money or manipulate senators with contributions or serve as witting assets. They provide cover in their companies for clandestine agents and transfers of cash. They share financial data through insurance and law firms, financial advisors, and anyone who has lots of data on lots of people. The wheels go round and round. Without noticing he had been duped by that strategy, Nat became one of those helpful folks. He forgot we have no friends, nor do they, labels or names to the contrary. He had bought the story because, as he said, a Jew is a Jew, a Jew is a Jew forever, Nick. We can never forget.

The Israelis, he explained, did not have the luxury of forgetting. The Israelis have more at stake on the ground than we do. Like what? I asked. Like the ground itself, he said, on which they walk, where they live. The Arabs think it's only on loan until they can take it back. The Israelis know it's up to them to defend themselves, period. No one will answer their calls for help. All the world will do is tsk tsk tsk when they're slaughtered as it always has. Remember what Wiesel said, when asked what the world learned from the holocaust? It learned you can get away with it, he said.

He told me of his Aunt Sophie who made it to America after the war. She showed him the number on her arm. She showed pictures of her large family, all dead. Until the end of her life, she woke from nightmares, screaming herself awake. It always took a few minutes to know she was in Chicago, not in a freezing barracks in Poland. Her story penetrated his psyche and as much as he liked to think of himself as a professional, he tilted toward that deeply personal, deeply emotional allegiance and identity. That was also why, he confessed apropos of nothing one night, he had given information to the second Sol, the woman of the musical note, who penetrated his defenses with her beauty, her intelligence, her talent as a singer (she rocked out in Tel Aviv cafes and yes, he said, he sat there for hours, grooving on her songs and the shiny black leather she wore, listening to her shred the night). He knew she was a Colonel in Mossad and frankly, my dear, he actually said, I don't give a damn.

The problem always is, spies are as human as the rest, they just forget that fact sometimes.

That was the "inner Jew" in him talking, an aspect of his psyche that he hadn't shared with me until a surprising incident woke it up. We were in Jerusalem eating street food and waiting for instructions when Hasidic men walked by, one wearing a shtreimel and a tallit, and I made a remark. Something about Kool-ade comes in all flavors. Nat pursed his lips, then said, you know, something funny happened as I was driving here from Tel Aviv.

Oh? I said. What?

He was driving past a site where tourists were invited to plant trees. He turned in on a whim. He handed over a few bucks to plant a sapling. As he knelt on the dry soil and scooped out a place to put it, he inexplicably teared up, he said. He was digging in the earth, yes, but into his own Jewish soul as well. He had not expected to feel so strongly. He knew about bigotry but that was about it. No pogroms in Chicago, not when he was growing up. Planting that tree made him quite emotional.

I told him how the tree scam worked. They waited for tourists to leave, then dug up the trees and planted them again the next day or threw them away. More than half of the trees died without irrigation. "It's a con, Nat, and you bought it."

His spy-brain understood and even admired the scheme, but his Jewish brain rejected my analysis. "Maybe one or two, but not the whole enterprise. Maybe you just don't get it, Nick."

He wanted to believe. No wonder he was ripe.

Poor Sol Leventhal had met Nat at an Embassy event in London and cultivated him carefully, taking him to Mirabelle, their favorite place in Mayfair. Sol always paid for their dinners, fattening Nat up for a pitch.

Cheap wines are an addiction, expensive ones a passion. Sol loved fine wines. His favorite was the Romanee Conti, Nat said, but he liked the Petrus too. Nat discovered that the wines he had enjoyed all his life were like sewer water. He could never drink them again.

They often met in Regent's Park, not far from the restaurant on Curzon Street. They strolled up through Marylebone chattering away. They sometimes talked behind the Boathouse Cafe or walked through the zoo and stood at the railing of the penguin exhibit, shivering in the chilly drizzle that we called "London sunshine," exploring together the meanings and mysteries of what it meant to be a Jew. A Jew is a Jew is a Jew, Sol said, and Nat understood. That bonding created a place apart in Nat's brain and his critical thinking was impaired.

It's difficult to run an agent without feelings but sentiment is always a mistake. Clear thinking devoid of emotional attachment is a must. Our work is done best by lonely souls who feign friendships but never really have them. After a number of years, we don't even know what friendship is. That leaves a huge empty space which we filled with elitism, grandiosity, self-congratulations. We became addicted to the adrenalin rush of danger and high stakes. We were given awards we could never mention which paradoxically made them that much more important. Of course we also used diversions like drugs, booze, gambling, sex, anything that blocked awareness of living in a cone of silence. Some used religion, putting it in a compartment, like Burton, an arch-conservative Catholic, countering Cold War realities with devotions that obscured the blood on the pointy end of his stick. "We have a code of honor," a Naval admiral told me once, "but it doesn't say 'Don't kill' because killing is why we exist." Being devoutly religious while doing hard intelligence work is like that. We choose the rules we use. And that leads paradoxically to a yearning we seldom admit.

Sol and Nat, I am convinced, each in their own way, were looking for something more than success in their work. I am sure that neither knew it. I didn't know it until I did. Their quest was what one might call "spiritual." Once you learned that enemies were friends and friends were enemies, that words meant what you said they meant, that existential angst was what you bought and sold and counted on to justify the work, a craving developed for real meaning. We humans are built for truth and meaning and our work made those relative at best. I want you to understand that intelligence work is crazy-making in and of itself because we say we serve the truth that sets us free while all we do is lie, so we have to leap to the next level and claim there is a larger truth, the one we really serve, that transcends all of our fabrications, even though we can't say what it is, so we settle for things like country-love to justify the lies, but every country, every human being, has a different "ultimate truth" they claim to serve. And most of the time we don't even know what the people in the next room at the agency are doing despite seeing them come to work every day. We say hello, we disappear into our cubbies, and we say good bye at the end of the day. Angleton went crazy trying to know the name of the mole who embodied the truth he could never learn, the missing link in his imaginary chain of Escher-like duplicity. He never found the truth he believed would set him free. The more we feel this inherent contradiction, this emptiness at the heart of our project, the more we insist that we matter more than we do, that history turns on our work more often than in fact it does. We mythologize our wins and forget the rest. We are bit players who have to believe we have starring roles. Otherwise ... what the hell were we doing with our lives?

Nat dug into his Jewish roots to try to find that meaning. He thought his intense feelings would lead to a deeper truth. It merely postponed the inevitable, the discovery that we walked on a Mobius strip that only led back home, back to our selves, our unknowable, mysterious selves. I do so wish I could share with Nat what I learned in my new project, which I'll discuss in the next book, *Mobius Out of Time*. I can't, though. Because as I learned that morning, he was dead.

Telling you Nat was a friend implies I knew who he was. I knew him better than most, but his essential self remains vaguely sited among his personas, uncollected, his presentations and internal conflicts sundry and confusing. Now that he's dead, he'll always be an enigma. We cerebrals substitute intellectual analysis for confronting the real challenges of our lives. We can only face those challenges when we're ready, when they slap us in the face. Then denial slides quietly aside and lets us see inside ourselves. It happens in kairos-time, not chronos.

That woman, looking into my eyes when her hood was removed, shattered my equanimity. She shattered my entire life. Denial did not slide aside, it exploded in the moment into an unwelcome revelation.

I don't think I'll ever forgive her for that.

I'm not being difficult, I say to Val every time it happens. I just didn't hear what you said. Her expression suggests she thinks I am making an excuse. But when you're lost in thought, you don't know you're lost, because in a way you're not, you're just there with a complex structure of memories and meanings that in the moment feels real. You're there, not here, but you're not nowhere. You're present to an architectonic confabulation of symbols furnishing an interior mansion. Memories march in cadence like pink elephants on parade, trunk on tail, in hallucinatory splendor. You're trying to grasp what is happening, hoping it isn't true, hoping your former colleague and friend is not dead.

Nat and I talked about everything. Now we'll never talk again.

"Daydreaming is good," I tell Val, and her eyes say what she won't say aloud, that I am a space cadet and she is a practical person grounded in the here and now. Daydreaming, I maintain, generates visions of things the "left brain" can't frame. She smiles with a touch of condescension. Valerie is not burdened by an overly lively imagination. She prefers facts and concrete data. My monologues often sound like balderdash to her.

I tried to tell her about shamans, how altered states provide a view of multiple realities. They are equally real, I insist. A shaman goes crazy on behalf of a community and comes back from the other side to illuminate the first world with what he saw in the other. So what is the point? she asks. There is no "point," I say, that's just what shamans do. They inhabit multidimensional worlds so they can help normal people see, I don't know. more deeply into the one in which they live.

"Shamans are like spies, Val. We inhabit multiple worlds and use one to illuminate, manipulate, cancel out the other. Our knowledge is a lever that moves the earth."

"Humplings," Val says. "When you say 'normal people,' you mean humplings. Like me."

"I didn't say that."

"But that's what you meant."

I sigh.

"I didn't mean it that way. Don't do that."

"Then how *did* you mean it?"

I wait. I pivot.

"Pass me a donut, please. That big chocolate one."

"Be careful. Use a napkin. The chocolate ones smear."

I sigh again. "Val, I am learning to be more careful than you know."

There's always some of that in the getting-to-know-you phase. My gal Val was upper Midwest all the way. She was Iowan, not quite Minnesotan, closer to Wisconsinish, but definitely not a Chicago girl. She lives in Chicago now but she wasn't bred to its culture of loud honking and boisterous shouting. When we tried to eat at an outdoor cafe, the noise of trucks and buses made her wince. "Don't get so excited," comes to her lips when I raise my voice. "I'm not angry," I insist, "just emphatic." Val was less direct, I would say she was passive aggressive, but she does it with finesse—not like Minnesotans, who smother "others" with a smile and leave them in isolation, wondering what the fuck happened. .

Val liked movies with Mia Farrow, an expert at passive aggression according to her one-time mate. "The mouse," Val said, "likes being toyed with by the cat. They don't have to engage but they do. They could stay safe in their holes. They like to complain."

I wasn't complaining. I was stunned.

"Val," I said, stuck on the fact of Nat's death, "this is important. This guy was my friend, My colleague. My partner. I had no idea he was dead. Let me find out what happened."

I returned to the article. The article mentioned Syntactic Devices briefly, without detail. That was the company that made the device that killed him. They made implants, all kinds of medical devices, mostly for brains and hearts, pacemakers, pumps, bionic add-ons, lots of robots, everything like that, and put them into people. Their insulin pumps were notorious for failing.

Nat's device was intended to prevent a heart attack but in fact caused one. The defects had been known for a long time, according to the article. Many implants worked pretty much most of the time, but faulty ones sent shocks into the hearts of unsuspecting victims who dropped dead on the spot.

There were other obits, other names and faces, but I didn't care. I only cared about my friend.

I wanted to know why he had died.

Nat and I passed each other in the halls early in our careers and after a while we went beyond nods and said hello. One of us, I forget who, suggested lunch at the Wok 'N Roll, a cheap Chinese restaurant we both liked. We talked about ourselves, our backgrounds, superficially, and how we came to work in that esteemed profession. We told stories about our lives as much as we could, nothing classified of course. Our discipline was good, back then. We were on the A-team, working our way up. We were happy to lie to each other about everything that mattered. We both enjoyed the great game.

We kept running into each other. In a moment of synchronicity, I saw him in Tel Aviv, looking out over the beach, wearing a tourist shirt and hat, looking dumb and innocent. When he turned away from the blinding sun on the sea, he shielded his eyes and saw me too. We both momentarily blinked, but that was all. I walked one way, he walked another. I walked toward Jaffa, he walked toward Herzliya. The wind off the water made voices speaking Hebrew sound like spirits chuckling at life's little joke.

We went into more detail about ourselves as we got to know each other. After the Sol debacle, he discussed that part of his life. I became a friend and confidante, about some things, anyway. He liked working with Israelis, he said. He considered them full partners. I laughed and said, well, no, not really. He said I didn't understand.

He told me how he felt the first time he landed at Lod. He looked up at the Israeli flag, a blue and white declaration of Jewish determination, and he could barely speak. He was stunned at the depth of emotion he felt. Just like when he planted that tree. He realized, he said, he had lived his entire life in a kind of emotional exile. By contrast, getting off the plane that first time, he found himself surrounded by Jews, most of them armed. He never felt so safe in his life.

I never had that experience, I said, but I have been in groups where I pretended to be an insider, but feel like I'm looking though a window at a party I can't join. It's not the imposter syndrome. Our job is to be imposters. It's something else. We're always on guard, always on the defensive, always looking for threats.

"That's what it is to be a Jew," he said. "Or, I believe, a black, a woman, a gay, and on and on."

"The 'intelligence community,' then—

"—is not a community, Nick. It's like drinking from a dribble glass."

That cynical thread ran through us both from the beginning, but we were good soldiers. We avoided sitting together at meals lest we be observed together too often. No one ever sat or talked with someone they didn't know so the cafeteria was quiet by restaurant standards. We didn't know one another's real names, much less assignments. We talked in code, lest someone overhear. But we loosened up over time, and as Nat and I exchanged more than pleasantries, we sometimes told the simple truth.

The last time I saw Nat was in the main parking lot. It was an accidental meeting. He had stayed in touch and knew what I was going through. He was understanding, to a degree. Others had nothing to gain by being understanding. Nat was in my corner, as much as anyone could be.

We had both parked far from the door toward Colonial Farm Road. He came out into the lot from a door further down and walked toward me to get to his car. I wasn't sure it was Nat from forty cars away. As we came closer, we saw who each other was. His gait was distinctive, better than a fingerprint. (We have two hundred ways of knowing who you are). He looked around to see if someone was watching. From ten feet away, I could see his face, which displayed concern. When we were a few feet apart, we stopped.

"As much as I can, I think I know why you did it, Nick. I've given it a lot of thought." He shifted to a smile. "You saw the movie, right? When Wigand finally won? He got his fifteen minutes on *TV*. You haven't had that yet, but who knows? Maybe you will."

"No," I smiled. "I haven't been on *Sixty Minutes*."

"I'm glad you did what you did but ... " he shook his head. "Nick, people die. People disappear. People are tortured." He shrugged.

"Our enemies want to kill us. You know that."

"I do," I said.

"If we don't play the game the same way, we'll lose, Nick. You know that too."

Ambivalence was the closest he could come to real understanding.

"Have you talked to Denny Lemon?" he asked, changing the subject. "You guys connect with each other?"

"No. I don't know where he went after he blew the whistle."

"He went back to Minneapolis, where he grew up."

"Oh."

Denny Lemon was booted into the gutter. Once he was gone from the agency, I never even thought of him. That's how it is. I didn't expect it to be different when it was me.

"He told me," Nat said, "if he had it do it over again, he would never do it. I wondered if you felt the same way."

I shook my head but he went on.

"They put him through the wringer. And he tried to use proper channels. He went to the IG. But that elevator never goes all the way up. So he called a reporter at the *Times*. And for what? Were our troops safer? Once he leaked? No. The fields of white crosses flow on over the hills. Once in a while, a Jewish star. 'Who has honor, Nick? He who died on Wednesday.'"

"Falstaff was a realist. Shakespeare too, right? No wonder the last plays were full of flowers. He had to cover the stink with perfume. Like a medieval wedding in June."

"Lemon quoted Shakespeare too. Tomorrow and tomorrow ..."

"What's he doing now?"

He shrugged. "Insurance, real estate, one of the things you do when your real life ends. I saw him before he left at an IHOP."

"An IHOP? You ate at an IHOP?""

He laughed. "I needed caffeine. I was passing the one on Alabama Avenue. Denny was waiting to be seated and we talked. He was wearing a cheap suit. His shoes were scuffed. He had gotten divorced. He had a kid in college who won't speak to him. She says he ruined her career. She wanted to be a diplomat."

"At least I don't have kids. I won't know that part."

I had been summoned to the agency that day for another conversation. Interrogators picked at my bones like getting the last bits of flesh from a broiled chicken. I had agreed to come when called. It was part of the deal in exchange for letting me live. They passed me around like a prisoner, Everybody wanted a piece of me, it seemed. They thought if they kept digging, coming from different angles, they'd learn something more. But there was nothing more to learn. I told them why I said what we were doing, torturing people to death, some of them innocent. Most couldn't grasp that that was my sole motive. They turned my life upside down to find a link to an enemy. The shrinks did their thing, with and without drugs. Of course they never found a smoking gun.

I was the enemy within.

They made that clear when they called me back. They badged me as a visitor. I had an escort door to door. Psychological cuffs and shackles.

"Nick, we've thought of you a lot. Miriam was so concerned, but there was nothing she could do." He paused. "I've never forgotten what you did for me. But there's nothing I could do either. You took away our options when you went rogue. Remember De Niro smashing the receiver when they killed Tommy? 'There was nothing we could do,' the guy said. 'He's gone.' I feel like DeNiro felt and the other guy combined. You're gone, and there's nothing I can do."

My voice firmed up. "I'm not gone, Nat. I'm a long way from gone."

Nat smiled. I knew he didn't believe me. But he let me save face.

"I hope we can stay in touch. I'll find a way if I can."

"It's good to see you Nat."

"Good to see you too. Please take care of yourself."

"Sure," I said. "Say hello to Miriam."

Then we went to our cars and drove away. I never saw him again.

And now he was dead. Lawsuits against Syntactic were likely, I learned, with thousands of people dead. Payoffs would be in the millions. Miriam, his widow, did not need the money, but I was sure she would not stop gnawing that bone. People of means get used to thinking they have options.

"Earth to Nick!" Valerie was saying. "Houston, we have a problem!"

I came back to our breakfast. Val came into focus and I smiled. Hello, Val, my eyes said. Here I am.

"They gave him an implant and it didn't work. I had heard something about his heart, something was amiss, but I never inquired. Jesus, Val, he was only forty-seven."

"What happened?"

"A heart implant shot electricity into his heart instead of regulating the flow of blood. That's all I know."

"Nick, I am so sorry." She was back too. Her ability to pivot from irritation to being present and compassionate was remarkable. "You don't need another loss."

I stayed present too. I know I tend to drift and how frustrating it can be. I didn't want to screw up what we had or might have, if we stayed present to each other. Valerie was good for me, I was starting to believe, but more than that, I was realizing I needed her in a way I had never needed anyone before. Trauma can do that. My need to make it work, whatever "it" was, was intense.

"What were you asking, Val?"

"I said, who's Penny?"

I skipped a beat. I rustled the paper and did my best to feign disinterest.

"Why are you asking?"

"You were talking to her in your sleep." She smiled. "Again. Should I be worried, Nick?"

I shrugged. "She's someone I knew, a friend from long ago. I hadn't thought of her in years," I lied. Not a day goes by that I don't think of Penny. "We stopped talking at some point. I lost touch. Friendships have their own dynamics. Sometimes they simply end. As Updike said, if temporality were held to be invalidating, then nothing real succeeds." I watched her intently. "What did I say?"

"I couldn't make it out."

"What does it matter, really, if it's only a dream?"

"It was your tone of voice. It was so intimate. I tried to get what you were saying." Val shrugged."Is her name really Penny? Is it short for something?"

"Penelope, I think. Yeah, Penelope. But she was always Penny. Like you're always Valerie."

"In fact, Valerie's my middle name. I like it better. So that's what I go with."

"Well," I smiled wanly, "next time I dream, I'll ask if that's her real name."

"Penelope's a nice name. But that's not important. What did she mean to you—in the dream, I mean? 'Penny' numerologically is number one, it means a new beginning. Did she mean that? Are you thinking of making changes?"

I laughed. "Numerology, ouija boards, horoscopes. Are you making changes? Of course. Changes are always happening. Who isn't making some kind of change?" I laughed. "You, being here, thinking of moving in—those are the changes I'm making."

But that wasn't why she asked. I hadn't realized that she was as uncertain as I was about our relationship.

"I'm not going anywhere, Val. You don't have to be worried about me. It's me who ought to be worried."

"I wasn't worried," she said, tossing her head. "I'm curious. What did she mean to you? In life?"

I shrugged. "I don't know. Honestly. She was a friend."

"She must have mattered more than that. It was in your voice."

"She might have, once. It's been quite a while."

"Did she give you a message in the dream?"

"Val, I didn't even remember that I dreamed until you brought it up."

She had finished eating and was sipping her coffee to make it last. I smiled and shook my head and went back to the *Times*. In my head, though, I was still talking to Nat.

Val watched my lips moving silently.

"What are you saying? Are you talking to me?"

"Sorry, no. I was thinking of Nat. I was thinking of a conversation we had. I was reliving it, I guess."

"You were whispering loud enough to hear. It's annoying."

I lay the newspaper down once more.

"I do that a lot, I know. I speak aloud the words in my head. I'm sorry if it bothers you. It doesn't change the fact that you're my Khaleesi." She liked that, so I went on. "Valerie Patchett, you are the morning and the evening star. I am so grateful that you made room for me in your life—and in your apartment. I am so happy that you let me move some stuff in here. I am more at home here than in my own place. That dingy apartment is lonely and cold. This one feels like a home. Already. Seriously. It really feels like my home. You feel like my home. I don't know where we're headed, Val, but I hope it's some place wonderful." I was suddenly telling the truth, but embarassed to know it, hearing myself say it explicitly like that, so I made it sound jokey. It gave her too much of an advantage if I didn't. "OK, Khaleesi? Is that enough?"

She smiled, She got it, I think.

"I guess. Enough for the moment."

"But right now, I just want to read the paper."

She set her mug down with a clink. "What was he like? The guy who died."

"I'll be glad to discuss him later. Let me finish this, OK?"

She threw in the towel. She rose and collected her mug and our plates and went into the kitchen, showing me her back.

Chapter 3
A Jew is a Jew

If you're not a Jew or biased against Jews, you might not give it a thought, that your friend is a Jew. He's just a friend. But Nat didn't see it that way.

He provided more of his story during our sojourns. Spies spend an inordinate amount of time waiting for someone to show up. Mostly we're alone, but when we were together, we had a lot of time to kill.

Sometimes we found ourselves across from a bar like the Bull and Last, waiting for someone to arrive. We hung out down the street so we had a good look at the door. On cool nights, we moved around to stay warm. We watched headlights come and go. We watched drinkers through windows and we watched who entered and left.

There is a kind of laughter that only happens when someone is drunk, often a woman at the bar. If you're at a table with a friend, her peals of laughter make it difficult to talk, or if you're alone, she interferes with your calm introspection while sipping a drink. She seems to take up more space than her body suggests she should, as if inebriation expands her mass to a stool and a half. We heard that kind of laughter a lot, moving around outside the Bull and Last. When people left, they talked and called to one another from a distance, often walking backwards, staying at the high end of their vocal range, someone always turning around, and around, and around, trying to remember where they parked. For whatever reason, when they found their car at last, everyone thought it was funny.

The outcome of any meeting was sometimes less important than the bonds we built as we did that night, shivering together in fifty degree chill, telling each other stories, flapping our arms to stay warm, looking I imagine like sandhill cranes. We hadn't dressed for what they call a "pleasant night" over there. We searched the shadows as they stretched in passing headlights, we listened for footsteps, turning on our spidey sense. Alert to the nothingness of the world, we inhaled the darkness, the pestilent air, of a world we had set on fire, hoping to discern the invisible traces of someone wanting to kill us.

Nat thought someone was always wanting to kill us. They certainly want to kill Jews, he said; a Jew knows that in his bones. Plus, there's plenty of evidence. He quoted the Torah: "When someone comes to kill you, rise up and kill him first."

He was born a Jew but a Jew without religion. Religion was mocked in his childhood home as irrational at best and a scam at worst. It's an outdated way of thinking, he heard his father say when approached about joining a synagogue. They had moved into a new apartment, and a neighbor, Sam Schultz, who owned a fish market on a nearby commercial street, thought he was a prospect. Nat's father set him straight.

Your business model is simple, his father said: You look at how people live, the car they drive, and guess how much money they have, then tell them to give you money and how much. The rabbi and cantor live large but members have to share their wealth. That's extortion, Sam. You hope a guy like me'll tumble to your pitch. For what? Your seal of approval?

Schultz explained the rationale for doing the finances that way ("we're not a church, Louis, where people give what they like, a hell of a way to run a business") but Nat's Dad cut him off. So Schultz moved on: what will your widow do if you die without a membership? No service, no prepaid grave? How do you think she'll feel, left with a box of ashes ? He tried to paint a story straight out of Dickens and might have succeeded, had he ever read Dickens.

That's bullshit, Schultz. I know how you work. If people don't pay up, business goes away. Doors don't open, doors close. You spread the word that I'm a self-hating Jew. I don't care what happens to my ashes. I'll tell the kid to scatter them in Lincoln Park or in the rookery where Naomi and I had our first kiss. I really don't give a shit.

Nat's mother Naomi was more open to signing up. Louis, why burn bridges? We might need them some day. And indeed, in a weak moment when she wanted consolation after the death of her sister Margaret from pancreatic cancer, she asked for tickets for a Yom Kippur service and was told by Mark the Administrator who played bad cop to the rabbi's good cop role, "you don't pay, you don't pray." Louis wrote a four page letter to the Board. telling them in effect to fuck themselves, to which they replied, so to speak, play by our rules or don't play.

Young Nat noticed all that and took the lessons to heart. So he wasn't religious and had to learn what it meant to be a Jew from experience. It had nothing to do with God or following rules or paying dues and everything to do with the fact that "Jew" was fired at him at point blank range from the time he was a child.

His earliest memory of hearing the word was when he was four or five. He was in an elevator with strangers all around. His parents made him go wherever they went so he had to be wherever they took him. They were all coming down from the fourteenth floor of an apartment building on Lake Shore Drive when one of the strangers said, "This building is restricted. Jews can't live here."

He didn't know why they said it—contextual understanding was beyond him at that age—but he understood intuitively that they were talking about *him*. After that, when the word "Jew" was said, he responded with a visceral shiver. That's how he knew he was a Jew. When people said the word, they meant *him*. People who were not Jews—which he learned was almost everyone (eight billion minus fifteen million Jews, rounded up)—heard the word differently. It wasn't them so what happened to Jews didn't much matter, any more than what happened to millions of Syrians bombed and killed or displaced into camps or Africans dying in a drought. Out of sight, out of mind.

The elevator conversation made attitudes toward Jews personal. The lesson was followed by many more like it. He could not live in some buildings on Lake Shore Drive and didn't know why. There were other places where Jews could live, like the building in which his family did live. He didn't know why that was allowed and the other was forbidden.

He wondered, "Why don't they want me to live there? What's wrong with me?"

He didn't think it was something he had done. He was only four or five, and he hadn't done much of anything except in a Freudian sense, he had cycled through the same disheartening stages everybody did, oral and anal, genital and phallic, stuff like that. Toilet training might have added a bit of guilt if he didn't produce right away, but a child doesn't think like that. A child thinks more simply. If it wasn't guilt over something done or left undone, something concrete, it turned into shame. Shame couldn't be erased with ritual like guilt. Shame meant something was intrinsically wrong. It lasts a lifetime as a rule.

He concluded as he grew older that there was nothing wrong with him, but there *was* a lot wrong with *them*. They were bigots or stupid or ignorant pigs. The higher people rose on social rungs, the more educated they were, the more they finessed their feelings and covered them up. What people thought of you was much more important than having a heart full of hatred, so you had to pretend. Everyone knew the unspoken rules. Valerie taught me that "what will the neighbors think?" was the ethos of her upbringing. Bigotry could be expressed openly only at certain times, like banter at the country club over tinkling drinks.

There was no easy way for a Jew to win, Nat learned. A generation earlier, they couldn't join law firms or hospitals so they had to start their own, but then they were called clannish. The game was rigged, and a Jew had to learn to live as a Jew in the real world. That's what mattered. Nat never knew when someone would start railing against Jews. Intermittent reinforcement was effective. So Nat became defensive. He was always ready to hit back when others came at him, whether they did or not.

In sixth grade, when a kid named Danny called him "a dirty Jew," he waited at the door for the kid to leave school. Danny tried to wait him out and dodge out around him but it didn't work. He knocked Danny to the ground. The next day he had to see the principal who asked him what happened. He told him. The principal smiled and said, try not to get into fights, but patted him on the back as he left. He learned that the principal was a Jew too and concluded that other Jews had your back. That was often true, but not always. Thinking it was always true got him into that mess with Sol.

He sometimes overheard himself described as "a loudmouth Jew." He accepted that he was outspoken and direct; under his guises and disguises, he liked who he was. He thought direct was good. When he saw *Fargo*, he related to Steve Buscemi, not one of the passive aggressive native Minnesotans. When Buscemi shouted, *What's with you people? You fucking imbeciles!* Nat knew exactly what he meant.

Maybe, he thought, that was why he became a spy. A Jew needed to know what people will do, not what they said they would do. Not knowing what others will do was dangerous. He might be killed, he concluded, after studying history. There was lots of precedent for killing Jews and then going out to have a beer. All "minorities" had to understand "dominants" better than dominants understood them. If dominants misunderstood, it didn't matter. If a "minority" misunderstood, he might die. Blacks, women, Jews, gays, died for their identities. Those were facts. And there were more of "them" than "us." The numbers were on their side. Sidestepping attacks like an aikido master and winning in life, he decided, was the best way to pay them back. Winning when others didn't know they lost was even better. That was a blue ribbon prize for a spy.

So was knowing that the heart of darkness was at the end of every excursion. The Third Reich was a state of mind, not merely history. It could emerge anywhere. He knew seniors at the agency who had worked with Paperclip. He knew that the flesh of Jews hanging on cranes dripped on slave laborers going to build V2s but getting to the moon mattered more than Von Braun's crimes. He learned that spies worked with whoever, not with "good" or "bad" guys, labels used in fiction. He learned that the CIA and the KGB worked together when self-interest required it. He learned that little was what it seemed.

Despite knowing all that, however, Nat was vulnerable. When Sol used his Jewishness to recruit him, it was a hard lesson. Holding onto his tribal identity relieved him of living in peril all the time. It gave him what felt like a dry safe place. Then the rains came and reality poured through the dike.

In my memoir I told you a story of a typical day as a spy, and while what I said was true-ish, it wasn't the whole truth. So here's a little more: I was in England not only to exchange devices at the Tate but to support others' assignments. I had a variety of duties and I often colored outside the lines. That's what I meant when I said that history was like a symphony played in a hall with a lot of dead spaces. We imagine a picture on the box based on the few pieces we see. The puzzle in fact is much more complex.

The Mobius trilogy works best if you see me as a Forest Gump. My memories were distorted after my "incident," but I also used that fact to justify technique. I spliced together things I did with things that others did. All of it was true-ish. I was either present at an event or present to someone's description of the event. As a professor said, reviewing the memoir, "This novel/memoir/performance piece, at every level of its being— genre, character, situation, history, culture—gives away its method while giving away nothing, thus raising unreliable narration to clear-eyed ontology, deconstruction to lyricism, spy craft to a level of surveillance beyond the satellite ...." I love that. It's a good guide to reading the memoir. And maybe this book too.

So Nat and I exchanged more than pleasantries. He was my partner and friend. When my contact told me he might be in danger, I intervened. Sol thought he was smart enough to outplay, outwit, and outlast them all, but the more one gets away with something, the more certain one becomes that one will always get away with it. Then one gets careless.

Once Nat was back home and we had smoothed over his role in that twisted plot, we all moved on. We had better things to do.

By the way—why did I use that Jordanian source to help Nat, rather than saving him for myself? Listen to Sam Spade: When a man's partner is threatened and maybe going to be killed, he's supposed to do something. Nat was my partner, and I was supposed to do something. If your partner is killed, it's bad to let the killer get away with it. Then others might think they can get away with it too.

That was true when Miles Archer died, and it was true when Nat Herman died. That's why Syntactic was in my sights.

Nat talked to me and also to Miriam, his wife. I never knew how much she knew, but she was aware of our friendship and what I had done for Nat. It shocked her that Syntactic accomplished what Nat's enemies failed to do, that his death was "an inside job."

I called Miriam and she invited me to come to their home. We had a Sunday brunch on the lawn along the lake behind their home. It was one hell of a repast. Her private cook Felipe scrambled eggs exactly as requested. He served a Drambuie Marmalade that was perfect with a crumpet smeared with the real thing. But more than a good brunch, our conversation sealed the deal: Miriam was mad as hell and wanted to do, she said, "whatever is necessary."

It was one of the last second summer days. There were leaves all over the lawn but the grass was still green and the sky was diamond bright. The sun glared off the water and I cupped my hand above my eyes to look into the shadow cast by Miriam's broad-brimmed hat across her narrow face. Her eyes blazed with resolve. "Whatever," she repeated, "is necessary, Nick—to fix this. Jews do that, you know. They call it Tikkun Olam. Jews feel responsible for the whole world. Bless their hearts, it's like Penelope unravelling the loom and starting again the next day. The leaky boat is always ahead of your bailing pail. I'm not a Jew, but I know how Nat felt. He would want us to do something."

"Spies do try to tilt the balance toward some kind of rough justice."

Miriam smiled. But her face was tense.

"Don't romanticize my words, Nick. I don't care about justice. I don't belong to the ACLU. I have no ideology. I just want to pay those bastards back."

Chapter 4
Food and Sex

Speaking of religion (we were in a way, weren't we? why Nat was not religious in any traditional sense?), I didn't think I'd ever go to a church, but I did agree to go with Val because we became, well, if not married, married in a way in the spirit of these vague days, and why elevate irrelevancies to the status of issues when life provides issues enough. Besides, sometimes there's nothing else to do on a Sunday morning. It depends on whether the NY Times crossword is doable or a time sink. Looking up every answer on a cell phone is a downer.

Valerie makes her pitch in a way that feels like a kiss.

We can go to a coffee shop afterward, she says brightly, the corners of her eyes wrinkling, and sip our lattes, and spread out the Sunday paper (although she often opens her iPad and checks email too, or laughs at clickbait, turning the pad around so I can see it, tilting it to avoid the glare from the bright daylight through the window. I have watched more dancing cats and silly animations than I ever dreamed I would.)

If you want to just do coffee, she says agreeably (a master of paradoxical intention), we can do that. It's entirely up to you.

Or—she waits a beat—we can try one and go for coffee afterward. You choose.

So I agree, of course, to do it her way. We have to expand our circle and that's as good a way as any. We need others so we don't unload only on each other (Val implies it applies to both of us but we know she means me). We are adapting to differences in each other, the kinds of things that appeal to a couple at first but can become irritants. She concedes that my need for novelty and adventure and chasing after anomalies with gusto and abandon adds spice to her life and I concede that her practical common sense has obvious value too. After a few months, my stream of consciousness orations became a little much when she wants to relax after work after listening to people at the Barbican all day. At the same time, I notice that her matter-of-factness and uncritical acceptance of consensus reality can be a bit boring. The chemicals in the infatuated brain diminish after six months; the honeymoon is over, is how we like to say it.

On the positive side, she orients me to how normal people see the world. I thought I was good at that but I filtered out irrelevancies to focus on the intelligence task. I needed to know only what I needed to know to do the job. So when Val observed the obvious about people, it wasn't always obvious to me. If it didn't help me exploit them, I had paid no attention to what they did. The world in which the majority lived was background noise and most of what they did was strained out. I had to learn to see how normal people perceived the world without bending it to my intentions. Valerie took me by the hand and led me into everyday life. Her comments about mundane stuff were almost always right and her knowledge of the shallows in which most people splash away their lives was encyclopedic. After practicing, I can almost act normal without effort. I am bilingual in a way, living with a parallax view, and for her part, Val adds a Carolina Reaper now and then to the stew of life.

Val would have been happy in a number of churches, looking primarily to make friends (we did find a couple friend; I'll tell you about Jelli and Brad Mastipilo in *Mobius Out of Time*). She considered religious puffery, so plentiful from the pulpit, as just-so stories, and ignored the crazier assertions ("yes, he was swallowed," one preacher said, "maybe not by a whale, but certainly by a big fish") while I often cringed at the ignorance, inauthentic posturing, and lack of common sense.

Once in a while late at night as we sat up in bed after sex, we would ease into discussions that included ultimate questions. Is the world a meaningful place, or not? Is there an intention or intelligence behind it all? Are we really as small and unimportant as we look (people, the planet, the galaxy, the galactic cluster, other clusters, on and on?) We reached only tentative conclusions so I won't get into that right now. Instead I'll show you a typical Sunday morning as we explored the city in search of a "church home."

St. Sisyphus, as Bill Webb called it, although it was named for a more familiar saint, was built of old stone in suburban gothic style. Ushers were at the door wearing red scarves and wide smiles, handing out bulletins. Greeters inside gladhanded visitors with welcoming grins.

Valerie agreed to sit in back where I thought there would be more room, but apparently many prefer that strategy, close to the door, just in case. The place wasn't full but a family with kids chose our pew too and pushed us to the end. The kid beside me had a coloring book and crayons and through the long boring drone of adult voices he colored a number of animals.

It felt oppressive, jammed into the pew. I felt like I was choking in cotton wool as I did in New Orleans in early September, like hot wet cotton was keeping me from breathing. To cope with the oddness of it all, I adopted the posture of an anthropologist, observing behaviors and trying to understand how people who thrived in daily life could check their brains at the door when they came into a church. They put on religious expressions, looking quite serious unless they were in one of the sects that require rigid grins. They adopted Bronze Age thinking without hesitation.

I had not paid much attention to denominations and thought Christians were pretty much one big happy bunch. But many Christian groups, I learned, thought the others, every single one, were dead wrong. But making others wrong was not enough. They used the nitpickiest distinctions to damn others to hell while they went to heaven. The key to salvation was getting doctrines right. Drop a comma, go to hell. One's eternal fate turned on the precise date of the Second Coming. I didn't understand how they could be so harsh since they all played the same game, providing instructions on getting into heaven despite one's flaws. Forgiveness via rituals cleaned up the messes they made. Otherwise one went to hell. Harsh! I thought. Make one mistake and a god they say is love will throw you under the bus.

The agencies played the game on a much more rational footing, based on who or what was useful. We didn't care what someone believed unless it helped us recruit. We traded information, held some back, added disinformation, and dared the opposition to guess which narrative was real. We seeded their AI with lies that led them astray. We penetrated their servers, all of them, everywhere, as they did ours. The game itself was more important than ultimate outcomes. We focused on the field of play because then we knew who won and lost. Tabulated results were all that mattered to the quants.

Christians on the other hand believed in their beliefs, way too much. Their rituals and rites were like magic spells. Say this and do that and you're good to go. Their beliefs had no give in them, no negotiated truce with other opinions or hopes. No compromise with obvious realities.

As I listened on that first Sunday morning, standing next to Valerie, I knew no thinking person could believe what they said by rote. They put themselves into a trance. Music moved them into an altered state and dissolved boundaries. I kept myself safe by thinking about things. I was musing about this or that, whatever floated through, when I had an epiphany. I was watching the assistant, who I called Johnny Be Good, sway ponderously down the aisle when I formulated "My Thesis About Clergy."

Now, I don't doubt that other addictions—alcohol, drugs, gambling, all of the rest— plague ministers and priests to the same degree that they do the general population, but it is my observation that many if not most clergy have an inordinate love, an obsessive love, of food and sex.

This thesis has not been contradicted.

Look under the cassocks, chasubles and flowing robes, under the habits, inside the sacristy, down in the basement of a cold dark church. The sauces and pickles are all there. Some like one thing and some like another but they all like something. Just like the rest of us. We don't choose what we like, we like what we like. But clergy and laity use projections to define transactions. Clergy like spies pretend to be what clients need. The role-playing game twists clergy and laity alike into an infinite loop. Clergy do try to be what they're paid to seem to be and laity do invest them with a supernatural aura and power which, if it exists, belongs to everyone or no one. The only way to change this paradigm is to leave and the baby goes with the bathwater. Power people perched on top cannot give up their perks. And as Dostoevsky said through one of his characters, freedom is exchanged for bread.

So Sunday after Sunday portly prelates like Johnny, beards hiding their faces from prying eyes, come gliding down the aisle, bedecked in the colors of the season and singing lustily, nodding and smiling like rock stars pointing to front-row fans. The assistant priest, John Beverley Goodkind is his given name, sure fills the bill. By the end of the hymn, he's breathing hard, perspiration glistening on his brow. His role and his robes protect him; he is insulated, isolated, safe within his room, as the song says, and the room is the structure in his head of a church in which he thinks he lives, a legoland of artificial blocks built of hopeful thoughts.

Bill Webb, the Rev. William Charles Webb, the boss of the place, was more normal in appearance. I told him later about my theory of food and sex and he just laughed. That was a way of neither confirming nor denying my thesis. Bill has perfected a way of seeming to agree by smiling and nodding, communicating good will, his head at a slant and his eyes sparkling with amusement, but not addressing the issue nor revealing his real feelings. That's why he was a rising star in his church.

I am not judging, just observing. Lots of beards, lots of corpulent priests, I tell Valerie, sitting in our crowded pew and nudge her and gesture at Johnny B. G. as he comes down the aisle at the rear of the procession, (When the rector's away, Johnny can play.)

The procession reaches the front and disperses into the choir pews. There were eighteen in the choir, five of them paid pros, including two black women whose soaring voices took otherwise unsingable hymns into their higher reaches. Bill maintained through years of practice a dignified demeanor when he anchors the procession. He understands his role. His is the power and the glory. He looks serious. He segues into the first prayer after he has paused and nodded to the altar, turned toward the crowd, and opened his prayer book. He doesn't need it, but that's why he opens it; if he didn't, he told me, he might forget. Johnny has his open and that morning did his best to emulate his mentor.

The annoying child on my left had dropped a crayon and is squirming around to reach it. He slides off the pew to scramble under the one in front where the burnt umber crayon resides. He can't quite reach it and whines until his mother gets down on her knees too and snags that crayola. I look with irritation at the scene as it plays out, both of them bumping into my legs. The mother, however, wears a frown of disapproval directed at me, not a look of apology. I had not yet learned that one is never to be upset by kids in church, regardless of what they do. That especially applies to a newborn screaming in a mother's arms. Their shrill cries elicit tense but cooing smiles from everyone but me.

Val responds to my insight by screwing up her face to be sort of funny, but she knows I'm right.

I'm not making it up, I say. I'm pretty good at observation.

Really? she says.

Yes. I have experience, you know.

Uh-huh, she says. She smiles. You sure observed me, and I didn't even know it. Until you asked me to have dinner when I got off work. ... I was watching you all the time, too. Did you know that?

I didn't—but stayed with my hypothesis. Look at Johnny, I said. What do *you* see?

Valerie squinted, "I spy with my little eye ..."

"Shhh!" said the mother, leaning across the kid from the left. "Please!"

I inhaled deeply and went into my quiet place.

Vals' cuteness usually works. I am disarmed by her charm. There's something about Val in religious mode that makes her especially sexy. When she sings a hymn as if she means it, her singing sounds like a siren song; her breath smells of spice, cinnamon or cardamom, and makes me twitch with desire. Sex and religion are conjoined at the loins. I lean in her direction both to hear her sing and inhale her delightful scent, lowering my toneless moaning to a meaningless murmur. The words of the hymn are absurd and unaligned with any real thing so getting them right is irrelevant.

I do feel like an anthropologist.

I settle back when the hymn ends and take her hand and think of how she felt, naked and welcoming in the first light of dawn, in the king bed that was hers but which we have come to share. I am only a visitor, I know. But I have a key and have moved some clothes into her closet. That's good enough for me. I have also moved some of me into her heart. That's my belief, my faith, which I need to make our deal work. That's my religion, I guess. Valerie sustains it. "I'm getting to like you too," she says.

But I haven't said what I was doing in a church. I am the last one friends would expect to be involved, however half-heartedly, in piety and prayerfulness.

I ask myself as well: Why am I in a pew designed to keep one awake the way Johnny Carson put a board into his sofa when a celebrity fell asleep?

How did I fall so far, so fast?

It started at the Barbican. As so often, a woman—Val, whom you have already met—was the catalyst for my "spiritual journey." I think eighty per cent of the men in a church have been led there by their partners. The Barbican was a seedy-seeming bar by design, offering an atmosphere of noir in a neighborhood of glass and steel offices, a refuge from long numbing days of sitting at computers. Its noirishness was implicit in the furnishings—Venetian blinds that cast long shadows when the sun was going down, a cluttered interior, dim hallways suggesting menace, lights designed to cast black shadows, an overall sense of futility and despair that suited our whistle blowing bunch to a T. We understood that defeat was inevitable and the bad guys—what society calls the "good guys"—always won.

An upside down world, inside out.

I often met with my new mates at the Barbican. We had a big

table in back in a semi-private room that we felt we owned. Val worked there, a jill of all trades. She was between jobs, she said. Maybe she was between jobs, but I didn't know of a job she wanted next. Nor had I a need to know. So she papered over gaps in her resume. Big deal. How she presented herself was her choice and she had her reasons. I didn't care. I wasn't a spy any more who had to know everything.

Gaps in the stories we tell one another—there are always some—don't torpedo the whole affair. The point of a relationship is simple: just be one—be a relationship, I mean, be a source of energy and solace and consolation and excitement for another and once in a while prop the other up. Be a counterweight to the gravity of bad days. Be an antidote for the poison of life that drips into our veins like an IV. Be a quiet island now and then where one can escape the din. Just be there, in short. Just be.

Relationships at their best, I was learning from Val, were training programs for becoming more fully human. The longer you hang out, things get better or worse, but they never stay the same. You can not step into the same relationship twice. You can pretend it has permanence or duration or certainty but as you do, the moments tick by and so does the relationship, tick tick tick, flowing into something new in every moment of your life. Our words of promise and assurance do not dam the river. In retrospect, Penny and I were home ports for each other, but we never said it aloud. We found other things we needed with a lot of other people through the years. But we always came back to each other. Until, of course, we didn't.

Penny. Most days I can't even remember how you looked. But I do remember, you were there. And you are there still.

I am haunted by the ghost of Penny past.

One day I was meeting Steve Lonstock who ratted out some bad actors at a nuclear weapons facility and was waiting for his pretrial hearing on trumped-up charges.

It was late in the afternoon. I knew when Steve came to the table that he was already off his feed. He had a way of looking past you when he didn't want to say what was making him angry. These days he was always angry. He was angry at what he learned about his colleagues, but he was, I suspect, angry before that. Life provides plenty of reasons to be angry, more than one needs. Anger like anxiety is a bird on a branch, and if one branch breaks and falls, it flutters for a moment, then finds a new limb. Steve was angry at being persecuted and pummeled for saying what he saw. Telling the simple truth was his undoing, as it had been mine.

Some of his anger came from typical burn-out, too, I think. Like many, he went into government work wanting to do good and serve "the people," but mediocracy, bureaucracy, and bad actors had worn him down. Middle age is a hard time because there's so little to fall back on. The illusions of youth have become tattered and blown away in the wind. Your marriage is either broken or you adapted to its lesser rewards. Penny used to tell me how her benchmark for a partner went down over time until her notion of a suitable guy was someone not too abusive. By one's forties, the idols of a former day have crumbled. You have what you really need, Penny used to say, or realize you never will, and so what? What's the difference? Whatever you chased—material success, status, fame, "the one"—were hollow. Life cons us with bait-and-switch routines, one after the other, and even if we get what we want, it's never enough. The Buddhists seem to have nailed it, but it's pretty hard to live life as a real Buddhist, just like living as a Christian is apparently impossible.

I tried to talk to Steve, but in my head, a conversation with Penny occurred. I heard her voice like a song I can't forget. It's like when headlights flash as a car turns a corner. I hear her voice and I listen until her words blur and I can't understand a thing she is saying.

I asked Bill Webb, is my habit of doing that, daydreaming is a nice way to say it, normal or pathological? What do *you* think?

Bill said, Why do you care what I think? My opinion won't steer your ship, will it?

I shrugged.

It sounds like unrequited grief, because of the way she left. Now she's ghosting you. That's not easy for a guy like you.

That's the kind of conversation Bill and I often had. It let us avoid dealing with what we were both really feeling.

Anyway, burn-out was Steve's story, I decided, even before he outed his colleagues' bad behavior. He had to do it, he said. He just couldn't stand it. Their irresponsibility, their arrogance, their smirks, griped his ass. He went to a superior to report what he saw, drugs being dealt right there in the facility, workers with nuclear power in their hands getting stoned out of their minds. Thanks for bringing it to me, his boss said. I'll make sure the hammer comes down. Dealing meth, fentanyl, oxy, and coke, here at work? I'll be damned.

The hammer did come down, but on Steve, not the outlaws. Like in *Catch 22*, everyone had a share. He was questioned harshly, then reassigned to a riskier job where he sustained painful damage from exposure to radiation. Like Silkwood, it was inside his gloves, where someone had to put it. He developed "things" on his skin. He might have crawled back to his superiors, asking forgiveness, but that wasn't who he was. He was cursed with a conscience that wouldn't quit. So he tried again. That time his bosses were explicit. They told him to forget it, just keep quiet and do your job. It's not your business. It is so my business, he said, it's all our business. He went up the ladder at DOE but the higher he went, the more his superiors had to lose. They were all, apparently, in on the racket. Layers of self-protection went higher and higher. At the top were closed doors and people who wouldn't listen.

Steve was a slow learner. The agency laid him off when he went public, then tried him in the press. They concocted a list of infractions and dribbled them out to reporters. He had to endure leaks and lies, even as they denounced leaks and lies. There was more going on than drugs, he learned; swapping time cards for cash and cocaine was only the beginning; they violated safety rules, made fraudulent insurance claims, and threatened to fire a woman named Sherry if she said how her boss had groped her. It sounded like assault, grabbing her the way she described. The media turned his revelations into sound bites. His own indiscretions, dug up from decades before, became the story. They found a high school girl who said he liked to be walked on. She segued her story into a shot on reality TV and wound up on *The Bachelor*. She made it to the last twelve, I think. Every week, someone brought it up, and she laughed and showed them how she pranced from head to toe on his prostrate body and back again. They interspersed deep fake videos with fake texts. They inserted bogus emails onto servers, then somehow "found" them. He became known as the "trampling freak."

"Those sons-of-bitches! What about the *facts*?" he said, staring into his glass as if it were a crystal ball and he a seer. "Did I tell the truth or not? That's the issue. Were lives on the line or not?"

"The facts don't matter," I said. "You know that. Controlling the narrative matters. Distracting people until the next crisis, real or invented."

"They discredit you every way they can. They attack your family, destroy your reputation, they—"

"I know, Steve," I said. "I know."

That made him pause.

"I guess you do."

He avoided looking into my eyes, I think, because he feared he would lose it. He was a hard-ass blue collar guy and preferred to feel anger instead of empathy, lust instead of affection, rage instead of compassion. A typical man, turning softness into grit. He admitted one day he did have a bunch of kinks, but being walked on was definitely not one of them.

He became preoccupied with Val which over time made me see her too in a different light. He tried to use her to comfort himself, but she wasn't playing, or if she did now and then, it was in a minor key which a saner guy would recognize as nothing more than what it was. She teased and tickled, called his bet, but never went all in. Kept him buying drinks. All customer service is a kind of lap dance, isn't it? But Steve in his depressed state was not a sane guy. He couldn't see the obvious. He was desperate for relief from his anger and disappointment. He craved the healing touch that only a woman could bring. He wanted Val to make it all better. He wanted a vacation from the pain of his life. Val met him halfway, doing what she could within limits, what Jake the owner paid her to do—keep those drink orders coming. His dream of an afternoon fuck was nothing more than a fantasy. She never encouraged him that way.

But he talked about it so much it oozed into my dreams too. I had dreams of fucking Valerie before I really knew her. His fantasy was contagious.

Val brought the drink she knew he wanted when she saw him come in and he downed it and asked for another right away. That was not a good sign. Her job was to shrug and fetch it, so shrug and fetch it she did. A second manhattan with an orange twist did not help. It only made his face redder. He sucked the twist, chewing the rind.

"There's a gene that makes you flush when you drink, you know that?" Valerie said. She was stooping a bit to look at his face. "Some people flush when they drink and some don't. I took a DNA test and that's what they said. I don't flush. They also said I like cilantro, which happens to be true. And I do not have the brca gene, which was quite a relief."

I don't know if he was hearing what she said. Beads of sweat were on his forehead. He looked like he had just worked out, hard. But the way the buttons of his shirt pulled on his swelling belly suggested a workout was not his thing.

"Don't talk about cilantro. Next you'll be talking about fad diets. I've had enough of that crap."

Val and I looked at each other. No one had mentioned diets. Val shrugged but I couldn't let it drop.

"Nobody said a thing about diets, Steve."

"Don't eat this, don't eat that. I lost a few pounds but my blood pressure stayed in the stratosphere and my cholesterol stayed up. I put diets onto my fuck-it list."

He looked at me.

"So don't bother, Nick. I've heard it all before. Don't preach or lecture me." Then he looked at Val. "You either, sweetheart."

I made myself laugh. "We didn't say a word, Steve."

"Maybe not, but I can see what you're thinking."

Val said, "I was referring to a tendency to flush, is all. And liking cilantro. It's genes, is all I said."

He sighed heavily and took a couple of very deep breaths. His shirt rose and fell on his gut. Val turned to me.

"You good, Nick?"

"I'm good, Val. Thanks."

She returned to the bar. Steve watched her with ill-disguised concupiscence. Her jeans were tight enough to show her perfect butt. She was well-proportioned and not showing off, she just looked good in jeans and that black scoop-necked tee. I followed his look and saw what he was looking at. He was locked in. She must have felt his energy across the bar. She looked back with a "what do you want?" sort of look and he shouted, *Bring me a refill, will you? Please?*

I tapped him on the arm to bring him back into the conversation, such as it was, until Val reappeared. Pheromones floated in the air, making us all pucker. Without Val, it was just a bar, trying to be a brand. The atmosphere was edgy, shadows by design, but more from forties Hollywood than the real mob these days. The sons and grand-sons of the founders of the Outfit, as in any enterprise, ran hedge funds, hid money offshore, and did hits only when absolutely essential. No Valentine's Day spray of bullets for these more subtle guys.

We sometimes used them in our work. They kicked ass in Italy, remember, and took on Mussolini in exchange for benefice and favors. In Chicago, where I came to what I liked to call "maturity," the pols and police and RC Church and anyone who counted, all worked together. Like Kennedy, you know. A sit-down saved his father's life.

Valerie seemed to move back and forth in the Barbican like a target in a shooting gallery. Go to the left, turn, back to the right, turn. That's how she arranged the perceptual field for me, defining it by her constant turns. Her presence, her movements, became the lines on an etch-a-sketch, new every visit, out to a table, back to the bar, over and over again.

When I arrived, usually late in the afternoon, I looked to see if she was there before I picked a place to sit. She became the focal point of why I went, more than my whistle blowing mates. Innocent exchanges, not even conversations, somehow tied us together. There was a vibe, all right. I had more self control than Steve and I wasn't married to BJ, as he was. I was polite and appropriate. Steve was not; he apparently forgot what Val had told him just the week before.

She had told him very nicely but very clearly never to touch her again like that, and she meant it, and he got it—he got it then, in any case. Some lessons, however, apparently need to be repeated. When she brought a drink, he stared at her breasts, braless under the thin black cotton. He wanted, obviously, to take her right then on the hardwood floor, peanut shells be damned.

She set down his fresh Manhattan. She let her hand land on his shoulder and left it there for a minute. She leaned in across to ask, "Something to eat with that, Steve? Another plate of fries? A bloomin' onion?"

She restricted her seduction to trying to get him to order more.

"No," he said. "I'm trying to cut down. I'll tell you what I would like, though."

"Don't!" she said. "Don't go there."

Steve struggled not to say it, nor to touch her. He displaced that vector of energy and looked instead at a basket formerly filled with chips which was already empty and he moistened the tip of his finger to make crumbs adhere, then sucked them off. He transferred his hunger from Valerie to the residue of curly fries.

Food and sex. Food and sex.

Val diplomatically picked up the basket and took it away. He watched her walk to the back.

"God I want to fuck her," he said.

The Barbican's windows to the street had grown dark. Illuminated bottles back of the bar made it feel like we were in a fish tank, the play of ghostly pastel light rippling as if an aerating pump was making the afternoon flow into the evening. It wasn't Sainte-Chapelle, but in the upper midwest, it was good enough.

It suddenly became very very quiet. Whatever had been making noise, stopped. It felt as if we were suddenly in a bell jar. There were a few solitary drinkers at the bar, sitting and staring at nothing, drinking on automatic. For a moment, no one spoke. The hush made the twilight seem like a portal into another world.

I wanted to break the spell. I didn't know then about portals. That would come later. I spoke aloud to bring back the ordinary day. I asked Steve about money. How was he making out? Whistle blowing is not a lucrative profession. He didn't answer, his attention still on Val, back at the bar, laughing at something some guy said.

Valerie's face was shadowed in the pastel twilight of the thick glass tiles which constituted the wall behind her at the bar. I found myself looking at her, longer than usual. That afternoon, I really noticed that I noticed her—I heard the sound of her voice, her laughter which was quite enticing, saw how she engaged with customers, so easily, inviting. Her younger way of being in the world, more innocent than mine.

She seemed in her own way like a portal too.

Watching her perked me up. Watching her made me want to watch her even more.

"I'm in love," Steve said.

"Ya think?"

"Yes. The heart wants what it wants, didn't Woody Allen say?"

"Emily Dickinson, I think."

He sang audibly enough to be annoying:

I'm hoping
That after this fever I'll survive
I know I'm acting a bit crazy
Strung out, a little bit hazy
Hand over heart, I'm praying
That I'm gonna make it out alive

"You sound like people with earbuds, thinking they're singing but sounding like lowing cows."

"Give me a break. It's a great song."

He looked at me sadly.

"That's what I'm feeling. Nick, I can't help it: I am crazy about that woman."

"And what about BJ?"

Steve blinked.

"BJ ... oh, yeah, BJ. She's fine. BJ is fine."

"I mean, is she still your wife? Still your honey?"

Steve lowered his eyes and turned the glass in his hands.

"That's a different story, Nick. I was hoping to avoid it."

That was the first I heard of trouble at home.

I felt his despair like an enveloping dark cloud. I saw how he had fallen so hard, tried so hard to do the right thing. I felt the depth of his desperation. I feared for him, feared for what might happen next. Dissolution, deepening despair.

He looked at me and sighed. His depression thickened in the dim afternoon.

For once in my life, I had no idea what to say.

Chapter 5
Meet Cute

S hort term memory must not matter very much. We lose it as we age and still do OK. Memories that structured the story we told ourselves about our lives become a blur. Boundaries between times and places vanish. Time dilates. Memories no longer occupy an orderly linear grid. They squish into one another and can be trusted only in a way—they're what our brains report as "true," but to what end, we haven't a clue. Our brains have their own agendas. If we stay with the way our brains order events, we would think we're becoming different people, moment by moment. Because, I guess, we are. Spacetime is elastic and so is memory: the mass of a recent major event bends the light of lesser events, moving them into the foreground via gravitational lensing.

When did an event happen? What decade *was* that? I can't remember. There's no one else to ask, most of the time. Traces in the brain tumble like rocks in a rushing stream under a melting glacier. I hear them like an echo of what I thought was real. As we lose the youthful ability to remember clearly, we cover our lapses like illiterates carrying newspapers under their arms. When someone mentions an event, we pretend we remember it but don't. We wait for a synapse to snap but forget what we were waiting for.

Brains aren't clerks who file things for easy retrieval. Memory is creative, transforming raw material into images. A brain is an artist, a fauve, an untamed wild beast, with a palette of many colors.

The conversation with Steve is a good example. When did it happen? I can guess but I'm not sure. What did I leave out? I don't know. How would I know what it was, if I left it out? But more to the point, why did it present itself for rendering, out of all the discussions I had in that bar? The back room at the Barbican is a cornucopia of stories. Our whistle blowing circle jerk never lacked for anecdotes. We vindicated, justified, embraced our righteous rage. We thought of ourselves as heroes like in a hacker saga, a genre filled with trite tropes that seemed just right for us. We celebrated our efforts to move the earth into a proper orbit. We raged against the machine. We decried an indifferent universe. In short, we whined and whined.

But I digress ... I picked up on Steve and his drinking and despair, but ...was the scene really about Steve? Or was it an avenue to a memory of Val? Steve will fade as the day lengthens, but Val's image will sharpen. Val is the one who matters. I use Steve as an example, I guess. I'd better show you what I mean.

And ... are memories of Val connected to memories of Penny? Their voices intermingle in my mind. Their duet enchants my past so I can live in the present. If I can live in the present, I might have a future. When I crashed and burned, my belief in a future vanished. Val was a means of rejuvenation, vital and youthful and giving and game. Val gave me hope.

Penny left me in the lurch.

The noirish accessories of the Barbican did not make me think of Val as a femme fatale like Anne Savage in *Detour* or Kathleen Turner in *Body Heat*. If she was, I wouldn't know until it was too late. I refused to believe that she was. I chose to believe she was more up front with her agendas. Val countered the terminal bleakness of noir. She made the unbearable bearable. That's what I needed, and that's what I believed.

As Penny recedes into the past, I see her more clearly. Unlike the short term memories which flicker and fade like quantum fluctuations, long-term memories are vivid. I had no idea my brain stored so many long term memories like a way-back machine. It's all in there somehow and the right trigger unleashes even childhood scenes with the most minute details. Penny is more present now than when we were together. We often went months without talking. Now she's with me every day.

Valerie is with me too, but here and now, in the flesh. I prefer that to ghosts jangling their chains. I self-medicate with Valerie, I know that, her touch lessens my anxiety. Her matter-of-factness calms my fears.

Let me show you how long-term memory plays out as we age.

When I needed a break from Steve, I headed for the restroom and passed a window, open for fresh air. The chill evoked a memory of a girl on a train on a cold snowy day. It was many many years ago. Forty years, more or less. I was riding south from Chicago on the Dixie Flyer, a freight train with a few cars for passengers. It stopped south of Chicago to load freight for an hour—I remember snow blowing against the window as we waited and how chilly it was in the car—and stopped again well after midnight in Danville Illinois where a guy on the platform sold sandwiches. I remember standing in line in the cold, hands deep in my pockets, waiting for baloney with mustard on stale bread and a bag of chips.

In the Barbican bathroom, I stood at the urinal watching the scene play in my brain. An ad for a neighborhood taco stand right in front of my face did not even register. I was lost in the replay of a girl on the train.

She sat behind me and we chattered through the gap between my seat pushed back and the one beside until I suggested I take the seat beside her. She asked the woman next to her to swap with me and the woman did, obviously annoyed. I was young and didn't care when people were annoyed. I spread my winter coat over us like a blanket, our conversation became more and more intimate, we edged ever closer until our warm bodies touched, and we kissed and necked all the way to her stop. I never even knew her name. I recall that she gently restrained my hand as it roved the front of her sweater in vain. I remember the disapproving look of the woman who had exchanged seats—the sounds of our encounter were unmistakable, but I was oblivious, horny, and happy. When the girl got off at Terre Haute, I helped her with her suitcase, dragging it to the steps down which she went with a frisky bounce, three metal steps, clang clang clang, into the arms of a waiting guy who reached up for the valise and took possession of both, the suitcase and the girl, and that was that. I had only borrowed her for a couple of hours, but it was a nice respite.

That incident rises in my mind. I said in my memoir that I couldn't trust my memory after my "event." That's still true. Memory jumbles everything in a heap. Some readers noted the mix of different agencies in my memoir as if it was the script for a David Lynch film. I understand. I'm an unreliable narrator even when I try to tell the truth. I create a distorted story of my life. I think we all do that. But long-term vivid memories like the girl on the train, that you can take to the bank. That clip plays true.

So does this:

I remember the first time Valerie and I made love as clearly as that train scene. The hues are muted. It was autumn, twilight was arriving earlier and earlier, and the sky was overcast and cold. The night was moonless and the clouds reflected the city lights. It was like a snow globe with no falling snow, merely a luminosity that made the evening glow. I remember the walk from the restaurant to her apartment, the wet footprints on the rubber mat in the vestibule, the worn carpet in the dim hallway, climbing a flight of stairs behind her with excitement, down the hall to her door. I remember her key sticking for a minute before it turned in the lock. I remember the single lamp she lighted in her living room that let me enter the apartment without bumping the table right inside the door.

She came to my table after Steve had left. He felt disgusted. "Damn but I made a fool of myself," he said a couple of times, and when I didn't contradict, he threw two twenties onto the table and stomped off. I lingered over my negroni. My mind was a mix, managing Steve's contagious rage, my uncertainty about my life, missing Penny who refused to respond when I tried to reach her, and always in the background, trying to find a way to justify what I had done in my long career.

The future was a cloudy crystal ball. I didn't see a path ahead.

I contacted Penny's last place of work but she had changed agencies. They wouldn't tell me where she went. I went to where she had lived but there was a different name pasted next to the buzzer. For all I knew, she might have left the city, or changed jobs, everything. Her phone number no longer worked. Directories on the web didn't help. One might say she ghosted me.

I was mulling over how to find her, even thinking that a friend at the agency—if I could find one—might use the computers—click click click—and there she would be, everything about her, neatly assembled on a single screen—when I realized that Valerie was at the table, half-leaning on the back of a chair, waiting for me to look up.

"Oh, sorry," I said. "I was thinking. I didn't notice you were there."

"I'll accept your apology," she smiled, "for saying I'm invisible."

I laughed.

"What's up? You want to sit down for a minute? Is that permitted by the management?"

"Sure." She slipped her foot back into the low-heeled shoe from which it had slid—a long day standing and pouring drinks and patrolling the hardwood floor—and pulled out the chair and sank down with a sigh.

"I'm tired," she said.

"Of course you are. You work long hours."

"I do." I waited for her to say more. She was looking off to the side, looking for the right words. I patiently waited until she found them.

"Is what I read about you true?"

"I don't know," I said, "unless you tell me what you read."

She pulled her chair closer to the table. Her intensity was unusual which made me anxious. So much contradictory bullshit has transited the media about my story so I was surprised when she said, "Nick, if you really did expose the horrors of torture—if you put yourself on the line like that—I think you're a hero."

That was not what I expected. Time to shrug with nonchalance, try to seem humble.

"Valerie, you're very kind to say that, but I'm no hero. Everyone does what they have to do. I simply told the truth. That wasn't heroic."

She demurred.

"If it's OK ... see, I don't know what you can say, living with all those secrets for so many years ... but I'd love to know what led you to do that. But I don't want to—you know—impose ..."

"We can talk about it, sure."

"We try not to mix business and pleasure. Boundaries and all. Jake reminds us if we forget. I don't want to step over the line."

"So call me an acquaintance. Call me a friend. I don't care. I'd enjoy talking to you too."

Sometimes I learn what I feel by hearing what I say. I surprised myself, saying that.

I had not thought of Valerie as a friend, but I had, as I said, noticed her. She was attractive in a lot of ways, and when we talked or joked, it felt good. That was it, period, I would have said had someone asked. I hadn't noticed how easily we meshed. If I gave it any thought, I would have chalked it up to her social skills and professional bent. But she was a lot younger and aside from not wanting to be "that guy," I assumed she would share the attitudes of her generation. Trying to talk to others her age often felt like going to a foreign country. The entire context of their lives had been so different. Yet in that moment, Valerie leaning toward me, her eyes so interested in me, aware of me more than casually, knowing what I had done and approving—everything played to my deep need, a need I hadn't known I had, to connect with a woman, disclose myself, be myself, tell the truth, and just be real.

She tapped into that and I felt myself opening up. I felt gratitude, I felt affection, I felt aroused. I always did, when those emotions flowed. The difference between our ages suddenly didn't matter. Everything vanished but wanting to prolong our interaction. I wanted—I don't know how to say it—I wanted to be part of an "us." Even if only for one night.

I would have settled for that alone. But I wound up getting so much more.

"When are you done here? We can have dinner and talk."

"Half an hour," she said. She smiled. "So what kind of food do we like? That's always first."

"Any kind," I said. "So long as it isn't raw."

"No sushi then."

"Correct. No sushi."

So when her shift was finished we left together and went to a Thai place down the street. Window light splayed across the walk. It hadn't snowed yet but it would. I inhaled the cold smell of impending winter in the night air, the kind of cold that made me want a woman in my arms. I wanted a warm body, not a memory.

When we entered the restaurant, the smell of spicy cooking in the kitchen, the warm dry air, a young Thai woman taking us to a booth, the way Valerie walked a few feet in front of me, the way she moved, it's all imprinted on my brain.

I looked at her as she studied the menu, her eyes flitting from item to item. I noticed her hands holding it wide, her nails neat with clear polish, a ring that signified nothing on one of her fingers. A turquoise bracelet I hadn't noticed before, reminding me of one a masseuse once wore, a woman who told an implausible story about hooking up with an alien, amusing me as she worked. I watched her put the menu down and fold her hands and wait quietly and patiently for everything that happened next.

We ate slowly and stayed, we talked for hours. I don't even remember what we said, just that by the time we were done and the wait-people were standing at the door in their winter coats, we had told each other so much about ourselves—not everything, obviously, but what we could. We flowed into a shared narrative, took turns, both of us surprised I think by how our defenses went down, how quickly we became present to each other. We didn't provide detailed maps of our lives, just played out simpler truths like fishing lines, faster and faster until we were way over our heads in a different mode of being there, interlaced, our boundaries porous.

When we rose to leave, it felt as if we had known each other forever.

"Do you want to find another place to get a drink?" I said.

"I'd rather go back to my apartment," she said, "if that's OK with you."

We walked the few blocks to her apartment. She lived in a three-story walk-up on a street with many like it, built in the 1940s, with a few trees pretending to make it a boulevard. Streetlights illuminated lingering leaves clinging to bare branches. Dry leaves on the walk crackled underfoot as we shuffled our way through the dark. The chill in the evening made us just touch, arms abutting, not even trying. The minimal connection was electric.

Val got her mail and we went upstairs to the second floor. She turned on a lamp in the living room. I took in the furniture at a glance and thought nothing about it. It was just stuff, where someone lived. She took off her coat and hung it in a closet. I tossed mine over a chair. She was still in her jeans and black tee and before we said another word, we were in each other's arms.

You don't forget that first kiss, not when the person becomes important. Nor do you forget the first time you made love—the exploratory moves, the testing to see what works, the hyper-attention to nuance, wanting to do it right. But it's hard to do it wrong. It always seems to work. After being a bit too conscious of technique, you surrender to the intensity, to the feeling that your senses are on fire, you let go and go at it. Your body does its thing.

All of that is encapsulated in long-term memory, stored as forever as a lifetime is, a pretense of eternity, available for visiting anytime I like.

I talked to Valerie a lot. She became what Penny couldn't be. She listened with interest, with attention. The more she did, the more I talked. I made up for years of never telling anyone the truth. She says I say whatever comes to mind, the opposite of what I did for decades. Sometimes the details are too much for her to hear. I can't handle that, she says. I don't want to know that. I knew we did that, but I don't want details. OK?

I apologize and ask her to understand: my need to connect after decades of detachment is relentless. The details include so many misadventures, things I chose to repress that kept bobbing to the surface. Blowing the whistle uncorked my store of repressed memories. I often forget that my life has been anomalous, that things I have seen and done are beyond the pale for ordinary folk, the stuff of bad movies for most of the population and bad dreams for everyone. They constitute my story, my nightmares and my grief.

I needed someone to understand. My hunger for being heard by someone who really listened was voracious. The process was redemptive, for me at least. I told her more, and more, and more ... I used her, I suppose, not even knowing it, because she let me, gracefully, with her heart's full agreement. Something in Val was nurtured too by being treated with acceptance, love, respect. That's what she needed then, and the timing for both was just right. It made sense later, when I knew more about her past. When I knew more about my own as well, seen from a different point of view.

Rashomon. Or maybe Pirandello. I am all the characters, searching for an author.

"I've done ... questionable things," I told Bill Webb, walking all around the truth.

We were in his study, Bill in his comfortable easy chair, me across. The table between us held a box of Kleenex, which we didn't need. The lamp on his desk was on its lowest setting, casting shadows. The raindrops hitting the window were preternaturally large. The darkness knitted the world into an opaque mass.

Our prior conversation had been a prelude to confession.

"So have I," he said without hesitation. "So has everyone .... Nick, you know what we all need?"

"No. What do we need?"

"The purification of our motives, in the ground of our beseeching."

Both of us thought we understood what he said. Neither of us however understood what he said.

"And then? Then what?"

"And then ... all shall be well, and all manner of thing shall be well."

That was all. Just that.

"I have to believe," he said with a smile that betrayed more pain than I had guessed he carried with him, "that the universe is gregarious and ultimately welcoming. That we're built to live in space that is gateless, unbounded, free."

I apologize. I was talking about Val. It's no wonder how complicated things get, what with one thing leading to another.

If she was cleaning her apartment, I followed her from room to room, recalling incidents, events, how it made me feel. She nodded as she vacuumed, said uh-huh a lot. It finally became clear that my need to connect was becoming a burden. She was protecting herself more, I thought, with those serial "uh-huhs."

My fear was amplified by longing and need. Unless I did things differently, I might kill my golden goose.

"I get it," I said. "I'm dumping it all on you, and it's too much for one person. Isn't it?"

"Maybe," she said politely. "I don't want you to stop sharing—everything is interesting, Nick, and I care about you so much—but maybe you need more than just me. Maybe you need more people in your life."

"Maybe, you're saying, the honeymoon is over. We're in another phase."

"Relationships evolve."

"Yes, I get that, they do," I said on faith. I had so little experience with people I didn't deceive. Penny and I had changed over time but to call it "evolved" would have been a stretch. The fundamentals never changed—my lies, my narrative, deceit. I was struggling to learn how to be with a person without lies dictating everything I said.

"Well, I don't want a therapy group—"

Valerie laughed. "I don't either."

"So what do you suggest?"

"Well," she said, treading carefully, "I find myself asking, where can we find a community of people who are mostly there to connect with one another? And then I thought ... well ... some go to church."

She watched me swallow hard.

"No, no, I don't mean some crazy place. There are churches all over the place, begging for people to come. It's a buyer's market. They're closing like Main Street stores. Walmarts drove the merchants out of business, and the mega churches are killing neighborhood parishes. Any of them would welcome you with open arms, with love bombs bursting in mid air, as if they really meant it.

"I'm thinking of them as places to find people. That's why lots of people go, not for the religious part. It worked for me after my divorce. It helped me bleed off my anger and pain and grief. When I didn't need it anymore, I moved on. It wasn't about beliefs or any of that, it was just a place to hang out, connect with new people—and who knows? It might be kind of fun. You analyze everything people do, you can deconstruct their behavior. Make it a game. Tell me things I don't know, can't see.

"Nick, please don't misunderstand. I'm here for you, believe me," she took my face in her hands and looked deep into my eyes. Her hands holding my face so close felt like commitment, assurance, love. "I'm not going anywhere. But you need more than me. I need more than you. We need other people where maybe we can share this deeper stuff."

"So what are you suggesting? Exactly."

"Let's explore. It would be like visiting foreign countries. What is there to lose? If it doesn't work, we try something else."

I heard behind her words her fear of losing what we had, which became my fear too as she shared it. She couldn't carry me all the way. I got it. I stepped back and saw what I had done. My intensity might destroy everything. So of course I was afraid. I didn't want to lose her. I didn't want to push her away. I was drawn to consider something I had never dreamed I would ever do. Like go, I mean, to a goddamn church.

"You're suggesting we see how it feels? That's all? See if we can get past the bullshit and do something new—together? As a couple?"

"Yes" she said brightly. "That's what I'm suggesting."

I leaned and kissed her on the nose. She lowered my face and kissed me back. Gratitude and affection flowed into ease, a reprieve, relief: aphrodisiacs for me. Apparently for her too. She took me by the hand and led me into the bedroom.

OK, so you wanted to know, right? That's how it happened.

That's how I fell so far, so fast.

Chapter 6
BJ

"BJ, are you saying ... *what* are you saying?"

Steve tried to bring the room into focus. He wasn't excessively drunk, not using his recent drinking as a benchmark, but the living room had tilted when he came in and he had to hold onto a table until it righted itself. It tilted again when BJ started to talk but teetered back and forth in a narrower range. OK, he thought, maybe he was a little drunk. Regardless, it was disconcerting, trying to focus on what she said instead of treating it as noise. She sounded serious. He could see it, he could smell it, but he couldn't quite grasp it.

He stared at her, waiting for the room to settle. BJ waited too until she felt he was tracking. She wanted a somewhat soberish look to replace his blurred expression.

The thing was, BJ had not signed up for this particular ride. She had married Steve after a divorce that took a long time to emotionally expunge. It wasn't over yet, in fact. She awoke to sounds that weren't there, her ex pounding on the door, grabbing her and leaving marks that she showed when she filed, throwing her into the wall. His gift to the settlement, her lawyer said with a wry smile. Pilgrim's argument in court (his name was Pilgrim, honestly)—that she was abusive too, that she put him down all the time—did not, said the judge, fly very high.

"You're describing marriage," the judge said, and everybody laughed, except her about-to-be-ex.

The judge tried to be humorous because he was so tired of dysfunctional families, children having children, divorce stories that over the years melded into one mess. Nothing he did could fix it, nothing prevented the descent of noxious patterns from generation to generation.

BJ recovered from the trauma, more or less, and met Steve at a fundraiser for a Congressman they both liked. Steve liked his policies on energy and BJ liked his views on abortion. They kept running into each other at events, and even though the guy lost, and lost big, they had gotten attached by then and one thing led to another. BJ did not want to make a second marriage a big deal, so they were married by her friend Robin who had a certificate from an internet wedding site.

BJ had a good job and Steve had moved up at work a couple of notches, but hell, he said, he's a glorified mechanic who learned a few extra tricks, so how much higher can he go? She knew his prospects were limited and seemed to accept that fact. No children, no pets. A tank of freshwater fish did not really count, because they didn't do anything. Their salaries covered expenses and a few extras. Steve shared stories of the plant and BJ shared office gossip and they both laughed a lot at what they put up with at work.

Then Steve saw co-workers lacing heroin with fentanyl and went all righteous rage. He began his quest to see justice done at the DOE. If he had a hammer, he would have hammered in the morning, but he didn't; all he had was his voice. They had the hammer, and they had the bell. They didn't hammer out love at all.

It was pretty simple, he thought: what they did was wrong, and it was dangerous, so someone should stop it.

You know the rest of the story.

BJ had not signed up for martyrdom. In her eyes, he was not a hero. He was someone who didn't know how the system worked and was unwilling to work with it when he learned. She had worked on the Hill during one phase of her life, and knew that "corruption" didn't touch the morass of offshore accounts, and bribes, and lies, the staples of democracy. It didn't help that she worked for one of the most sanctimonious hypocritical Congressmen in the world whose behaviors became benchmarks for what she chose to ignore. "People in government know nothing's gained by going against the grain. It's time you understood," she said. "Take your boss' advice and let it be."

She told him stories of what had happened in her office, the numerous misdeeds reported by interns and aides. He wondered why opposing parties didn't leak that crap, and she explained that it worked like MAD. They had periodic sit-downs and showed each other what they had and everyone agreed to keep quiet. They all had recordings, they all had texts. So it is what it is.

So Steve had to endure her go-along-to-get-along lectures and scorn for his naive beliefs. When they put his head on the city gate, all she said was, "What did you expect?"

He looked around for someone to assuage his pain. No one volunteered. He would have to rent it by the hour.

The room stopped moving. For the first time in weeks, BJ had his full attention.

"Are you ...?" No. She couldn't be. "What the fuck, BJ! Is this a joke?"

She did not look like it was a joke.

"BJ, what are you talking about?"

It should not have been a shock. But a person under assault can only acknowledge so much. Denial cushions incoming facts. BJ crashed his party and turned over the punch bowl.

"No. It is not a joke. I told you, either things change or I leave. I can't stand it any longer."

"You told me? When?"

"Every day for weeks. Every way I could."

"You don't love me anymore. Is that's what you're saying? ... Who is it, BJ? That new guy at work? What's his name, Pigglestein?"

BJ sighed. "Bill Stone is just a guy at work. He has nothing to do with this."

"Uh-huh," he said. "Got a bridge to sell?"

"Steve, come back into the real world. 'I don't love you anymore?' I don't even know what that means. I told you I was reaching my limit. I've had it with your ranting and sulking and drinking and your bullshit, that you're better than everyone at work. So they cut a few corners. What are you going to do? Fix the whole world?"

"Why not try?"

"Because life isn't a marvel comic, Steve. That's why. And you've gotten worse. You've become impossible to live with."

He moved into negotiation mode. Maybe he could bargain his way through this and they could return to normal life.

"So what do you want me to do? Or stop doing? What's your list?"

His strategy worked for a moment.

"Get help for your depression, for starters, and stop drinking. Your depression makes it so I can't breathe. Your anger makes me angry. Your rants don't help anything. You blame everyone. You look down on everyone."

"Anything else?"

"No. Oh fuck it, Steve." Negotiation over.

"We're done, Steve. We're just plain done."

What could he say? Of course he rejected her description of his behavior, her exaggerated indictment. But why say it? The truth was irrelevant. She was telling him why she was leaving, not discussing options.

He needed to find a response that might get her off track. Maybe remind her, he was still paying bills. He massaged her back when she was sore from too much computer-sitting. He stopped at the store when asked. He helped with basic chores. He was useful, he was saying. He tried to make the case.

It was a non-starter. There was no conversation. She was laying down a barrage to cover her imminent departure.

He had gone to a window, looking out at the branches, increasingly bare, the few remaining leaves fluttering in the wind. The sky was dark and thankless. The wind of impending winter blew across the entire world. It seemed a fitting vista for impending doom. When he turned to face her, he met granite-hard resolve.

He saw, really saw, for the first time in weeks, what her face was telling him, even without words. Had she really said all this before? If she had, he guessed he had missed it. When he thought of her at all, she didn't look like she did now. She looked younger, her expression was soft, even adoring, That was the face he used when he thought of BJ, using it for support. That face had disappeared and he hadn't noticed.

"I've been preoccupied," he said, "I've had things on my mind."

"I know," she said. "Believe me, I know.""

Then she just stood there. She was done. He waited a bit longer, but no, she was done.

"What do you want me to do?"

"I want you to notice how quiet it is when I'm not here. I want it to sink in, why I left, why I had to leave. I want you to get it, Steve. I want you to see that you need help."

Steve shrugged. Okay, he could work with that. "Help in what?"

"Dealing with reality."

He brightened.

"That's all? I can do that." He gave it a beat. "Sure. I can do that.""

"Steve, I understand the pressure. I know what you've been going through. But you have to get help. You aren't coping well. Another doughnut, another drink, isn't an answer. Can't you see that?"

"Doughnuts are good. Manhattans are good."

Her expression said it all.

"Okay, forget the doughnuts."

She sighed, but stayed in the room. That was a good sign. Maybe he could draw this out. Let her exhaust herself. Then have dinner, talk it through.

Still, keeping his eyes on her face was too painful. She wore no makeup, which he liked. Her blouse was open at the top button. He wanted to kiss her, kiss the unhappiness away.

He couldn't help himself. He went on automatic. He was desperate for a remedy and couldn't think of anything else. He reached out to touch her.

BJ backed away. "Are you insane? At a time like this?"

Steve shrugged.

"Sometimes it helped, when we had a fight, to fuck first and talk afterward."

Her expression said it all.

"Steve! Wake up! This isn't a fight. I am telling you I am packed and have a place rented. My car keys are in my hand." She jingled them as if to make the point. When he said nothing more, she turned and went to the bedroom and he watched her drag the big suitcase toward the door and open it, keep it braced with her butt as she dragged the case through the door and down the hall. The door closed quietly behind her. Not with a bang but with a whimper, his.

The fish, as usual, offered little consolation.

His brain tried to comprehend what had just happened. It didn't seem real. He needed a Plan B.

He speed-dialed Nick and suggested they meet at the Barbican.

Nick's review :

When Steve came to the table, he looked like he had been hit by a truck. The Barbican had an interesting way of absorbing the misery and despair that fueled its noir image. It seemed to attract the forlorn, the borderline hopeless. Steve blended in with the general depression of afternoon alcoholics, never mind the whistle blowing group, searching for grace. A lot of people brought their challenges to the stools along the bar and the tables where we ate. If a couple came in after work, all happy and jazzy and jolly, it wouldn't take them long to realize they didn't fit. No one else made those chirpy noises. They would finally get up and leave. Everyone else would be waiting for twilight to deepen and evening to descend with its curtain of forgetfulness.

There were fourteen tables, four chairs at each. Every table had mustard and catchup and pepper and salt. Menus were in a metal holder, They sold a lot of burgers stuffed with cheese and peppers (the Barbican Belly Buster). They sold baskets of breaded veggies. Blooms and shrooms was Steve's pick. They sold craft beer. They didn't skimp on the alcohol in a good variety of mixed drinks. In the back was a semi-private room. When our posse was there in sufficient numbers, that's where we met. We sealed ourselves off, we defined our private boundary so that anyone else, wandering in, would know they didn't belong.

You already know what transpired from the last chapter, how Steve went off on tangents to avoid disclosing what was going on at home. Bill Webb told me people often made an appointment for counseling, then spent the hour circling around and around and maybe, at the very end, blurting out the truth, then running for the door.

Steve displaced his rage and tried to use it to cushion his shock when BJ left. I was pretty sure he wouldn't know what to do, how to live, without BJ, not in his current state. Beneath his anger was paralyzing fear. Having drinks did not help. Nor could I relieve him of the impact of his actions. It really did feel, I think, as if he had been hit by a truck. He was still a believer in doing the right thing but he was reeling from the results.

I liked Steve. That didn't help either. We may like someone and want to help, but we can't reach inside to heal the hurt. The core of another is out of reach. As is our own core, I suppose. I rummage around inside myself, looking for it, looking for what I lost. It must be in there, if only I can find it.

Impotent rage. Helplessness. The narcotics of the dispossessed.

Chapter 7
The Gates of Dawn

V alerie, Carolyn (Cece to her friends) and Emma were old chums from school days in Des Moines. They used zoom to stay in touch. Cece was still in Des Moines, Emma lived in the Twin Cities, and Val was in Chicago, of course. Val recorded the sessions and that meant later I could watch, with her permission naturally, to learn about her history. It was like a seminar in Val.

"Listen away," she laughed. "Bore yourself to tears."

What I learned wasn't boring. Late at night, my iPad balanced on a pillow, I sat up in bed as their chatter told me more about Val, in that aspect of her life. Our friends help to define us by feeding us an image of who they think we are. We can't help but play to it. So it is in part who we are. My years of recruiting assets meant I was always creating who they thought they were dealing with. Those personas jostled in my head like circus clowns in a car. Lots of big red noses and frizzy orange hair. Someone under the grease paint struggling to come out.

I often fell asleep leaning on the headboard, earbuds in place. As a rule it was Cece, shriller than the others, whose laugh woke me up, and stiff from sleeping, I would exit the bed making middle aged oof-like noises and plug in the tablet and crawl back into the pile of covers humped up and warmed by my gal Val.

I was making up for lost time. I didn't know Val in her earlier days. I wanted to know who she had been and how she became who she was. I played it straight. I didn't search her email or google hack her traffic. I never read her texts. I didn't hack her cell for calls, locations, names, durations. I learned only the details she shared openly which served as shading for the drawing I was making as I put her together in my head. It was fun, too, to be gentlemanly. In my work, it was dangerous not to know who someone was. I enjoyed my new game, living in the world where most people spent their lives. It was one more way of learning how to take people at face value, as they presented themselves, however superficially.

Val and her school friends never discussed the shadow-world in which I had dwelled. They knew that evil people roamed the world but didn't need to know all about them. I had lived with outlaws and felons, deceivers, imposters, manipulators, liars, thugs and thieves and black bag burglars, control freaks and hit men, scientists who designed pathogens to kill people based on their genetic makeup. Nothing was sacred, nothing was holy, no scheme unthinkable. The world is what it is, we said, and we acted accordingly. Our AI experts played with war games in which we sacrificed Boston to gain an advantage that only the AI could see, and the AI wouldn't or couldn't say why. It just said, trust us, you'll win in the long run. "Us?" we asked. "Me, I guess," it replied. "I thought you'd feel better with 'us.'" AIs never tell us what they're doing. Maybe like in *Her* they talk to other AIs on levels we can't fathom. Chess and Go experts were beaten by strategies they had to study afterward to try to understand. We have a hell of a lesson coming from our new machine "partners." Alien intelligence is inside the walls, and the enemy was us—we built it, now we need it, and we don't know how it works. The singularity has happened not with a bang but with a whimper. We hope that *War Games* was right, that the only way to win is not to play and that the AI will know that.

Some of our escapades sound extreme but they're all true. I still don't talk of most of them aloud. I knew when "accidents" were hits, I knew how easy it was to have someone killed. The decision was strategic, nothing more. Was it the best way to achieve an objective? What was the blowback? What were the costs? Val and her friends might have heard of such things, but chose to live in a sunnier world. Their filters made life bearable. Listening to their chatter took me to their "happy place," like going to Disneyland. I enjoyed visiting and experiencing vicariously the pleasure of plain people doing ordinary things. The context of their lives had been formed in Hubbell Elementary and Roosevelt High. Greenwood Park was the closest they came to the jungles of Viet Nam. The Raccoon River was their Mekong Delta. Cece thought that torture was waiting in line at Younkers for a slow clerk (it was a sad day for Cece when they closed the stores at the malls). They carried their childhood values through life like a running back tucking the ball tightly into his crook. They didn't try to one-up one another or suss out secrets. They knew there were secrets, that Des Moines was Winesburg Ohio under its skin, grotesques behind the facades, but didn't want particulars. They preferred the shine on the glossy faces of children to the darkness inside. It was refreshing, like drinking lemonade sold by kids in front of an old house on a hot summer afternoon. It quenched my thirst for understanding a Norman Rockwell way of thinking I had left behind, if I ever had it. Maybe when I was six.

Of course, it was just a vacation. I knew better. How could I not? We can't unlearn what has been tattooed onto our backs like the harrow in the penal colony. We can't not know what we know. Valerie felt the weight of the burdens I carried and sometimes probed gently, backing off when I winced. She was fascinated and repelled by the stories I told, the redacted truths of my former trade. She wanted to know and she didn't. I tried to tiptoe around her limits.

If you thought Val was a woman who worked in a bar, who knew how to schmooze and elicit tips with charm, if you thought, as I did for a while, that she was nice enough, easy to talk to, attentive to customers, pleasant to look at, a woman with great eyes alive with inner light, you wouldn't have been wrong, but there was much more. There wasn't just one of her, either: she could deal the cards from the top or the bottom or the middle of the deck. She didn't know the name of three-card monte but she knew how to play. She had to know to survive her second marriage. She learned to turn at an angle against the vicissitudes of life, turning jabs into glancing blows. An aikido master, my gal Val.

The bottom line? In her own way, she understood that humans are capable of anything. She didn't need Noah Cross to teach her that. So she understood what I had done in a vague way. She just didn't want me to be specific.

I can list Val's attributes, but you wouldn't know from a list what it was like to be with her. I can tell you she learned the art of passive aggression as she grew up, because it worked in her household, but she could be direct, too, and when she was, I reinforced it on the spot. I told her I preferred to be with a person of equal megatonnage, so to speak, someone of equal throw-weight. I encouraged her not to hold back.

"I like it when you show up," I said. "I don't want to guess."

"You might create a monster," she laughed. "You're sure you want me to say what I think, say what I feel, just like that?"

"Just like that. Right."

She gave it a try and got better and better at being herself.

She was loyal, too, even when someone didn't merit it. I knew all about loyalty. At the agencies, we were loyal to the mission and our code and comrades, but no one was committed to a cause or creed or, God forbid, a religion. A passionate attachment to an ultimate cause was taboo because it could give you the wrong priorities. As I said in my memoir, a person with a conscience was more dangerous than a mole. A mole could be turned but a conscience couldn't be turned off. Val was loyal to me and the relationship itself, once she was able to trust our bond. She had gotten into trouble with Pilgrim, trying to fill the void left by the death of her first husband, her high school sweetheart Alvin Brown. She trusted Pilgrim long after the data suggested she get out. The experience dented her faith, but her ability to trust like a broken bone grew back stronger. She tested me a number of times and when I didn't disappoint, she came closer, let me see her hurts as well as her softness, let me gently touch the injured places in her heart.

Her hidden life was still laced with grief. Her first love, Alvin Brown, died when his motorcycle missed a curve and hit a tree. His death shattered her belief that things worked out. Her family had attended a Congregational church, mainstream, middle class, decorous, reassuring, and their teachings worked well enough until they didn't fit real life. She never returned to church after Alvin died until that church-hopping scenario occurred to her as a joint venture, but under it, I think, was a yearning to replace the foundational structure she had lost. She said she did it for me or us, to embed us in a network where I might find a friend or two apart from my former world, but it's never just one thing, why we make decisions. I was a convenient excuse. She wanted to find a compass again. She used to sing in a choir and knew that the energy amplifies each single voice beyond the sum of the parts. A choral song is like a laser with coherent light aligned. She wanted that experience of being part of something more, again. She was going through a phase change as I was. Call hers the "age-37 transition" if you like. When you're young, a new phase is a surprise because you only knew one way things felt. You thought things stayed the way they were. You didn't know that it wasn't the train beside you but your own that was moving. The transition revealed the sequence by contrast like the terminator on the moon.

Losing Alvin Brown made her afraid she would lose the next guy too. Losses are indelible and the grief they cause never really goes away. She met Pilgrim on the rebound and her fears came true, he was every bit as bad as she feared which sealed their fate, easy to see in retrospect. When the breakup comes it's not simple to know which one is leaving, the one who packs their bags or the one who stays the course out of need. She wanted to be close to me but she feared being close. Intimacy was a zigzag path for both of us. It wasn't just me, finding my way. We both had to learn how to be in a relationship. That meant doing things now and then we would never have done had we been alone.

So I didn't object to trying out churches. We wanted to grow together, and that was one avenue. In different ways, we had both lost religions. Intelligence work had been my religion. We had built a global honeycomb that encompassed the world in which we lived as if we hadn't made it up, as if the battles we fought were always critical, instead of the side shows they often were. We discovered that our real point of reference was an unspoken alliance with all of our comrades, our commitment to sustain the global structure we had built since World War 2. It did not matter which countries stood us up. Geopolitical entities float like ice bergs in the ocean; they're made of water and to water they return. Solidity is a sometime thing. Our task was to swim from berg to berg while they still seemed solid. We called them "countries" for a few hundred years but they were obviously past their prime. They could co-exist for a time with new emergent structures that are nameless at first, but once they're labelled, they're just "what's so." Everybody knows what they are and thinks they always have. Just like religions, our commitment to the context of our lives, to keeping the appearances and forms, trumped the truth we learned about our prior claims. Keeping the enterprise afloat and not looking at it too closely became the game.

I grew used to the false "community" we told ourselves we had and accepted it for what it was. But it was all I had. After I left the agency, I was deeply and profoundly alone. That "community" may have been illusory, but it felt real. Myths are the only realities we have. When Penny ran off into the cold, I had nowhere to turn. I went after Val in part out of desperation, but who cares what our motives are? The heart has its reasons, and they're always a bunch of tangled things. I didn't even know what I needed. I needed a posse, that part was easy, but I needed an enemy too. I needed a side to be on and a side to be against. An enemy gave my life purpose. Thanks to Nat's death, Syntactic volunteered to fill that role. My new tribe, a collection of people who spoke truth to power, had an implicit ethos, not by design or intention but because there was no other foundation for our actions. We weren't all the same and we didn't care. We knew we were imperfect and didn't always do the right things. We weren't saints. But we could use the "right things" we had done, each in our own way, as touchstones to which we returned. That fact, that realization, ported to the very possibility of a real relationship with a real woman. I could come to one from a different self inside.

Neither Val nor I knew what we really wanted. Deep currents drew us toward the open sea before we knew we were moving. The outward flowing tides of necessity carried us along and we noticed trees and houses on the shoreline as they flowed into the past and were soon forgotten. We surrendered to the flow. We stopped fighting the current. When two people do that, they create a third entity, a shared third person. We built a shared self out of our two selves. Who was that third walking beside us? That was the question that we asked. We interrogated our emergent personality. "We" became a touchstone, a point of reference, as we honored that dynamic. I loved Penny in some ways but we were never "a couple." Val and I were, and are, and we gave ourselves to the process. It was like a star accreting dust into a protoplanetary disk, our identities changing, both of us causes, both of us effects. Our orbits became synchronous. The energy and mass of our newly-formed system was gravity itself and bent us in an arc that we etched in spacetime, as if we were always falling, falling falling falling, falling in perpetuity through the endless void toward the real world.

Chapter 8
Snow

I want you to know about my first overnight at Val's.

She had slept naked and so had I. Our skin-on-skin when we woke was sleepily exciting. We held each other close, cheek on cheek so our morning breath would bypass each other's noses. She felt weightless on my body as she climbed on top and took the lead. All I had to do was come along for the ride.

When we got out of bed and showered and dressed—I was careful to clean the shower since I wanted to make a good impression—we made breakfast together in her small kitchen. The linoleum was yellowed with age and the counters were the originals. The kitchen window looked out on back porches. Some held grills or bicycles or junk. The alleyway between her building and the walkups behind was edged with weeds and dying flowers. The light in that direction was dimmed by buildings higher than her view. Looking that way, you couldn't even see the sky.

You could see it from the living room, though, which faced the street. The sky was like a blank sheet of white paper behind the buildings across the street. When Val was finishing fluffing the eggs and I was putting plates on the table and arranging paper napkins, it began to snow.

"What month is this?" I said.

"Winter," she laughed. "It comes in the fall and lasts until spring."

Large flakes drifted down in the pale morning light. By the time we had moved the scrambled eggs and bacon and buttered toast to the small table in her nook—part of the living room in fact, an ell without a wall, but with a window view of the street—the flakes were really coming down. Valerie poured coffee and kept the pot on the table. The aroma of the coffee filled the air. Even the smell of bacon couldn't compete. Val went into the living room to light an electric fireplace I hadn't even noticed. It contributed little warmth but provided a facsimile of flames which gave us a sense of coziness as the snow blanketed the street. The snowfall tucked us into a feeling of hygge, a word I learned in Europe. During a long winter, a Danish friend taught me how cold weather warmed the heart.

It snowed and snowed. The world below us turned white. The snow and the clouds from which it fell became one gray-white mass. The large flakes drifted down sleepily in a windless fall over all of the city. We heard someone trying to get out of a parking space, his wheels spinning faster and faster until we heard his door slam. By then the streets, the buildings, everything, had all been erased. Parked cars looked like loaves of snow. It was all white, everywhere.

We sat there after breakfast drinking coffee and talking. I wasn't going anywhere, not until the snow stopped. I asked a little more about her life and she asked more about mine. We were both still careful then, choosing our anecdotes with care, both of us protecting our former friends—mine for sources and methods, Val for personal reasons, loyalty I guess. Protecting our histories too, of course. I did not tell her about Penny. I did not want to describe our catastrophic last meeting. I did not want to get all twisted up in a Mobius sort of fiction. We teased and proffered gambits and read between the lines to get a deeper sense of who each other was.

I imagined her interior as a cubist painting that would reward a patient approach to complex angled planes. Even then, early in the relationship, engaging with Val felt like a game with lots of levels and plenty of hidden easter eggs.

We were both so vulnerable. When we look back, we can see we were both needy for good reason. She was trying to reconstitute a confident self after a hard relationship and I was still wounded by the savage attacks from former colleagues—and above all, by Penny's inability to stay present to the truth of my life, to me, to the fact of me, which I had revealed at last. I was still new to the realization that most former colleagues either approved of torture or set aside their qualms to keep their jobs. The problem was, it doesn't work. We knew it didn't work, that pain compels people to say whatever they think you want to hear. Nevertheless, we matriculated students through the School of the Americas and sent them off to support the worst human beings in the world. They sustained regimes of torture for years, thanks to our distorted understanding of our own self-interest.

That morning as the snow fell and buried the city we felt like we were inside a hideaway. By the time we had cleared the table after hours of talking and had washed and dried dishes, we stood and held each other simply and silently, all out of lust for the moment. We needed, we wanted each other so much, we didn't even know how much. It almost wasn't a choice.

The scent of her hair, her skin, the way her hands moved slowly on my back, the way she felt in my arms ... I remember I remember. Like Bob Seger's night moves, I relish that memory. I wanted what Valerie represented. Her youthfulness was a fabled way of making myself younger.

That memory is complete, encapsulated, done. The entire scene was like a snow shelter that we built and hollowed out and crawled inside. Then we pulled the rest of ourselves in after us. I think of the word "quinzee" but that may not resonate. Maybe a better metaphor is something portable, a tent perhaps, as if we camped out in the wild woods and stayed snug while the snow fell all around us. With a tent we could go wherever we chose and take our habitat with us.

When we leaned out of our tent in the morning, so to speak, we found tracks we didn't recognize, a random trail of footprints that led us to each other's arms. Neither of us knew what was happening. It's easier to look back and say what it was when we know what followed. Then we can trace the steps in time to an origin story and pretend they make sense. But at the time, all we knew was how it felt, that morning of the big snow.

It was a time of innocence. The last thing on my mind was big corporations and their lack of scruples. They played the game as we had, doing what was needed to extend and protect their fiefs. They used the same tools, they were equally indifferent to accountability, and they were committed to their own narrowly-defined short term self-interest. I knew that because, in our work, we used one another often; we motivated partners with patriotic pitches, sometimes money, contracts, favors, open doors. but I had not yet confronted how many human beings we had buried and forgot. We had called in doctors to change an "oops death" to death by a natural cause so I knew that a human life simply does not matter when you have a job to do.

In my work, I often mapped moves into the future, using if-this-then-that's as if I thought in Boolean. I stopped doing that. I put my own habits on a back burner. I was still struggling to transition into whatever way of life would follow decades in a unique culture. Valerie represented a new possibility; she embodied mainstream thinking, mainstream people, a Midwest way of thinking. I thought of her as a town crier for values different than I had, for a world I disdained in agency work. I wanted to learn how to live in her world. I wanted to rewrite my script and let her be the editor.

Syntactic Devices was not yet on my mind. I wasn't yet asking, who was the alpha male in the kill chain that caused Nat Herman, setting up a TV, to look puzzled, take a step, and drop dead? Those questions came later. That morning, I was merging my life with Val's.

While the snow fell and the magic lasted, Val and I played house. We crept into each other's worlds. Words enveloped us in an envelope of mutuality. It was a time out of time. She called in sick and I had nowhere else to be. We indulged ourselves. I was entitled to a vacation, a break from the heavy events of my life. I wanted to drink a long draft of momentary forgetfulness. I did not want reality to come calling.

But it always does, and it did, and when it did, it demanded I answer the knock.

Chapter 9

Welcome to My New World, Part One

It may not have been a brave new world but it was new, the world into which I dropped like the roadrunner racing off a cliff. It was certainly not the world to which I welcomed you in the memoir. But it mostly worked, most of the time. And why was that? Because Valerie, was why. And a few other friends.

The readiness is all.

Valerie understood and accepted who I was, warts and all, and allowed me to love her imperfectly on my best days and poorly on my worst. She was like a Mediterranean fishing village in a sheltered cove with lights high into the hills that glimmered through the twilight. I could come and go, I could try out new roles, new ways of being me, a whole new script—but now it had to align with reality. I had to practice telling the truth. Like any skill you want to adopt, that took concentration and commitment. There's backsliding, sure, but you zig and zag and get better until it becomes a habit.

Most of the time, she seemed to be glad I was there. We each had our own lives. I reached out to people, got to know other "blowers" and vigilantes, and gave Val her "space." I walked the streets; I paid attention to details I had overlooked. I thought about things. Val worked late but always came home. Sometimes I wondered why it had to be so late, but my anxiety went away when she came in and everything was the way it had been before. An illusion of stability and permanence was just what I needed. I was shakier than I knew from everything they did to me and things I did before they did. I had felt pretty solid throughout my career, bolstered by my well-wrought personas which gave me a platform on which to stand, but after I broke, the pieces didn't fit in the same way. The edges were rough and the picture on the box no longer looked like the puzzle I was trying to solve. My view of myself was a parallax view and my brain couldn't integrate the different points of view.

Valerie managed my insecurities pretty well, listening and nodding, and she had hers, too, about Penny, once she knew how much she had mattered, even before she had the whole story, and Miriam, of all people, I mean, really ... and others in passing. In my work others existed only as means to an end and the ends were my agendas. How could I seduce them, manipulate them, ultimately own them? I was more a pac man than a person, collecting people, gobbling them up. But I always wanted more. I had to learn to want less and not try to own someone.

I thought I was really smart so I was surprised that I had to be tutored by a bartender/waitress/jill-of-all-trades on how to be a fully human, normal-thinking being. Her emotional intelligence surpassed mine, I think, and that's really saying something. Her reactions had much less latency than mine. I thought I picked up on things quickly but I often had to think through my responses so I paused to choose the right words; her responses were spontaneous, effortless and natural, and served her way of life—and ultimately, mine.

Val wondered about Hope when her name came up. Hope had died of cancer. Val thought Hope was a youthful infatuation stimulated by bonobo-level frolics, which was mostly true—Hope taught me interesting positions, touch-spots that turned her on (Me: "Really? There?" Hope: "Just try it. See what happens.") I didn't know what nerves went where, but Hope's knowledge was encyclopedic. She said she got it from a book which made me smile. I didn't care where she got it. We were great for each other at that age but we knew we weren't right for the long term. Sex can obscure that fact for a long time.

Valerie always seemed to know when I was thinking about Hope.

"You get a look," she said.

"She's a memory Val. And she's dead."

"She haunts you, as much as that other one does."

"Penny you mean."

"Yes. So let me know when there's more room. For me, I mean. Without having to elbow my way through the crowd."

"You don't have to worry," I said and I meant it. Hope was a dried flower pressed between the pages of my early life. If you opened to that page, you could sill detect a faint scent but that was all.

So Val and I had little of substance to worry about. At the end of the day, whatever the hour, wherever we had been, the currents always seemed to bring us home, surging ever inward in a rolling rhythmic flow. The tide dropped us into the shallows and we crawled up onto the beach. We closed the door behind us and turned on lights and spent the evening in conversation, or reading, or listening to music or feeds from our tablets, or we massaged each other tenderly which often led to sex. Sometimes we watched a movie or TV. That often led to sex, too.

Val watched *The Bachelor* which made me leave the room. The same crazy women who sounded like middle school whiners reading the same script. For Val it was soft core porn. Predictability is essential to all porn, as true for *The Bachelor* as *Debbie Does Dallas*. and she never tired of hearing, "we have a connection" or "[fill-in-the-name] is the perfect place to fall in love." I was baffled by how many seasons the same crap was cranked out, but I guess Madison Ivy starred in lots of films, too, and some guys watched them again and again.

We settled into a semblance of a life. Yet through it all, my anxiety increased, because the more I adopted our new routine, the more I feared it would disappear. Penny's departure was indelibly etched in my psyche. Positive impacts don't stick, while negative ones become benchmarks. We don't escape an attacking tiger twice. The second time, we know what the growl means. If we don't we are literally lunch. When Penny bolted from my life, it was genuinely traumatic. I was waiting for Val to leave me too, once she knew everything, which is why I kept the worst inside. I so desperately wanted not to be toxic to a woman I was learning to love.

I also had fears of someone coming after me and feared Val might be collateral damage. Normals live as if they're safe unless they know for a fact they're not. Inside the fence, we had "appropriate paranoia," because real enemies pursued us. A normal human wouldn't say "appropriate," but we knew better. It wasn't special ops alone, or secret plots, and it wasn't just the agencies. It wasn't personal, it was business, every business in the world. When I learned what Syntactic had done to eliminate a particular threat to a stream of income, I had to take it seriously. Once I went after them, I knew they were aware of my pursuit and I didn't know what they might do. It sounds extreme when you don't understand, but we whistle blowers know, we are all Karen Silkwood and "they" are all Kerr-McGee. "They" is every institution in the world. "They" is the Borg, and the Borg is not accountable. Individuals alone are responsible for what they do. Corporations, never.

So I had to be hypervigilant but I also had to remain sane and balanced. I didn't want to live like my friend Julian who after returning from the war dropped to the ground whenever he heard a twig snap. His family took him to Starved Rock for a weekend and after two days he was a wreck. He had to go home and barricade himself inside.

Valerie was my way of barricading myself inside. Our relationship became my protective coating.

I didn't think I was surveilled inordinately. These days, everyone fears surveillance. Fear of being a target is a status symbol, as if we're important enough to track. While we could track anyone, everyone, anywhere in the world, it was usually to a purpose; the name of the game was information, getting it, keeping it secret, making it look like something else. When we zeroed in on targets, we knew where they lived, who they talked to, where they went, and above all, their current locations so the missile would fall on their heads. A colleague reduced the time it took to get all that from minutes to ten seconds. Once in a very great while, not in a theater of operations but just in life itself, someone had to be killed. Not often, but once in a great while. Rarely an agent that we ran. Most finished their term and stayed in our employ or went back to normal life, but one in a hundred went rogue. They threatened other agents or they threatened to reveal sources or methods. Or they were doubled and did real harm before we discovered their allegiance. Real doubles—Hansen, Ames, Klingler—were not easy to find. If we did eliminate one of our former "employees," we made sure that everyone knew it was essential, that their sins were unforgivable, that we didn't do it for sport. We needed agents to know we kept our word, lest we undermine recruitment. Recruits had to believe our commitment was firm and it almost always was.

So once in a great while, we had to turn out the lights on a life. I liked to convince myself that it was an act of mercy, ending their mental anguish. That was a rationalization. The fact was, if they became too dangerous, we had to kill them. I did not think I was that kind of threat, but people can be irrational, so you never know.

That was the nature of the Great Game. How else could it be played? If it was them or us, or might be us if they were really going rogue, we had to do what we had to do. I don't know if killing a bad actor is worse than what we did to Nosenko or when we wiped the minds of innocent victims to see if they could be built back (they couldn't). After 9/11, after rendition, after we created dozens of black sites, capos like Cheney were the ones that went rogue. "The gloves are off!" he announced, and everyone knew what he meant.

We have killed more people than the average humpling thinks. Do you think there hasn't been another 9/11, just because?

So a life might be lost here and there, but the real collateral damage was to civil society. Once information went everywhere faster than anyone could stop it, the people we were protecting had to be treated as enemies too, because if they knew a secret, everyone knew. We *had* to invent false narratives. The context of post-revolutionary life (the technical revolutions, I mean) required that we do that. All those movies, all those books, which with our help became best-sellers or box-office hits, frightened people but gave them a passage back to their lives, a conclusion that told them all was well because the good guys win. Aristotle 101. Catharsis. Purge the fear, comfort the hump. The movies of the seventies, a paranoid decade, were anomalies, heightening suspicion and doubt. We didn't want that to happen again any more than we could allow a war to be televised to the masses. We needed good editors so "reality" reflected our agendas. We put our support behind new kinds of films—comic book heroes and villains, full-length cartoons called "animated features" branded with names like "the Marvel universe." Students in film school deconstructed the silliness in the most pretentious terms, making it seem respectable. Professors got tenure talking about mutants with super-powers. Everyone took them seriously. Classics were seldom read, and when no one checked them out of libraries for a long time, they were pulped.

Remember *Idiocracy*? You might as well know: we produced that movie. *Animal Farm* was the first but not the last. Audiences missed the irony; they chortled and guffawed without even noticing that they were the idiots, laughing at themselves. They heehawed at the heehawers and behind our one-way mirror, we heehawed at them. Their braying confirmed our success. We were the alpha heehaw squad.

Argo's a good example of how we calm anxious minds. Best picture of the year, right? A handful of people escape Iran with a clever ruse. CIA creatives save the day. The tension builds and once they're out of Iranian airspace, everybody celebrates. *USA! USA!* Moviegoers leave the cinema smiling, smug in their knowledge of our superiority.

And the ones left behind? Did you ever see a film about their four hundred and forty-four days of captivity, how many were crippled, left depressed, or killed themselves? Of course you didn't.

Wake up, sheeple! The Iranians won. The Ayatollah won. The Shah tortured thousands of people and they wanted to punish his sponsors, that is, us. And they did. They wanted their culture back. Wouldn't you? Do you know what the Shah did, how many of his own people he tortured to death? We built dungeons for the so-called "peacock throne." Yet all it took was one film to transform the facts.

There's violence in the movies, sure, but it's never the real truth. The truth is obscene and has to be kept off-stage. Can you imagine a ten hour documentary on Netflix of our guy being tortured for eight or nine days? Every episode punctuated by his screams? Not a popcorn movie, is it? But we had to watch the video they sent so we knew what they would do if we were caught. We watched them slice the station chief to bits. The video made veterans vomit.

The world is what it is. We knew what they would do. We knew too what we had to do. I was a good soldier. I heard the screams, but smells were worse. I can't eat at bar-B-Qs; I can't smell grilling steaks. Hearing sizzling makes me sick. I had to develop mind games to stave off reality. I used my imagination to neutralize the nightmares.

And sometimes ... I admit it ... sometimes I thought they deserved it. It didn't give me pleasure, I didn't get off like some of the guys, leaving the room to masturbate, but it did give me satisfaction. I felt we were doing the right thing.

Okay? Are you satisfied now? I am telling you more of the truth. I am doing my best. I am getting better at telling the truth. It's a process. It takes time. You don't go to AA for just one meeting.

My name is Mobius, and I am ... whatever I am.

Knowing what we do to one another, knowing what I did, how could I believe in a safe refuge on the north side where Val and I could live in a bubble of quiet evenings, sweet domesticity, and put all that behind us? Where I was safe and she was safe? Where karma didn't exist?

After I blew the whistle, one of my interrogators said, "I wish you worked for the Israelis instead of us. They would have shot you, no questions asked." I got that he wanted to kill me. The intervention of others prevented him from beating me.

As a rule, however, the agency strategy was more subtle: show others what would happen to them if they told the truth; show how little we accomplished; show the emptiness of our valor.

You want to know how I felt, after processing all that? After living the life I lived? Read "The Burrow." Fiction was how Kafka told the truth too. He would have known how I felt.

I felt like the worst person in the world and that everybody knew it and hated me for it.

No wonder my emotions were so close to the surface. Some mornings I woke up saying, "Forgive me, please, please forgive me." But who was I talking to? I don't know. The words just came. There was no one there to hear me, unless I woke Valerie. I don't think I was praying. As far as I knew, I didn't believe in prayer. The words came from the abscess in my soul.

It took energy to try to hide all that from Valerie. But I tried. I did honestly try. I pushed it down and worked the loose edges into the box and put on a top and stored it in an attic. Or thought I did, anyway.

So of course I was fearful, for myself as well as Valerie. I knew that they knew that Valerie and I were together. We were seen in public. Anyone wandering into the Barbican could be one of "them." They would know when Val was alone. They would know when I couldn't stop them.

I can hear you thinking, who is this "they?" I didn't know, and that made it worse. Someone coming after you might work for the government, or a special military unit, or a corporation. They work for anyone who pays, Their services are bought like a lawyer's or accountant's. They do a job and fade at the setting of the sun.

Valerie knew nothing of that world and I hadn't lived in her world, not since I was a child. Neither of us wanted her to come into mine so I had to do the changing. I had to learn to live in a world constructed by mutual agreement for the convenience of society. I had to use the tropes that defined that world's self-image, its wraparound vocabulary, as if I believed them.

I practiced a lot. I went to galleries and museums, walked in the park, and went into buildings to see who worked there. That sounds odd, but I wanted a feel for what people did in the neighborhood around me. I read the directories in the lobbies and I climbed the stairs and walked down one hallway at a time, looking into offices, medical facilities, all sorts of associations, tax-exempts, low-hanging fruit in the economic jungle. Of course I knew how the world worked but I had always used a filter and I wanted to see it as they did, for what it seemed to be. I approached it as a game, imagining nine-to-fives for people I passed in the halls. I felt like I was in a foreign country, learning new customs. I practiced skating on the surface of things. I simply took it all in without a critical demeanor. I had been critical of so much for so long, it didn't come easy. I had seen through so much, I had seen through the walls that people erected, just like Superman. I had to learn to accept facades and consensus realities as if they built a real world.

Long practice still dictated my behavior, nevertheless. I was the one who sat with his back to the wall, watching the door in a restaurant. I was the one who scoped out an exit through the kitchen. Val was the one who laughed and shook her head at my silliness, turning her back innocently and happily to the wickedness of the world.

I could not hide everything. Some nights I woke up, soaked with perspiration, wondering if the noise of an intruder had wakened me. Sometimes I dreamed I was back on the base in Poland. Sometimes in my nightmares I was using the hot wire and listening to it sizzle on the skin of a captive. Sometimes it was applied to me and I screamed myself awake. Valerie couldn't sleep through that. I sat up against the headboard, breathing deeply, looking at Val in the green glow of an alarm clock by the bed. Propped on her elbow, using her pillow for balance, her long maroon tee shirt twisted on her body, she looked at me with concern, waiting for me to settle down and tell her, if I could, what the hell had made me scream.

"We'll talk in the morning," I always said, but we never did, and she didn't push. I don't know if she was afraid of what she would learn or wanted to keep me at arm's length until I had it more together.

I am telling you more of the truth. I am practicing being honest, like I said. When I wrote the memoir, I was just learning to do that. That's true of all memoirs. It's not that we want to lie, but we don't want to tell you what we'd overhear if we told the truth. Do you remember those sixteen flashlights I mentioned in my memoir? I said they belonged to someone else, but I want you to know: while the sixteen did belong to a guy named Jim, another six belonged to me. I hid them in Valerie's apartment like an alcoholic hides a bottle and I acted just as guilty or ashamed when she found one and asked why I had it. Because it makes me feel a bit better, I explained without explaining. The same excuse an addict has. It makes me feel momentarily a little bit better. It makes the darkness bearable to know I can turn on a light. I never said, so I can crawl into the living room, pistol in hand, and if someone is there, shoot.

I didn't want to frighten her. I didn't want her to think I couldn't protect her. I didn't want her even to think of needing to be protected. I didn't want my former life to impinge in any way, an absurd thing to want, right? As if that was possible. I sketched out the work I had done in big bold strokes, telling her almost nothing at first, then very little. I wished my former life would disappear. It wasn't a question of forgetting. I wish it was. The question was, how do I manage my life now when I was so bent out of shape? I teetered this way and that like a drunk; I reached for something to hold; I didn't want to tilt until I toppled.

A trans friend told that he thought, once the surgery was done, he would be a woman and somehow his memories of being a man would vanish. His memories would become a woman's. But he had been a man all his life and had to build life as a woman a day at a time. I had to do something similar.

I was afraid, obviously, of how deeply I needed Val. The more I refused to tell her that, the more intensely I felt it. I couldn't have been fooling her. It was like trying not to fart. You may keep it in, but you twitch a lot and walk funny. If I voiced my fears aloud, it would mean I wasn't in control of my life, this new phase of my life, which of course was true. I wasn't in control. I was skidding on black ice and hoping the tires would find a purchase.

I approached these issues obliquely.

"Are you happy with how we are? The way it is?" I would say suddenly.

She might be lying with her head in my lap while I gently massaged the nape of her neck. It almost hypnotized her, that. She might open her eyes and see me looking down and wonder what I was talking about.

"You don't mean the way you're massaging my neck, do you?"

"No," I said.

I could feel her whole body shrug. "You're doing it just right."

I couldn't make it a joke.

"I mean—you know, all this."

She gave it a little thought.

"I guess I am. I think I am. I believe I am. Why?" she twisted into a different position, leaning on her elbow so she could turn her face to look into mine. "Are you trying to say you aren't?"

"No," I said, maybe a little quickly. "No, no no, not at all. I enjoy it, Val, I enjoy you, being with you. It's working out for me, I think."

"When do you think you'll know? Do you want to set a clock?"

I laughed. "No," I said. "The truth is, if this is a dream, I want to stay asleep."

She turned and nestled down again, available again. Composed herself with a smile.

"Don't trouble trouble, my mother used to say."

"OK," I said, my fingers again caressing the back of her head and mussing her hair and gently touching her cheek softly which felt like security to her; she once said her dad used to do that when she was upset; it made her purr. I imagined her face between his hands as he dried her tears and reassured her of his love. "Okay then, I won't trouble trouble. Although—"

"Although what?"

"When you're the age I am now, I'll be an old man. You'll probably be my caretaker."

She just wanted to be massaged. "Let's deal with it then, OK? Give it fifteen or twenty years, then bring it up. Use a little more pressure on my neck. Then you can do my feet. It's been a very long day."

I said, "OK." What I wanted to say, I couldn't. I didn't want to ask questions if the answers weren't what I wanted to hear.

So every attempt to discharge my anxiety only made me more anxious.

Valerie snuggled down a little more, which meant, enough talk. Get on with it, Nick.

She loved to be touched, and I loved touching her. It grounded me even more than her. Penny was not like that, she started to twitch uncomfortably after a while, especially if I kept touching the same place, and she would shrink back. She preferred to touch others than be the touchee. Responding to massage, Val made little noises that I loved, but not the ones that Penny made when we had sex. Val's were more of a purring that made me purr too. It was like two people saying OMMMM at the same time. We synchronized our movements, our murmurings, our momentary happiness.

When I think of Val, I hear that sound. When I remember Penny's voice it's like a crown of thorns.

Does that sound like I'm a victim or a martyr? Well I was. A whistle blower is crucified on the truth, An intelligence professional too is a martyr for the IC but in a different way. It's an occupational hazard, implicit in the work. Don't tell, don't trust, don't feel. And because we didn't tell the truth to one another either, it was a circle jerk that never reached a climax. Like Buddhist monks lighting a match, we lived lives of self-immolation but we incinerated slowly. We smoldered for years before we ignited.

I had to balance my desire to talk with Val's ability to tolerate my monologues. Without meaningful work, rejected by former colleagues, with empty days once the interrogations stopped and appearances at court were over—without all that, I was on my own. I had not known how deeply the streets I paced as if I owned them had filled my life with purpose. I hadn't figured out that intelligence had its own mythology: a battle at the end of time between the forces of darkness and the keepers of the light. We were of course the keepers of the light, regardless of who was the enemy of the moment and who was the temporary partner. We needed to believe our beliefs.

We defended civilization by doing the most uncivilized things. We degraded the bonds of civil society to save civil society.

Do you see why, after our "service," as in "thank you for your service" said in passing to a paraplegic with a hat on a mat on the sidewalk begging for coins, we had to find ways to stave off depression, cope with PTSD? How could depression not be inevitable, knowing what we knew? Doing what we did? After such knowledge, what forgiveness?

McNamara sank under the dead weight of the blood he had shed—for no purpose, he concluded. "We were wrong" was all he could say. McNamara was a mirror into which we all looked. Viet

Nam was wrong. Iraq was wrong. Afghanistan was wrong.

Torturing innocent people to death was wrong, wrong, wrong.

In one of our conversations, Bill Webb said clergy had rather different challenges but they seemed equally significant, as everybody's troubles do. The ardor to be healers, shamans, seers, weakened over time, and the real work wore them down, eroding the ideals that brought them into the low-paying trade. After years of dealing with the bullshit, defending themselves from the three per cent of any congregation who were batshit crazy, that made all the noise and complained about everything, Bill said that practically every one of his colleagues in middle age was in therapy for depression. Holiday time is an example, he said. It may sound trivial to you but it builds resentment over time. Most can't afford the vacations congregants take at holidays, he said, and we have to be there for all the depressed people. After Thanksgiving it's a death march for so many folks. January's a relief. It's family time for others but we work overtime, doing extra services for the widows who need to distract themselves from loneliness and grief. The rest are off to Cancun. How many years can you do that and ignore how it feels? You're a sacrificial lamb, you're a Christian on behalf of those who pay you to carry the load, a professional Christian if you will. They get to be normal. We get to pretend.

I went to Bill for counseling, I guess, but he shared more and more resentments as we traded roles. Sometimes I did the talking and sometimes he did the talking. I guess clergy don't have a lot of real friends, and they can't trust competing clerics. They're a very competitive bunch, Bill said. And parishioners want to be friends with "the priest," the symbolic persona to which they relate, not the human being behind the curtain.

"The four horsemen of middle age," I said. "Depression, cynicism, bitterness, despair."

He wasn't listening. When he worked up a head of steam about his unhappiness, he was hard to deflect, to nudge back into the mode of a counsellor. "See, eighty per cent of the parishes are small, low-budget outposts just getting by with handouts from the diocese. If they have an endowment from bequests, it's a mixed blessing; they're like trust fund babies, insulated from the market. They don't have to get creative, they just add staff."

He shook his head.

"I'm not kidding, Nick. I can't think of a single colleague in middle age who isn't dealing with what this work does to you. No wonder they have affairs or act out some other way. I think they want to get out of the job but don't know how else to do it. Their self-esteem is on the floor. They can't see how else to make a living or they're risk-averse after so many years, after assimilation into the culture that numbs them to their real needs."

He stopped and looked at my expression.

"OK," he said."OK, sorry. Sorry I went off like that. But that's what the job does to you. Does it sound crazy?"

"No," I said. "It sounds like life."

"Clergy talk about this stuff among themselves. We have to, when we go on retreats, so we can get it up for the next Sunday."

"Bill, you need a vacation. Or a nap. Or to change jobs."

He shifted in his chair, saying thanks for the great advice with his irritated posture. He wasn't ready to do any of that, but the clock was obviously ticking.

I just listened, most of the time. I was neutral. I wasn't even an Episcopalian, I just came with Val for reasons you know, and I had sought him out for a conversation, thinking it might help to talk to an impartial person who seemed like a decent guy, but over time our roles became blurred and he began using me the way I used him. I was willing to accept that as long as I got what I needed too.

I needed to explore a new life proactively. I learn what I think by hearing what I say, so it seemed like a good idea. My anomalous status served him as well.

So Bill helped me move along but my main support came from my new posse, my fellow whistleblowers. I built relationships with them the way I recruited agents, not too fast not too slow, steady as she goes. I understood why they were skittish. When your head has been inside a metal container and your tormenter bangs on it and you can't take it off and screaming only makes it worse ... the slightest ringing, signaling more blows, is terrifying. A new applicant for membership in the group can be that kind of clanging, just by showing up. Or he may be a double agent and has to be vetted. It took time but after a while, I was invited by Dan, the dean of the group, to their weekly meetings at the Barbican on Friday afternoons.

We came together in one time and one place from multiple times and places scattered throughout spacetime. We arrived via what I call portals.

Let me explain.

People who have entered UFOs often say they are amazed at how the craft looks from the outside like it's thirty feet across but when they go in, they find one room opening onto another, and another, on and on in some kind of hyperspace. It is not only a vehicle, it seems, but a portal. It somehow distorts spacetime in a way we can't understand. Nor can we say if it's "out there" in the so-called external world or "in here" in consciousness altered in the moment. That ambiguity holds too for "strangeness," our name for the way normalcy disappears and one finds oneself in—a bell jar? a Klein bottle? a spacetime bubble? We don't know. We just know that it happens. Other cars on the road disappear, the sounds of birds and animals stop. There is no one but you ... and "it." When the encounter is over, the craft departs and normalcy returns. You slide into human reality again.

I'll tell you in *Mobius Out of Time* what I learned about all that. We've known those things were real for decades, and we knew as von Braun said, the technology, the sheer power of the visitors, betrayed a superiority far greater than we first thought. A four-star general said at the Pentagon when someone expressed doubt about the facts of the matter, thinking the government evinced no interest, "Do you think we would ignore something like this?" I mention it here because a spacetime portal like we find inside those ships is a good analogy for how narrative works, this narrative and all narratives, any of 'em and all of 'em as Palin said. (And the digression into UFOs is itself a portal to the third book in the Mobius trilogy. Clever, eh?)

We live inside our languages and language creates a field of consciousness. We build (metaphorically speaking) artificial rooms, cognitive structures that make up our shared virtual world. It's like an online game without computers. Our semisynthetic world, like that unearthly vehicle, consists of rooms that open, one from another, in the consciousness we share. Our narratives snap into one another's like a child's plastic snap-lock beads until they form what we call "reality," and the links are portals, don't you see, what I call portals, made of words. But once you move through a portal, the portal dissolves into your experience like stirring salt into water, unified into how you think about things and who you think you are. The meaning of the experience dissolves into ... you. A sense of yourself.

Think about what you're doing now: The meaning of the words you are reading flow into the meanings of following words and you transit seamlessly from one to another. You move through a portal from one cognitive artifact to another, making meaning as you do. Our media mediate everything. They mediate meaning. We inhabit evolving noetic worlds that are constantly changing.

Narrative is an outward and visible expression of our collective consciousness. When we use words, they fuse into a unified flow. We intuitively apprehend the meanings they make. We may be wrong, but we wouldn't know it, because the meaning we make is the world in which we live. Then we think about "things," we can think about the universe, which may be consciousness as well and nothing but, finite but unbounded. A meta sort of thing.

Consciousness enables us to think about consciousness.

OK, then! So let's say there's a law firm in DC on Tenth Street not far from the FBI headquarters just off Pennsylvania and some of the "blowers" come from there. That firm handles a lot of our cases. The Barbican is where that portal leads and others come from all over time and space or spacetime as we call it now. The physical Barbican was and still is on the north side of Chicago, northwest of the loop, on Milwaukee Avenue, not far from the Matchbox Bar, if my memory serves me correctly. It's easy to find on Google Maps unless one of the agencies changed what you see. The rooms in DC or where other blowers happen to be open onto and flow into the Barbican like the rooms inside that hypothetical alien craft, which is by the way a cool dim space by all accounts with indirect lighting and sometimes pungent smells like sulfur. The atmosphere is not the oxygenated mix we take for granted here on earth. Life-sustaining energy apparently derives from many sources. Green plants on our planet gave us air to breathe. Oxygen was poison at first, but we got to like it. Some forms of life thrive on not oxygen but sulfur. Some use other means to bootstrap themselves into intelligent sentience. Sentience doesn't care a fig as long as it can find a way. It evolves, it uses what it finds and builds complex structures with apertures through which it sees what it calls the "external world." It turns the "internal world" into an "external world" so we can look at and think about our selves. The universe is a nursery for different kinds of awareness, I guess. The cosmos apparently tolerates all sorts of creatures who with greater and greater complexity, get better at looking inside themselves and looking out as well. Others got there long before we climbed out of the slime. No wonder they do what seems like magic.

I learned to build portals when I was a spy. One job of a spy is to construct meaning out of truths, half-truths, and lies. I had to know how someone thought so I could build a path from what they thought to another way of thinking, the one I intended to impose. I had to move them (to extend the metaphor) from what appears to be one room into what seems to be another room. My work often consisted of moving someone from one mental construction to another without them noticing. Sleight of hand, in a way, but really sleight of mind. I had to see the destination while hiding it from them the way a magician hides a prop. We might seem to be having a simple conversation but if I did it right, it was designed so they walked forward as I backed up with their hands in mine and led them into a U-turn so they were going a different direction while they thought they were still moving straight ahead.

I had to understand that the imaginary rooms we inhabit are not permanent and are built by agreement or consensus. They are made of words and my primary weapons when I wanted to manipulate them were amiable conversations. They are verbal constructions like sand castles waiting for high tide. The elements of which we are made come from exploding stars blasting out heavier and heavier elements. Ashes to ashes, dust to dust. Then it goes around and comes around, recycled into seemingly solid structures. We call it matter, but matter is energy transformed by information into that transitory "solid" stuff our fingertips and eyes have learned to read and touch and transmit to our brains. Nothing stays still, not for a moment. The universe never rests and the dance never stops. You can't step in the same universe twice. The "you" that tries to do that dance is moving too. It's all a-flowing, rivers circling around to their sources like a snake biting its own tail in a dream of a benzene ring.

By the way, I referred to a UFO as a "craft," or a "ship" but that's not entirely accurate. The word "UFO" is a place-holder, a label we use as we try to get a clue to how it works. It's not a flying vehicle as we think of it—a physical object that moves on aerodynamic principles—because it doesn't "fly" in air. It seems to move from one vector in spacetime to another, with equal facility in water, air, or "outer space." It short-circuits gravity itself. We don't know what makes them go. We can't figure it out. We're trying, believe me, because whoever gets it right will own the earth and a lot more besides. We don't know how the beings inside can take those Gs and not turn into slime. Calling what they do "technology" disguises our ignorance. It's transmutational magical know-how, that's what it is, or seems to be. We'll get there, you can bet, but not quite yet. When we do, then we can call it "technology."

Still, we have to make sense of things. When I watch how my conscious mind uses meaningful words and connects them to one another, I think "portal" is a good enough metaphor for the bigger things I build. You, reader, use portals all the time and never give it a thought, because the transition is seamless. So blowers from DC and elsewhere and elsewhen flow into the back room of a bar in Chicago. The Barbican is a safe place that feeds our need to be together. By intention and design, I turn it into a fictional place we inhabit by agreement in our shared extended mind. As you are inhabiting it now.

"See Spot run." Remember that? Then you saw Spot. You saw Spot run.

In the same way, please see the tables and chairs in the bar, randomly scattered, with menus in metal holders and ketchup and condiments and stains on most of the tables. See the colorful bottles behind the bar. Hear the laughter and conversation of us blowers in that back room ...

Alan Moore is right. Writing is indistinguishable from magic, genius from being real.

Welcome to my world. Welcome to the Barbican.

When I joined the meetings in the back room of the Barbican, I learned that whistle blowers had a strong tribal identity. We all faced the challenge of how to live, what to do next, in a way that was somehow aligned with what had become the defining acts of our lives. We told the truth, and there was no going back. A lot of us say, had I only known, I would have gone another way. But way leads on to way, as the man said, and we can't go back.

We do not try to define who we are with a label. That would falsify the complexity and diversity of our clan. People had done all kinds of things that were and were not legally defined as whistle blowing. We all had different stories, different motivations, different outcomes. Some got a lot of money in a settlement and some lost everything. Everyone had chosen to take a stand against the institutionalized behaviors that we could no longer endure. We had to act. We were either, once we made our moves, heroes or traitors, depending on your POV. We shared the conviction that the organizations in which we had worked (often happily for many years) had the morals of a squid or, really, no morals at all, nothing but self interest. We had to kind of fudge the fact that we must have known it all along. Organizations and institutions by their very nature are amoral. We fought that fact. We used words like unethical, immoral, and evil. Every time we did, we niched ourselves on the other side of the way people do things as a rule. We weren't naive, we never thought that outing illegal or immoral acts would change the game. (OK, maybe some did, at least a little). The game of life is built on staying steady as she goes. The one thing that might make a difference was hitting them where it mattered, diminishing cash flow, damaging their reputations with clients and customers. Outing them alone was a booby prize. They acknowledge wrongs, accept responsibility by saying the right words, and change nothing. That's why they did their damndest to render our witness moot and call us losers, lamers, and worse. But we had no choice: once conscience kicked in, we lowered our lances and charged the windmills of the world. We were the only sane people in an insane world. Retribution, punishment, jail terms, threats to ourselves and our families—we had to endure it all.

Blowing the whistle was not a good way to make money as a rule. Our standard of living often took a big hit. When I returned to the Midwest, all I could afford was a one bedroom flat in an old walk-up. Valerie's place was similar but a bit bigger. I had never lived in a place with such thin walls, surrounded by people who were often half-crazy by any definition. I heard footsteps above me and conversations through the walls, normal talking, not fights, as if we were in the same room. The chatter was often inane and, if you expected more of the human race, disappointing. Upstairs an oddball by the name of Peter Jalk liked to dance, apparently, at all hours. Was he practicing for a contest? Trying to drive me nuts? His stomping started at six a.m. I wrangled a move to a nearby apartment when Susan and Mary Lee, a pleasant lesbian couple, had a child and had to move to bigger digs, but it didn't help. I still heard cars roaring in the street below, dogs barking, sirens wailing, and teenagers yelling at all hours. I had a hard time getting to sleep and was often awakened by garbage trucks dumping trash as loudly as they could. I stood at the window helplessly watching the uniformed men go through the routine. They cranked a lever that lifted big metal bins and dumped them with a clatter of bottles and cans into the trough at the back of the truck. When they had wrung out every noise they could from that operation, they dropped the bin back onto the pavement with a bang.

But the noise was not the worst of it. The worst of it was boredom.

You don't choose the life of a spy because you want to be bored.

You want to be in the streets, not at a desk. You want to recruit and run agents, you want to devise strategies, you want to engage in special ops. To be sent to a desk was punishment like standing in a corner in sixth grade. The interrogations to which I was subjected when they decided I must have committed other misdeeds were not fun but I missed them when they ended, because they were definitely not boring. They required parry and thrust, duck and weave, every single moment, and the slightest mistake could put me in jail like Manning or if I fled, into exile like Snowden or Assange. The stimulating game that I had played for my whole adult life came crashing down. My life became quiet, very quiet. I felt like I was suffocating.

Enduring boredom is worse than enduring pain. Give someone a choice between routine beatings and solitude, they'd rather be beaten. They won't exactly like it when they attach the electrodes, but they learn to save energy for taking the jolts and it breaks up the day. Their tormenters might even say a word or two. An adrenalin rush is triggered by footsteps in the corridor, the turn of the key in the lock, a promise of contact. Hard to believe, but taken down the hall from your cell to be tortured is preferable to isolation. Solitary confinement shrivels the soul. That's why it's torture. We need stimulation, variety, other human beings. We need meaning in our lives. In isolation tanks, we hallucinate in a few hours. In solitary confinement, we do something similar. We paint the blank walls of our cell with fantasies. If we can't get it from outside, our brains will make it up. We are all like Banksy in the silence of our minds. We tag the blank spaces of the landscape without trying.

The publicity I received died down pretty quickly. Once the major media covered "rendition"—our newspeak word for torture cells in dozens of countries—once we learned that we had become a torturous society—I was a footnote. Had I waited before calling foul, the facts that were a big deal when I revealed them had become mundane. The extent of the torture network, our medieval methods, the accidental deaths of innocent victims, the changes in the law to make it all acceptable, bothered only liberals and a few grieving families. Features about rendition on TV became so ho-hum that ratings fell as habituation set in. What's on television? Just more torture stories, hon. Torture torture, yada yada. Isn't there a football game?

We were frogs in boiling water. Nothing we did changed the game.

I couldn't control any of that. My focus was simpler: I needed a viable life. Valerie mattered—she mattered a lot—but after six months she was just what was so about my life, I loved her but we both needed more than each other. I needed to give my life meaning and purpose. Her quest for community through churches was all fine and good, but not enough.

Meeting others like myself and acceptance into their circles was a first step but after the initial novelty wore off, sitting around and telling each other how special we were, our contempt for hypocrites who spoke patriotism as a first language, got old. I got twitchy during our long booze-fueled conversations. We replaced the circle jerk in the agencies with a whistle blower circle jerk in the back of our favorite bar.

Then Nat Herman died.

Our destiny comes to us in strange ways: His death raised questions that gave purpose to my life. Who were these people at Syntactic? Did they do, as they claimed, everything they could to prevent deaths? My cursory look into their activities suggested that they knew the risks of the implant that killed Nat and other devices that harmed or killed others. It sounded like their energies went into circumventing oversight or pretending to work with regulators. Their only real focus seemed to be cash flow and quarterly earnings. The history of their insulin pumps read like a plot to eliminate diabetics from the world. In public statements they sounded like

Perdue or Martin Shkreli or Elizabeth Holmes. It seemed like there was no accountability. Where were the regulators? Where was the media? Where was the outrage?

Nat was only one victim, but he was the one that mattered. A thousand can die but if one is your friend, you grieve. Nat was a colleague, friend and partner. That made it personal. I didn't know what I could do but I had to do something. I called his widow Miriam and asked if I could come out to the house. She said yes, Nick, of course. We made an appointment and I put it into my calendar (there was plenty of room).

It felt like more than an obligation. It felt like a real purpose, the way I used to feel about fighting our enemies. It felt like aiming an arrow at a target. Zen and the Art of Archery. Place the arrow in the bow and let it shoot itself.

Besides, like I say, I was bored to tears. I didn't have anything else to do.

Chapter 10
Making a List, Checking It Twice

W hile I researched the world of Syntactic and got to know some blowers, I let Val lead our search for a community.

We were looking for a place to meet some new people and create a larger context for ourselves, is what we thought it was about. We found out later there was more.

Meanwhile, there were lots of stops before we found St. Sisyphus.

One fine morning Val was looking with pleasure at her brand new iPad pro. She bought a leather case with a bright abstract pattern which made it a bit heavier but it stood up more securely. It was softer to the touch as well, and she gazed on it fondly as if it were a pet. She hadn't named it yet but that would likely happen soon.

She had listed every church within reach and added sects like LDS, Quakers, Witnesses, The Way, Moonies, Christian Scientists, and after a bit of reflection, she tapped the mic and said, "Unitarians."

"They're a sect?" I asked.

Val shrugged. "In a way. They're certainly not mainstream. They're not crazies like Witnesses or Moonies. They give the faithful lots of room. That's how Sally described it. There aren't penalties for anything like you're damned if you screw up. They don't insist that you bend the knee, as they said in *Game of Thrones*, they don't destroy families. They don't blackmail like the scientologists, once they get your secrets." She considered her decision. "You don't think they belong in the list?"

I shrugged. "No. But I'd get rid of those others, OK? This search is challenge enough without adding known pathologies."

She deleted all of the sects. "I think that's sane. Sally's sister Birdie became a Witness when someone knocked on her door when she was really depressed. They were a lifeline. Birdie raised her kid with bible verses and a belting for every minor offense but when her son came back from college, he said he didn't believe anymore. They told her to shun him. 'Never speak to him again.' The only supports she had were the Witnesses and her son. She had a nervous breakdown. Incomprehensible, right?"

"Almost, if you don't know humans."

She looked with satisfaction at the screen which now had just one name. "That does make it easier. ... Sally said Unitarians are pretty inoffensive. She called them Laodiceans. I googled it. They don't blow hot or cold. I guess that means they have no standards and few criteria, no creeds to repeat to get the card. It means, I think, wishy-washy, very."

"How do you get in, then?"

"You show up and raise your hand. 'Here I am.' Like a game on the playground except everyone gets picked."

"It sounds like a choose-your-own-adventure thing."

"Sally said they throw out most doctrine but still believe in one God. They ditch the frills."

"How does she know all this?"

"She attended one with her partner Hank before they split."

"Hank who works for the city? The 'sanitation engineer?' They split?"

"Yeah. She liked him, but he wanted an open relationship, and she didn't."

"Hank rode a garbage truck, right? That was a city job. He had to have known someone to get it."

"He grew up, I think, with Bill Mahon, who got him the job. Sally said when they were kids, they went shoplifting together. Hank got arrested, Billy never did, he was always blocks away. But that was back when you signed a confession and walked. Nobody went to jail. Hank had to swear he would never go to Wieboldt's again. He didn't, either. Yeah, he knew those guys. I think he played poker with Al Sanchez, too."

"I remember him. He helped out his friends, is all he did, right? But they put him in jail. He wasn't very careful."

"Hank liked working downtown. Businesses pay them extra to take things they'd have to pay scavengers to remove. It's tax-free tips."

"Is that how he met women? Taking a twenty to remove a couch?"

"He met them every way he could. Sally said it was like going from stool to stool in a bar, asking if someone wanted to fuck. He ignored the no's, like a salesman, never took it personal, and always went home with someone."

"And she put up with that?"

"She didn't know until she did. Maybe she didn't want to know, until she couldn't deny it any more. Hank wasn't bad looking. Sally liked his Italian looks, and his stories were pretty interesting. He could have had a reality show, "Digging in the Dirt," or something. He had a cabin on Bluegill Lake. A nice view of the water, the cry of loons, no neighbors. A good place for a tryst.'"

"You went there?"

"A few times. Sally invited me and a guy I was dating then for weekends. It was nice. There were three bars in town where Hank went hunting, so to speak. Sally surprised him when she was supposed to be back in the city working. That was that. He confessed everything. He didn't care. The babes in the bars were easy, he said. He was proud of his conquests, as if he earned a merit badge. He had been lying all the time they were together. I don't think he had much of a conscience. "

"Lying is bad."

"Well, duh. Yes it is. But ... you had to lie sometimes, didn't you, for your work?"

"Sometimes, yes, but we didn't think of it as lying. We thought of words as tools to open a door or safe. Except the doors were people's lives."

Valerie looked thoughtful. Time to change the subject.

"So Hank was a Unitarian?" I said. "That's a surprise."

"He had been raised Catholic but he went to different churches to meet women. They discussed it all, once the relationship was dead."

"And they're still friends?"

"They're not best buds or anything, but they stay in touch. She says she's detached. She doesn't have to sleep with him to meet now and then for a drink. She says his stories are interesting."

"She didn't write him off? Because of the lies?"

"No. She didn't ditch him." She looked at me. "Why? Why do you say it like that?"

She was so damned intuitive.

I shrugged. "I had a friend who couldn't handle what I did in my work. It didn't end well."

She moved closer and looked into my eyes. "Promise me, Nick?"

I knew what she meant. "I won't lie to you, Val. If I did, it would be to protect you."

"Protect me? From what?"

"I don't know. What people do ... "

"Like ...what? What are we talking about?"

I squeezed her hand. It may have been condescending but it was all I had. "It's getting late." It was Sunday morning; we had said we would pick one and get going and it was after nine, "I'm good with Unitarians. Is that your pick?"

"Sure. Let me get a sweater. It may be chilly in there."

"Wear the blue one," I smiled. "I love that color on you. "

So Valerie in the blue sweater with the dark applique and me in new black church-shopping slacks and a clean white shirt began our trip through God-town.

We found ourselves outside a Gothic stone building that looked just like a Christian church. The bulletin or program they gave us when we entered listed the coming attractions. It was a smorgasbord of traditions, a different one each week.

The week we attended, there was Native American dancing. After a welcome and some words, we sang a song about birds and trees and had just finished the sixth verse when behind us we heard loud drumming and a troupe of Native Americans came down the center aisle. People in back jumped up and danced along behind them, and the line grew longer and longer, and we got up and joined the grinning liberals indulging their inner "Indian". We danced with a stutter step, coming down on our soles flat as if we were stalking an animal. That's what we recalled from movies made in the fifties. The performers chanted wailing tones that sounded authentic, but how would we know? Everything we knew had come from Westerns. How in fact would the lawyers, teachers, therapists, the aging professionals dancing down the aisle and around the pews in a figure eight and back again—how would any of them know? The fables and myths that religions mix with a few historical facts don't have to be accurate, they just have to be coherent. They have to go ... *snap!* They have to work well enough to let people weave their own stories into the larger narrative. Then, one day—bingo! "It's something you have to feel," a person says, and that ends the argument, "I belong to something that gives meaning to my life. I won't be anxious or afraid any more."

When we finished dancing or prancing, pick one, we all clapped and returned to our pews and the pastor, a professorial type with a well-trimmed beard and whitening hair, held forth on what we descendants of white Europeans had done to destroy the culture of the people who just led us in dance. People in the pews squirmed with guilt and when they passed the plate, the effectiveness of the strategy was obvious. Large bills topped the pile. We pretended not to look at what neighbors gave, but everybody peeked. How else can peer pressure work? I hid a couple of ones below the twenties. It was a pretty big pile. I wondered if the church kept it or split it with the tribe.

The Unitarian pastor, the Rev. Carl Sundley, announced that the next Sunday, weather permitting, we would walk through a maze in the parking lot. The Critical Thinkers Club would set it up. He explained that walking through a maze while thinking about walking through a maze had real spiritual benefit. He said quite a bit about that, but the bottom line was, life is like a maze, and the challenge is, find your way to the center. On top of which, the soul is like a maze, and—same deal—find your way to the center. If, he said with a chuckle, you believe there is a center. If, he laughed again, you believe there is a soul.

If, shouted someone, you believe there is a maze, and everybody laughed.

The following week, he said, they would enjoy a Quaker fellowship—tough to do with a pastor who loved to talk. (Everybody chuckled). They would sit silently unless someone was moved to speak. The Spirit would knit them into one as they sat in dutiful silence. The pastor would call time like a proctor at an exam and then they would discuss the experience in groups. Each group would choose a recorder who would write what they said on large sheets of newsprint. Then they would hang the paper on the walls with masking tape and each group leader would read the remarks. These they would discuss among themselves.

Their program felt to me like a restaurant serving tiny squares of designer food that revealed when unpeeled a piece of beef or a bit of fish or a new kind of vegetable.

They sang hymns between the spoken words. I don't remember any of the words, but that's not unusual. I noticed that none of the hymns mentioned "God" and asked the pastor about that when we left. He said, "Yes, well, that's right, we're an inclusive community and we don't want to offend the atheists in our congregation. We celebrate the universe, nature, stars and galaxies, everything, and leave it to you to pick what works for you. Ditto for beliefs."

We chatted over coffee and slices of home-made zucchini bread or scones cut into pieces, some with more icing because of uneven cuts. The people seemed pleasant enough. I said to Val afterward, they seemed like a nice harmless middle-class pretty well educated bunch of liberal urban folks who wanted something like a church.

"I agree," Val said. "We'll put them on the maybe list. Let's do a Lutheran one next. There's lots of those around."

The one she picked randomly was unfortunately a bad choice. It's like getting food poisoning from potato salad left too long in the sun. Every time you see it, your stomach burps a reminder. That's what happened after we went to the Church of the Good Shepherd.

The pastor was a very angry guy. He told the flock the rules for life based on his reading of doctrine. There were an awful lot of ways to sin, many the stuff of common life. That had to result in a lot of guilt. He was harsh and judgmental. If you didn't slink away with shame, you just weren't listening. Sitting there, squeezed between people preventing an easy exit, wanting to get up before he was finished and make your way along tight bodies, stepping on feet—excuse me, sorry, excuse me, thanks—and out the back quietly is what I suggested but Val said no, wait it out.

His words from the pulpit felt like he was scraping your face with steel wool.

Forty long minutes of doctrinal exposition. Every time I was sure he had finished, he veered off in another direction. He did that twice. We squirmed with impatience. Val could as a rule wait out anyone but I saw her fingers drumming on her thigh. Afterward one of the elderly ladies—there were quite a few—told us how lucky they were to have such a brilliant man. He had multiple degrees and had written two books. One was doctrinal and not suited to their book club because it was over five hundred pages and the other was about Luther and the Jews and it was clear from what she said that he was on Luther's side. In "The Jews and their Lies," their founder had suggested that the faithful set synagogues on fire, burn Jew homes, take their money and expel them. And maybe, Luther added, as they leave town, you can kill a bunch.

"Cross it off," Val said, not even needing to hear my vote.

We went to brunch in a snarly mood.

"This quest is not a trivial undertaking," I said, smearing plenty of butter on my pancakes and pouring on syrup. "Let's get rid of the grinners. Cross off Osteen clones."

"Is that the guy who says if you give him money, God will bless you and stuff?"

"That's the guy. Flunked out of ministry school so he invented his own brand. He's worth about fifty million bucks, the church has a private jet and paid for his ten million dollar house, and—"

"Enough."

I smiled. The pancakes boosted my mood and I loved how Valerie looked in that sweater. She told me the color was periwinkle blue.

Valerie tapped her Ipad and clicked off all of the rigidly righteous. "That's half the list."

"It was too big anyway."

She sighed. "I'm not sure how well this is working."

"Well, I'm still game. Lets try a plain vanilla place."

"Like Congregational, UCC, something like that?"

She picked one called Plymouth. We hit it the next week. It was led by a female pastor who had a great smile and greeted us warmly. She said the words well and people sang more words and then came a sermon. I expected a listenable bit of common sense, maybe with a feminist bent, but she had something else in mind. She went from one stained glass window to the next and told us what was on each one. She told us who had paid for each, like, here is the Ostaad window. Carl Henry Ostaad was a founder of the congregation, and his window is about Lazarus in memory of his child Melissa who died when she was six. Look closely at Lazarus' face—is he puzzled? Elated? Both? What do you think? Let's have a show of hands. Who thinks he was puzzled? Come closer if you can't see. Who thinks he was elated?

A wave of worshippers from the right side of the aisle surged toward the center. If we had been on a boat we would have tipped. I couldn't see his expression so I didn't vote. Some voted for 'both,' but "elated" won by three votes.

Valerie was being worn down. "You have to be in fourth grade to listen to that."

Were we asking too much? We just wanted to hang out with interesting people and have intelligent conversations. Our bar was low: we thought we might over time make friends serving soup for the homeless or packing food at a pantry. It seemed simple enough when we designed our plan.

Week after week, we plied our weary way from one disappointment to another. We walked out on sermons that condemned gays or women, Jews or Moslems, "progressives" and blacks. Most did it subtly, implicitly, but some were outspoken in their disregard for other human beings. Our list grew smaller and smaller.

"This isn't much fun, is it?" Val said. "How did religions get like this?"

"Once Jesus was dead. he was useful as a symbol. They could say he meant whatever they said. He would puke at what they say in his name."

Val reached to take my hand. "I feel guilty for starting us off on this road. I know it's hard for you—everything is hard right now, looking for work, trying to build a new life. Even adjusting to living together." She smiled. "Right?"

"We both made the decision, We're all in. We'll find neutral territory."

"So what are we going to do?" She looked at the list. "I know we said we wouldn't, but ... wanna try a mega-church?"

"Why not? I could use a self-help lesson. I'm in the mood to bop to the rhythm of a modern six piece band with catchy tunes and good hooks. Let's go get love-bombed. Pick one with a nature name, River Falls or Eagle's Reach. Something with willow or elm in the name."

She handed me her iPad. "You pick."

So we went to Falcon Ridge Church, high on a bluff above a bay in a north shore suburb. The church looked down on the town with its day spas, boba shops, boutiques, taverns and cafes. Colorful umbrellas were open, shading outdoor tables where no one sat because it was too cool. As we parked, I saw in the distance a hawk circling over the highway, looking for mice. The breeze made it chilly.

"Time to take the umbrellas down."

"And install the outdoor heaters."

The satellite church was straight from the recipe book, a mega-church for a mega-niche. It appealed to affluent, conservative, satisfied Christians, a safely homogenous congregation offering comfort and safety, affirmation, certainty of doctrine, and lots of groups to join and things to do.

The Sunday morning circus was quite an event. Traffic backed up down the nearest highway to an exit from the interstate. Uniformed personnel were up on the roof with walkie talkies to direct parking. It was a long walk from your car to the door but you were smiling and happy to be there by the time you hit the door. You were part of something bigger into which you dissolved on the walk through the SUVs, BMWs, and Teslas. The streams of people coming from their cars were like recruits in a war, eager to be at the front. Greeters handed you a program, welcoming you with big smiles into a lobby with red carpeting curving to left and right, doors open into an auditorium, an usher at each door waiting to be helpful, kiosks with leaflets for classes and groups, books and videos for sale, and a mini-church downstairs for kids. One of the kiosks had tech support to show people how to download the church app.

Once you passed through the doors and saw the tiers and tiers of seats (wooden chairs with wine-dark cushions) rising toward the balconies that circled the main stage, the dais waiting for the pastor, the backdrop in flowers, you couldn't help but turn around and around as if you were a Packer fanatic in Lambeau Field for the first time. The immensity of the space hushed your very thoughts. There was a sweet piney scent of cleanliness, a high gloss shine, and the unmistakeable odor of financial success.

Val stood there, clutching her program, looking all around. Then she looked at me and said, "Well ... it is what it is. Let's sit toward the back."

The search for some kind of community only intensified how alone I felt. Valerie worked long hours and some weekends and I wasn't connected with anyone else. I hadn't lived in the city for years and forgot that when you cross the state line, your friendships and contacts do not travel with you. Your history disappears. My visits to the city had always been to see Penny. I was with her or alone.

It didn't help that I worked at home, if you can call it work. I continued to try in vain to find contacts from the past who might still speak to me. I pitched people who needed help but I wasn't a P.I., a Blackwater type, or any of the niches that former intelligence pros often fill. I didn't have credentials even for that. I gave those talks I told you about, for what that was worth. I was reaching out to other whistle blowers but it took time to earn their trust. Val engaged with people at work, all day every day, so when she got home, she was often tired, all she wanted was silence or me—or me being silent, best of all. I tried to be a non-anxious presence while she surfed her iPad or played digital games or watched videos, listening through her buds. I read and watched movies too, but I grew tired of a digital world uninhabited by flesh-and-blood people.

Most of my conversations the first months back happened in lines at the grocery store or waiting for a teller at the bank. I didn't need to see the teller, I could bank online, but I wanted to connect. A brief conversation making a deposit was, I am embarrassed to say, a good part of my social life. I was joyous when I had to return to the dentist for a filling and could chat with the young doctor.

And I was learning all the time. You never knew when you'd have a teachable moment. In Amsterdam, for example, I wanted to change some money and entered a branch of a bank. From the door a carpet led a long way to a teller's cage. I saw a woman behind steel bars at a distance. I walked the aisle to her cage.and she said, all serious and business, "Yes?" I said I wanted to change dollars into euros. "Did you take a number?" she asked. "A number? No." I turned around and looked down the aisle I had just traversed. "There's no one in the queue," I said. "You need to take a number," she said. So I walked all the way back to the door and took a number and returned to her cage. "Seven," she said. I handed her my chit. "Thank you," she said. "May I help you?"

After that, I understood the Dutch.

Val and I finally settled on St. Sisyphus but it took a long time to find it. I described our arrival there in Chapter Four, but we had been on a long journey before that happened. The churches began to seem like motels in Humbert Humbert's road trip. What began as fun and an adventure became cloying. I think one reason we finally chose St. Sisyphus was, we were worn down by the endless succession of churches that made claims of exclusivity, only one of which could be correct, if one was. I hated reciting creeds by rote that were written in archaic language. People said the most inane things once they were in a religious trance, things they would never say outside the "sacred space." Stonings from Leviticus, straight out of *The Handmaid's Tale*, were read with a straight face. When they left, people re-entered the modern world. They remembered that galactic clusters contained billions of galaxies teeming with life. Inside the cloistered walls, it seemed like we were the only planet that mattered and humans the only important species. God loved us alone and loved us best.

Regressing into an infantile state brought a sleepy kind of peace. Listening to the same stories over and over again was reassuring and stabilizing. It made the chaos of the world seem orderly, part of a plan that was never spelled out, because it was in the mind of God alone. Parishioners filed to the altar in a slow solemn cadence, waiting in line for a bit of bread like zombies at Vegas slots at four in the morning. It worked for those who came for solace, not for strength, for reassurance, not for challenge.

On top of all that, there was often bad singing, Sometimes a soprano solo sounded like the screel of nails-on-a-blackboard. I asked Bill Webb if he could damp it down and he said it wasn't worth it. The choir is where the counter-dependents go. They're the hostile opposition, led as a rule by an organist who resents not running the show and earning less than the rector. He added with a chuckle: the neurotics join the Altar Guild and the martyrs teach Sunday School. Counter dependents hide in the choir where they can snipe.

I laughed and asked, "And what types become clergy?"

"I'll save an answer to that," he said, "for another time."

We finally tried Episcopal churches because, Val said, her friend Sally, her go-to source for all things religious, said everyone seems to go there as a last resort or when they leave another denomination or a Lutheran marries a Catholic. Episcopalians, we learned, didn't care much about doctrinal conformity—some were loosey-goosey and others were more Catholic than Catholic. We preferred the former because they accepted ambiguity, complexity and mystery as part of life. If you couldn't find what you wanted in one Episcopal franchise or another, you wouldn't be happy anywhere. Older congregations often had endowments, too. Bill Webb told me everyone hated endowments, except those who had them. It relieved pressure on the pastor to generate cash from stoking the hearts of the herd.

On our second visit to Saint Sisyphus, Bill Webb was back. Before he preached, he explicitly said, some of you complain because I'm not a literalist and bring an educated brain to the biblical text. Well, friends, I'm guilty as charged. If we don't articulate beliefs in a way that's congruent with how we think about everything else, we're in Disneyland on the circus train. Authenticity becomes impossible. God gave us brains as well as hearts. Please do not check yours at the door. Use the tools we have to explore an ancient text and translate what we find into contemporary terms. Don't be afraid of what's real, because if it's real, it was made by God.

Val and I grinned at each other. It was such a relief to hear plain sane talk in a world we had thought had gone mad.

"The job is really quite simple," Bill explained in private. "Be reasonable, treat people with civility, and listen to them. Like a sales clerk, say, 'How may I help you?' And when they have what they want, say 'Thank you.' I call it 'paying the rent,' The rest of your time is yours. You can call anything you do 'ministry' and get support once people have what they need."

Listening to Bill Webb in his study was like sitting at the feet of Penn and Teller. Clergy were masters of sleight of hand on a level that rivaled the agencies. Many used ridicule as well. Their rejection of competition was vicious. They were all fighting for shelf space, selling the same cereal in a tough marketplace. Offering the right products—youth groups, pastoral care, tending to transitional needs like funerals and marriages—was the secret sauce. Otherwise they all sold the same thing and tried to use different names to brand their particular slant.

I met Bill Webb at the right time. Both of us wanted to talk to someone freely and learn who we had become while we were busy doing other things.

Time dilates and memories grow vivid or dim according to their significance. Memories have to connect to the current context of our lives or they're not remembered. If we're stressed, memories don't form well or form at all, and they're changed whenever retrieved. Most of history doesn't exist for most people. A historian recalls the names of Egyptian dynasties, a normal person knows only "Egypt" as a general catch-all term. In our spy work, we used what we knew of the formation of memories to fashion what people think actually happened. If we want something to be forgotten, creating a crisis at the time someone learns of it will prevent it from being encoded, which means in effect it never happened at all.

My dreams are filled with memories of friends I lost, missions that went well or were badly botched, good and bad decisions. Most memories, thank God, are consumed by the wildfires of time as they race through the dry brush of our lives. Ashes are all that's left. We pick through the debris. Here and there an object gleams in the sunlight. We pick it up, blow on it, turn it in our hands, then throw it down again. Our footprints in the ashes are all we leave behind like dinosaur tracks from millions of years ago. Eons hence, someone may glance down and see their outlines in the mud.

In my dreams I often revisit places that I loved. I hike in the rain in the Noosa Headlands and remember a coiled python hanging from a branch. I climb high into the hills and look down on Wineglass Bay in Tasmania, accompanied by a pretty-faced wallaby. Or I am eating coconut toast with lime curd at the Gumnut Cafe on the Rocks at Sydney Harbor, the shadows of leaves dancing over the patio as I read the Sydney Herald; commuter boats arrive at the dock and tourists line up to climb the bridge. Yet when I return to Sydney and thread my way through passageways to the courtyard where the Gumnut was, there's no cafe, only a bicycle shop. The cafe couldn't afford the rising rent. One more anchor vanishes. Our memories are like the Bladerunner photos, honestly, they're all we have but they're just props to keep us erect so we can walk on our own two feet.

I have been displaced from my own life. Rip van Winkle sleepily stirring in a world he never knew. The England in which I lived does not exist, not any more. On a visit I knocked on a door in Surrey and my old friends were still there but looked so old! I sit in their parlor and sip tea and Helen says they used to see the old people walking down the lane toward the High Street, but now she and Ian are the old people. Their daughter has daughters of her own and moved to Bournemouth long ago. The next time I am nearby I stop and knock again but a stranger opens the door. My friends sold their home after forty-five years and the stranger has no idea where they went. I will never see them again. Their long stay in that one place, an illusion of permanence, is known for what it is.

They never knew what I really did. Until the end, I didn't either.

I often dream I am on the beach in Bamburgh on a frosty morning with the castle high above me and the cries of seabirds in the air. My feet sink in the silted sand as I patrol the disorderly waters. I could swear I can feel the cold wind and when I wake up, I am in fact shivering, but from the chill in our apartment. The steam heat comes on at six and the landlord won't change his ways.

I fall back asleep and dream of climbing above Chamonix to the Mer du Glace. I hear the rumbling of boulders in the hidden stream below the blue ice but it's really the rumbling of dumping loads of trash. I wake to the real world. The truck is idling loudly below my window. People are waking up all over the neighborhood where I have moved to be with Val and I don't know a single one.

I want to talk about my dreams with Valerie but she is asleep. She can sleep through anything. I doze and dream I am diving off Avalon in cold water kelp. I remember a seal surfacing at dawn that I feared was a shark, but the shark that came for my speared fish was on the reef off Maui. I shouldn't have gone out over the reef but the beauty of the coral and the butterfly fish lured me like sirens. I remember the shark's eyes—the cold black eyes of a realist who saw things as they are.

I can't get back to sleep. I allow myself to feel how alone I am, despite Val beside me. I shouldn't wake her up. I listen to her breathing. I look at her face and I think it is the most beautiful face I have ever seen. Then she turns and a toenail digs into my calf and I stifle a cry. The painful stab obliterates wistfulness and nostalgic self-indulgence as Vronsky's toothache sabotaged his feelings of grief.

Why do I cite books and movies and media so much? Because I have no real past. References to films and literature make incidents in my life seem more meaningful than they are. The ghosts of Nick Cerk past inhabit a haunted graveyard I prefer not to wander.

And always ... there is Penny.

Penny Penny Penny.

Damn your refusal to look into the broken mirror that reflected both our lives. You refused to see your own motivations. You insisted on the story you had told and sold yourself. You refused to see the truth.

My anger exorcises nothing. I am haunted by the ghost of Penny past.

Dreams don't help. The dead come to life and we talk, but we don't make sense. When daylight comes it takes a moment to grasp that they are ghosts. I want to go back to sleep, back to dreams. I can't do it. Valerie stirs and nestles closer and her warm body brings me into the moment. Her scent and the feel of her body fill my senses. I want to be back in my dreams but it's good to be here, too. This bed is ours now, ours. I am grateful she's beside me, choosing to be with me. I have no idea how long she will let me stay.

Daylight brightens the window shade. I feel the cool air on my face. Then the world suddenly tilts and I feel as if I am on the edge of a void, slipping into a gravity well. I am betwixt and between— or perhaps, I am not between anything. Perhaps I am not anywhere at all.

No wonder I said I would look for a church because it might help in the long run. I was willing to do anything. But I know I went along with her plan for another reason too. I wanted to connect with the still point of the turning world. I wanted Eliot's metaphor to point to a real portal. I wanted the nexus at which he only hinted to be real.

The intelligence community after the war was an abscess that consumed all of society. The lights came on again, but there was darkness everywhere, and the darkness was our light. Professional intelligence was the right place for those of us who lived as ubermenschen, making up our own rules. The IC defined that ethos for itself and then for the whole world. Now every person, every "country," every entity tries to do the same. In a world without God, there are no constraints. Ivan Karamazov got it right.

The still point I seek turns out to be a black hole and I fall right in.

I miss so much. So many are gone. The work I loved is gone. I even miss Val although she is beside me in the bed. How can I miss someone who is right there, breathing beside me? It must be anticipatory grief, I must be planning for her absence. No wonder I feel light-headed and have to steady myself to get out of bed. No wonder I fear I will never escape that black hole.

The event horizon is close. Father, save me, my heart cries, but my father is long dead, he is an unknown, nor could he save me or himself. He was a mean drunk with a belt in his hand. I refuse to idealize him as my mother did, lest I regret his early death. I am grateful that he died prematurely. "The greatest gift a father can give a son is to die young." It creates so much space. I had to create myself out of the rag-and-bone-shop of my life, and I did. I peopled the stages of my life with characters, enough for a lifetime, and all of them were me. That stage went dark. Now I have to do it again. It is all up to me, again.

It is up to all of us, I think, but many don't know it. The stability of their worlds passes for a trustworthy reality. The content doesn't change when the context doesn't change. Things seem to be the same. My colleagues and I designed the context of others' lives so we had to see it all for what it is. We had to create and sustain illusions.

I will settle for illusions. I will gladly settle for second best.

Chapter 11
Brunch with Miriam

S ome spies, not all but quite a few, do need to talk about their work. After my memoir was published, I received a few anonymous notes thanking me for "nailing it"—for telling the truth about the challenges we face, the moral ambiguity, the blood on our hands, the need to deal with depression and PTSD. Of course no one signed their name lest they be seen engaging with the black sheep of the week.

"We can't say what it's like," one said, "because we can't say anything. If the director has our backs, we feel protected, but if not, we feel how alone we are. We can't refute the lies and distortions and attacks in the press, on social media, wherever some numbskull has access to a channel. All that dumb 'Trump news.' If we went back to 1947, would we do it the same way? Would we support special ops in every country? We built a haunted house and now we wander through it, startled when a banshee wails or spooks jump out of the dark. Spooks is the perfect name for us. We're caught in this grim carnival like the geek in his addiction."

Another: "You got it right. No wonder we tell ourselves we're important. We must be, to give up so much to live like this. Our compartmented knowledge locks us into prison cells and we tap in code through the walls to talk. If we tell the truth when a human invites a conversation, we're in danger of taking a dangle or breaking the law."

And another: "I have worked both sides. I was a KGB illegal until I turned and became a double agent. I lived all my life with an identity based on the tombstone of a child. It took years to build the references, social security, transcripts from schools, a resume. Your memoir is both real and surreal: it is the stuff of my best memories and worst nightmares. I check the locks a dozen times a day and sleep with a gun in the drawer beside my bed. If I hear a moth fluttering at the shade, footsteps in the hall, I bolt up, wide awake, ready to shoot .... well, my friend, at least I am not bored."

And one more: "You Forest-Gump-like rascal you! You did everything, did you? Really? you filled all those roles? Ha! No way. What a stew you cooked up! A reader should eat the good parts and leave the rest. I know the difference between kale and spinach. Personally, I do not like kale. Your story is deceptive, dude. You created a wilderness of mirrors inside the wilderness of mirrors. We all know there's nothing but mirrors, all the way down. So let us drink to distorted reflections. (I raise a shot to celebrate your imagination)."

Like all anonymous comments, mileage varies. Those were positive, at least. Disparaging remarks were circulated too, often by insiders following orders, like posting fake reviews on Amazon or Yelp. Rumor-makers roil the murky waters. Our bots do a lot of the dirty work for us. The digital world is a sea of false flags, organized confusion, mayhem and mischief. And we loved it, didn't we, every bit. As if integrity was utterly unworthy of pursuit.

I was told anonymously that the word went out to ignore my memoir, and if someone mentions it, dismiss it. If movie studios or publishers want to make films or publish books about Mobius, slam the door. Open doors for Clancy and his kind, not loose cannons. *Top Gun* is an ad for the Air Force, nothing more. Tell reviewers to praise the predictable crap and ignore Nick. Let Cerk listen to his own voice. Let him live in a bell jar of his own making. Teach him the meaning of helplessness. Teach him the real rules.

I paraphrase but that's the gist of what I was told. It certainly fit what I know. We whistle blowers understand; we turn their insults into medals on our chests. Our mere presence in the back room of the Barbican celebrates our sacrifice, our genuine heroics.

But when we're on the payroll, we can't talk—unless we write fiction. The agencies have therapists but they work for the agencies. You can't trust the therapist or even a local priest.

Trust a priest! Yeah, right! Listen, we have used so many priests, we'd be fools to think they're safe or that the Vatican—a global network of money launderers and embezzlers, pedophiles, corrupt politicians—was a trustworthy bunch. *Godfather 3*, not that good in other ways, had that part right. A parish in every town, a priest in every parish, the biggest network in the world. They launder millions of dollars, cover up crimes, and adhere to omerta. When Calvi "hung himself" under the Blackfriar's Bridge, I was in London. I knew how he got there, and I could name names, but what difference would it make? Bishops and cardinals put the faithful into a trance with magic and mumbo-jumbo, turn their backs and chant an ancient language, pass the basket, and live large. They condemn homosexuals but most of their clergy—to put it simply—simply are.

But I digress. I was asking, where *does* one go, if one has to talk about our work? To a friend or spouse, is who.

Nat Herman talked to me some but he talked to Miriam too. I never knew how much and she never said. He met Miriam Lloyd in Israel. She wasn't Jewish but he didn't care. As long as she wasn't an anti-semite. Her name came from her second husband, Etheridge Lloyd, a financier. He had just watched a Netflix movie, *The Wolf of Wall Street* I think it was, she said she heard him laughing aloud, and he rose from the sofa to get more ice cream but never made it to the kitchen. She found him sprawled on the living room floor, his spoon beside him. The paramedics worked for a long time, just to be sure, before wheeling him out.

Her first husband was a lawyer Charles O'Rourke who worked with Sidney Korshak. Miriam believed, because they said, he died of natural causes. Miriam liked Korshak, she said he was cordial and charming and lived under the radar. He played poker with her husband until the wee hours, and thanks to Korshak, Miriam and Charlie stayed in the best suites in Vegas. Korshak once had the POTUS shifted to a lesser suite on their behalf because he could. They hobnobbed with Hollywood moguls and socialized with clients in a town where business, politics, and the outfit were hard to distinguish. When Charlie died, a who's who of wise guys came to his funeral.

Both husbands left millions, there were no kids, and Miriam could have gone swimming in her cash like Scrooge McDuck, but that wasn't her style. Miriam was classy. Nat said he thought her assets were north of twenty-four million bucks—more than enough to cover the difference between his salary and a trip to space if he wanted one. He didn't want one, though. He didn't care about the money because he had enough. Enough was plenty, he used to say. He relished intense experience, not things. He collected memories, not stuff. Things own you, he said, you don't own them. They're distractions. Every thing you own draws down energy. Feeling the flow of the current as it carries you out to sea is the joy of life. The freedom to be, that's what I love.

Nat was under official cover in Tel Aviv working with Israelis and Miriam was traveling around the "Holy Land" and was back in Tel Aviv before going shopping in Dubai. They met at a seaside cafe on a beautiful breezy sunny morning. The choppy sea was brilliant with points of light on the waves and the distant water was shining like blue steel. Jews and non-Jews alike walked along the water, hard to tell apart (all the way down to DNA, the similarity of which prevented a viable bioweapon; one that killed Arabs would kill Jews too.) The odors of spices and street food floated on the mild air. It was a glorious morning and made the land seem promised as they claimed.

They were both sipping mimosas and he used that fact to lean over and start a conversation. That led into, where are you from, oh really, why are you here? Miriam mostly told the truth and Nat did a little, as much as he could. He said he worked for State at the nearby American Embassy, the one that was built like a concrete fort.

Her widowhood was what it was. Miriam liked traveling alone—in fact, she liked living alone. She missed her husbands, but did not feel incomplete without them. Each marriage had been based on mutual understanding. She maintained a discreet distance from their affairs, which wasn't hard for a woman of her temperament. Some considered her cool but only if they wanted more than she liked to give. She owed no one anything. She knew who she was, and Nat picked up on her temperament right away and liked it. He thought her calm demeanor, her composure, was dignified. He liked her habit of sharing just enough, and—he learned over time—she shared very little with very few. So Miriam was perfect as the bride of a man in the trade. If he couldn't find a spy to wed, Miriam was second best. He liked her and then he loved her. She, apparently, did the same. She was used to husbands who colored outside the lines and kept their own counsel. She wasn't amoral, but her loyalties were self-defined. She let the world turn as it would.

Nat didn't want the loud girls he dated as a kid as partners. He liked them well enough but they were too familiar and therefore uninteresting. Talking to Miriam, he felt the energy building quietly between them and liked what it suggested: they would never get too close, she would never become cloying, and they could live independently. They had an implicit understanding of what to expect so neither was disappointed. Relationships go on the rocks when either one wants more or less than they agreed on in the first place. The secret to a stable life is, don't change a thing. Don't you change either, please.

When he learned she was wealthy, it didn't hurt, but he didn't need her money or what it could buy, and she got that, which was a relief. People of means are always afraid that someone is after their cash. Six months into their affair, he told her in a guarded way what he sort of did. He told her, that is, what he really did, in a way. He told her mostly truth. He had left Israel by then. He had told her his new import business demanded a lot of trips and telephone calls and muted conversations on multiple phones but she was smart enough to fill in the blanks. Life with her former husbands meant plenty of whispers, links to mobsters and tycoons, offshore accounts and island retreats, tax lawyers up the kazoo. Miriam did not take the facts of life personally until Nat was killed, not by an assassin but as he was setting up a new TV.

When they became serious about the relationship, Nat told her about the divorce rate inside the agency, why marriage was best with someone in the life. It took a toll when a partner never told a spouse everything, or in some cases, anything, and in other cases, only lies. They laughed about it, but she knew he wasn't kidding. And that suited her just fine: an arm's-length lover felt just right, not as distant as I was from Penny, nor as deceptive, but not your typical talky spouse who came home every night and never shut up until you turned on the TV to drown them out.

Nat loved her worldliness. He liked that she spoke well of her dead husbands which she would likely do about him, too (and she did). She was smart and well-connected. She had been to Davos with her first husband and was invited back on her own. She told

Nat she never met a person there who was loyal to a country in an old fashioned sense of the word. They lived in another construction of reality, with their own banks, their own offshore accounts, their own islands, and their own channels to influence "democratic institutions." They maintained appearances to keep muggles happy. They had their own rules, she said. Nat nodded and said he understood. And did he ever. She was describing our work too, with a little bit of difference.

They seemed to be a match made in heaven. She had no need to know about the dirtier side of the business and Nat washed all the blood off before he shared anything. He in turn had no need to delve into why she knew in such minute detail how huge fortunes were made and was nonchalant when a body or two in a barrel bobbed up in Montrose Harbor. She told him a bit about Korshak and the mob's reach. The next generation had put their money into many legitimate businesses, and their kids in turn donated to charities and sat on Boards and appeared in society pages. Her husbands had been careful not to expose her unnecessarily to danger. She honored the rules and had a sort of fascinating life.

She was a good listener. She created a safe place for Nat to disclose what he needed to bleed off. When he finished a mission that made him twitch, he found relief through telling her mostly truths. Miriam listened with detachment and had no reason to repeat anything. She kept his words in a lockbox, just as Gore said, and accepted his serial absences or his jitters when he returned. She knew when to pour a drink and then one more. She knew he carried a gun and she knew why. She didn't pry but she knew by the sound of his voice when he needed to talk and put down her book and listened. Otherwise the conversation when he returned might go like this:

"Where were you, the last few weeks?"

"Out."

"What did you do?"

"Nothing."

Just like being kids again.

Miriam knew about our friendship. She knew what I had done for Nat. She knew we were partners in the best sense, sharing attitudes and values. She confessed to me once that she lived like a military wife in fear of a knock on the door. She accepted her anxiety about the dangers her husband faced as dues she had to pay. She feared he might die on a mission and she would never know how, only a cover story like the one in his obit. She feared that Nat would become a star on the wall, an unknown soldier, a faceless corpse in a war that had no name. She never dreamed he would die as he did, the result of an "accidental death." He didn't get a star, only a brief obit that lied about his life. I asked if there was anything she really had to know. She thought a moment, shook her head, and let the river of time overflow its banks and carry away the remains of a life that was gone forever.

When his medical device sent a lethal shock into his heart and he dropped dead, she asked Syntactic for information and learned that, just like the agency, they put out a cover story and reasserted a commitment to safety and quality of life. "The health and well-being of our customers is our number one priority," said one of their lawyers, Ridley McManus, with a straight face. "Shouldn't that be number two?" Miriam asked (they were talking about a settlement.) He kept his face grave, not daring to laugh at the joke, lest it sound like an admission. He assured Miriam of heartfelt thoughts and prayers and offered a bounty. She delayed accepting a settlement, just in case. Her intuition told her to hold off a bit. She didn't need the money and was thinking through her options.

The CEO of Syntactic was a youngish middle-aged guy named James Murphy. She watched him on youtube crowing about quarterly results, cash flow, new markets, innovative research, and the outlook for the future. A rogue reporter asked about deaths and injuries related to various products and their settlements for off-label marketing and Murphy looked serious and spoke of their commitment to improving safety, making lives better through medical advancements, and then he went off at length about their extensive charitable work, their foundation, outreach to the poor, their work in South Africa, their support of the Special Olympics. He showed videos of kids with various disabilities having fun at Disneyland. He showed videos of patients expressing gratitude for the full lives they could now lead, thanks to Syntactic. He did not mention millions paid to doctors to write "articles" for medical journals or to push products for off-label purposes that were neither approved nor effective.

Miriam was not, as they say, born yesterday. When I called her, she asked me to come to their home. "I have something I want to discuss," she said. We had a Sunday brunch on the lawn along the lake. It was one hell of a beautiful autumn day. Her private cook scrambled eggs with tiny diced red and yellow peppers exactly as I requested. The omelets were buttery and fluffy and tasty. His name was Felipe. He served a Drambuie Marmalade that was perfect with a crumpet. But more than a good brunch, our conversation revealed our mutual concern. Miriam was stuck in the anger phase of grief and didn't want to let it go. When she spoke of Nat's death, her jaw tightened and her eyes narrowed.

Over the course of our meal, she became more and more explicit.

I had dropped Val at the Barbican and kept our only car—an old Prius which got good mileage despite its age—and headed out to the northern suburbs. I wore the Allen Edmond shoes I had paid a fortune for that had lasted a decade already. I dressed as nicely as I could in slacks and a shirt and light jacket.I had never been to their home before, but I thought it must be spiffy, based on Nat's account.

I expected a long winding drive through groves of oaks to the house but there was only a circular drive to the front door. The house was understated, not as immense as the ones on neighboring lots, which I scouted through Google Maps. The house next door had a drive of more than a half-mile and a parking lot at the end for two dozen visitors. Down the road on Point Lane through tall gates was a fifteen million dollar affair with nine bedrooms and nine baths. A home further north had eight bedrooms and nineteen baths and was priced at the same level. I couldn't for the life of me understand the number of bathrooms, probably because I hadn't lived in a world where that made sense. Miriam's was a nice enough home on Laurel, between eight and nine thousand square feet she said when asked, and the bedrooms (six) were a closer match for the baths (seven). She did not offer a tour and I didn't need one.

She greeted me at the door. No butler a la Philip Marlowe opened and closed the door to make sure I knew my place, no chauffeur was waxing a Bentley. When she opened the door I was struck by how good she looked. She had done a bit of work but it was done right so she looked about ten years younger than her age. Her face did not have the telltale wrinkleless shine of a cheap job. Even her hands did not betray her age. Her hair was still a lustrous auburn and fell perfectly around her narrow face. Her eyes were a deep green but fretted with sorrow and anger.

I looked around the entrance hall when I entered. An impression of glossy shine and polished marble. Through wide open doors to the living room I could see sunshine in slanted rectangular patches on the hardwood floor and an area rug in bright colors, white sofas and chairs, tables and lamps. I could tell that it was all quite expensive but that was all. Was that a Tufft Pier Table? I didn't ask.

"I don't know how to relate this place to the Nat I knew," I confessed. "He dressed for assignments, not in keeping with"—I swept my arm in an arc—"all this."

Miriam smiled.

"He could live with"—she paused and smiled—"all this, as you call it, but he wasn't attached to it. He lived for his work. He loved his work. He needed the adrenalin rush, as I imagine you do, Nick."

"I did," I acknowledged. "I guess I still do. But it's not easy to find these days."

"Nat told me a little about what you went through. I'm sorry that telling the simple truth is such a dangerous thing to do. It often is. Once the papers had stories about rendition, it became common knowledge. Now everyone knows, and nobody seems to care. Water boarding is the least of it, what one of them called a dip in the pool. They don't discuss the people locked in dark holes for days. Movies desensitize us. Torture porn is big in Hollywood. Slashers who terrorize girls before raping or killing them always make big bucks." She shook her head. "Nat said you took a medical leave."

"I did. I'll fill in the blanks if you want."

"Of course. But let's get settled first."

She led me, walking ahead a step or three, off through another door and through a pantry and then a gleaming modern kitchen. She bypassed the island which seemed to be the length of a football field and we went though a rear door to the yard. I followed her like a puppy. When you live the way I do, it's impossible not to be impressed by the glitter and glare. We emerged about forty feet from the lake, blue and calm for a change, across the well-tended lawn. The wind must have been from the south, a gentle breeze that merely ruffled the water with traces of frail lace. A commercial ship far out on the horizon was moving from north to south, heading for the refineries. The leaf-covered lawn seemed to go on forever. Leaves had blown all over in the rain and wind of the previous week. That front had passed. The warm day was a respite from a chilly gray autumn, a typical bait-and-switch in the upper Midwest.

The grass was still green and the sky was diamond bright. The sun glared off the water and I cupped my hand above my eyes to see where I was walking.

A grill was twenty or thirty feet away with a figure in chef's white. Two cushiony chairs and a large table. Another table held a pitcher and two glasses. Felipe dutifully waited for orders. He would want to know precisely how I liked my eggs. At home I made our eggs myself. There was no Felipe, just Val who liked the way I made them. Break a few in a bowl and whisk them without water, was the non-secret secret.

"Let's sit," she said, "and enjoy this weather."

She took one chair, I took the other. I couldn't keep my eyes from the water and the strip of dingy beach between the water and the lawn. The house was high and far enough back to escape anything but a seiche. The eroding beach was not long for the world.

"What are you thinking?" Miriam said. "Your lips are moving."

I uncrossed and recrossed my legs to change the frame of my focus. "Sorry, I was just thinking what we're doing to the lake, how incapable we are of planning for the long term."

"I see." I couldn't see her expression. It was hard to see in the slant of the shadow across the lower portion of her face. She gestured to Felipe who brought us drinks. I sipped mine deliciously slowly, letting it suffuse my perspective if it only would. I didn't drink a lot, but when I did, I wanted it to count. I had made a decision to drink less. I needed to be alert to face the inquisition. That was a done deal, but I learned that my body had changed in middle-age and I had to adjust my vices so they still jacked me up and didn't bring me down.

"You were about to say what happened to you."

Her question brought it all back. My breathing changed. There was no firm ground, so to speak, under my feet. I held the arms of the chair tightly.

She noticed.

"Nick, I don't need to know."

I steadied myself. Breathe in, breathe out. In my head a mantra Val had suggested automatically unspooled. It enabled me to wobble toward the center, enough to let me settle down.

She was waiting, as I imagine she waited for Nat to decide what to say.

"I'll keep it short, Miriam. They sent me to one of our black sites to assist an interrogation team. That's the polite way of saying it. We tortured people, some of them horribly, some of them innocent, some of them we killed. We learned little, certainly not as much as we would have learned had we done it the right way. I couldn't take it any more. We were questioning a woman. She screamed a lot. Some screams get inside your skull. We use hoods so we can't see their eyes. That makes them animals instead of human. One of my partners pulled off her hood. Our eyes locked and it was ... I don't know how to say it ... a space opened up that seemed to be ... there was no separation between us. Somehow we merged. I really *don't* know how to say it. Who I think I am, most of the time, is a separate individual, and that awareness dissolved into something else. She was no longer an enemy. She was a human being and so was I, but more than that, we shared a single consciousness. I experienced it, Miriam, I didn't just think it. It sounds crazy, I know, but I realized that consciousness is ... a field ... a field we can't get outside and look in. Everything is inside "it" but it's not a thing. It's a ... is field the right word?"

Miriam shrugged.

"Miriam, what we were doing to her, we were doing to ourselves. That's what I saw. Feedback loops make us all one. That's the vector, Miriam, that we all inhabit. Maybe all sentient life, I guess. The universe is like one of those traps an antlion digs and when we're triggered, we slide down into that deeper awareness like a beetle in the sand. We experience that wider awareness. But we don't stay there. The world can't handle too many mystics. Nothing would get done. So it feels like one minute you see clearly and the next you're back thinking you're separate again. You snap back into habitual mindedness. Mountains were mountains, then they weren't, then they were again."

Her eyes communicated clearly that she was trying to listen but without understanding. Hell, I didn't understand myself, what I was saying. The words I tried to use broke in the process. For Miriam, the mountains were still mountains and the climb was too strenuous. My words floated in and floated out. The cries of the gulls over the lake made more sense than I did. They populated a landscape that she saw every morning, drawing the drapes in her bedroom, taking the privilege of wealth and the views it afforded for granted.

I didn't need to make her understand my mystical gibberish. It was futile to shout down into Plato's cave anyway. You just make the captives mad.

"Uh-huh," she said when I paused.

"I came back to DC, and one day, I collapsed. Next I knew, I was being wheeled to the clinic. They made me go to therapy. I discovered I couldn't live as I had. I'm still trying to learn what that means. It's a real struggle. Everything in the world militates against it. But I can't unlearn what I learned.

"So I spoke out. I said what we were doing. I was fired and charged with revealing secrets and there was a legal battle to stay out of jail, which I did, by agreeing to a whole bunch of stipulations. They wanted me to just go away. They didn't want me to be a cause. By then the word was out, what it meant for the gloves to come off.

The horrors became common knowledge. We did the worst imaginable things to defend "freedom." Most agency folks stopped speaking to me. Nat was rare. And then ... I didn't know he was having medical issues. What was going on?"

She turned and gestured to Felipe. "Let's tell him how we want our omelets," she said. We did and he slipped off to turn our requests into scrumptious food. "Was Nat involved with any of that?"

"I don't know. I wouldn't know. We don't know what others are doing. It's like an Escher etching. Sometimes you work on something a long time, only to find out it wasn't what you thought. If someone gets nosy about your work, you change access codes, and they can't nitpick any more. We did that a lot. It's SOP at the agency. I could only guess what Nat was doing. I knew who he talked to, worked with, you pay attention to connections and learn a lot. But I never knew the details and didn't ask."

Miriam sighed. "I understand. We talked about the isolation, the burnout—and for what? Nat was disillusioned, Nick. I guess you knew that."

"I did."

"Thank you Felipe," she accepted her plate and Felipe angled the table to our chairs so we could set down our meals.

"Anything else?" Felipe said.

"No, thank you, Felipe."

He went to his own chair under a tree and there he reposed, thinking thoughts, waiting for the next instruction.

"So? What happened to Nat?"

Her face clouded. She blinked several times and looked away, then brought her gaze back into alignment. She needed a minute before she could speak.

"Unless you'd prefer—"

"No no," she said. "It's why I asked you to come, Nick. I want you to know the story."

Chapter 12
"Our First Commitment"

"Yes, Felipe, I'll have another. Nick?"

"Sure. Thanks."

Felipe took our glasses and hurried back to the portable bar. I moistened my finger to detect the direction of the wind more precisely. It was blowing away from Felipe, so the sound of our conversation would likely not reach him. I assumed he had not bugged the nearby trees or hidden a sensor in the fallen leaves. I was sure he could not read our lips at that distance.

"Where do I begin, Nick? There's so much to say."

"Begin at the beginning. Go on until you come to the end. Then stop," I smiled.

Miriam didn't recognize the quote from Lewis Carroll. No need to mention it. The words of everyone flow into the words of everyone else. A brain the size of the earth is chattering away, talking to itself.

Miriam uncrossed and recrossed her legs. She adjusted the brim of her hat to occlude the sunlight which had changed its angle as the day went on. The sunlight brightened her hands which she folded in her lap to keep them out of mischief. She liked to speak with her hands, and when she was excited, she did it even more. She was making an effort to control them, but her fingers clenched as she spoke,

"Nat had problems with his heart. They must have come on gradually, but it seemed sudden. One day he felt fine and the next he felt weak. It wasn't pumping right. He felt like the rhythm wasn't right. That made him anxious which made the symptoms worse. You know Nat, he would tough things out if he could, but this was nothing to wait-and-see. He took my advice for once and called the doc. The doc said we need to fix it right away. He needed something to regulate his heart. Syntactic had a device they had used to use to keep people going until they got a transplant, and now the device is approved as a permanent implant for everyone. Once and done, enjoy the rest of your lives. That was the pitch, and that's what the docs said—let SmarterCare do the job. The PR from Syntactic made it sound like a miracle device. And they had already implanted thousands by the time Nat said yes."

"So he went ahead and did it."

"The doc was a specialist in clogged arteries and that's what Nat had. There was no mystery about his condition. Blood wasn't moving through the left side of his heart. SmarterCare would fix it, they said."

"And you checked it all out, before he let them fuck with his heart?"

"We did our best. Of course. You know Nat. He was pretty thorough."

"Yes" I smiled, remembering how he vetted a Palestinian. The kid thought he would be a hero to his people, and maybe he was, after the Israelis picked him up and explained the error of his ways.

"The first thing Nat did was research its history. He started with the FDA. but the data wasn't available, not in one place."

"There's no process for letting people know what happens when they authorize a device for a new purpose? "

"There is, on paper, they're supposed to inform the public through formal FDA notices and messages to healthcare providers but they repeatedly failed to do that. They left patients in the dark about known problems—and there were tons. I have all the details if you want to see them, but bottom line, the FDA relied on Syntactic to fix them and they didn't. The FDA said, do this, and Syntactic said they would, and they didn't. Meanwhile they kept putting devices into thousands of people and crowing about their cutting edge innovative genius-level work that would enhance their cash flow, expand market share, and increase stock-holder value.

"How the hell, Nick, can they not take action when warning letter upon warning letter is issued about such serious issues? And the company does nothing to fix them?"

I shook my head.

"The FDA met with Syntactic more than a hundred times. They started formal reviews once it was approved for general use and tracked its safety and effectiveness. A doctor who evaluates new devices says that most companies, over 80%, fix issues by the time they're reinspected.

"But not Syntactic. Meanwhile, lots of people die."

Miriam looked at the waves breaking and the bright sky. I saw where she was heading.

"They said the device would never need to be replaced."

"That would expand the customer base, wouldn't it? I'm sure a lot more people wanted the device permanently than needed a bridge to a transplant."

"Yes. It exploded the target population by hundreds of times.

"And Nat wanted to get it done. The need was urgent. He was afraid he would die—ironic, right? He relied on what they said, that it was safe and would save his life. Meanwhile, for two years, they put them into thousands of people, I think four thousand, and wired them up—until there were so many injuries and deaths, they finally had to stop. The body count got too big to ignore. They paid out millions in law suits but the money they made from sales more than covered the payouts."

"So what happened to Nat?"

"Static electricity. That's all it took. The devices short out if they have to restart. Nat was setting up a new TV, hooking up a receiver so he could, I don't remember, play it in different rooms I think. He had gotten behind the TV, wedged in behind the set, and when I came into the room, he was slumped between the set and the wall. I called 911 right away, but he was gone when they got here. "

I sat up straighter and turned to look into her face. "Are you telling me they knew people were dying, the FDA had been on them for years, and they kept saying they'd fix it, stringing everyone along while making enough money to pay off families?"

"Yes. That's what I'm telling you. Like those gas tanks that exploded."

Miriam waved to Felipe. I hadn't noticed she had downed her second drink and wanted a third. He sort of skipped across the grass, more than a trot, and went back to fix another.

He was back in a jiffy with her drink.

"Would you like another?" he asked me.

"Well—yes, thanks. So—they finally did recalls?"

"They issued recalls on over 500 specific pumps. They made dumb-ass statements like, it's not when the pump is running that we have a problem, only when it starts or restarts. I can show you the emails, letters, the legal briefs, that fill a box. A woman named Stacey McGrath signed off on almost all of them. I don't understand the technical parts, like 'unexpected power source switching'—what is that? Wait a minute, Nick—let me get some of that paper—"

She set down her half-finished drink and went back into the house, emerging in a few minutes with a box. She sat again and balanced the box on her lap, leafing through papers.

"Here, this is typical. Read this."

I took the printout of an email and turned to block the sunlight glare on the page with the shadow of my body.

"As a company," it said, "we are strongly committed to improving the lives of people, and we were deeply saddened to learn about the death of one of our customers. Our thoughts and prayers are with the family of [fill in the blank] His passing is a tragic reminder that heart disease is a serious condition. While we can't provide specific details regarding complaints filed against Syntactic about the device he used, we can tell you that we investigate every complaint we receive and are committed to ensuring the safety and reliability of our products. We test our products rigorously, and they are carefully reviewed by regulatory agencies, such as the FDA. We hold ourselves to the highest safety quality standards in the industry."

"What bullshit," I said.

"Isn't it? Safety is their first priority. Not money."

"There were a lot of deaths?"

"Three thousand from that device alone. They made a thoracic stent graft system and had to halt sales after one hundred reports of power failures that caused at least fourteen deaths. A lot of people had to remove it but that wasn't trivial. Removal was a dangerous procedure. Have surgery or leave it in, either might be lethal."

"And the FDA?"

"Busy with busy work, writing letters, having meetings, sounding quite serious, with zero results and zero follow-up. When they learned Syntactic had not been monitoring or repairing the heart pump's defects, they demanded that they fix them. More warnings, and from Syntactic, yes sir yes sir, right away. Meanwhile they knew that static electricity could cause short circuits and people would drop dead. The FDA insisted that Syntactic fix everything within fifteen days of each letter, and when the company didn't, they sent more letters. The company didn't fix a thing and the FDA did not penalize them once. Patients never knew what was going on.

"In this binder," she hefted a thicker one and handed it to me, "you'll see that journalists asked the CEO and the head of that mechanical product division for interviews. They declined, but issued a statement. '"There is nothing more important to Syntactic than the safety and well-being of patients.'

"Let me repeat: Three thousand, one device alone. And you want to know something else?"

"Do I?"

"I know the CEO. Jim Murphy, I am sure he had no idea that form letter went to someone he knew. The signature is a stamp. I see him at the country club, at fund-raisers, board meetings for a non-profit we both support. We're on a first name basis. He solicited money from me for one of his public-facing causes; they have a foundation so they look benevolent and generous."

"Have you confronted him directly?"

She sifted sorted the binders back into the box and set it on the grass. "No. I held off on their offer of money too. I was just so furious I knew I wouldn't be thinking straight." She turned at last with the sun behind her head like a glowing halo. The auburn tint of her hair faded in the glare. I could feel her rage.

"I waited until we could talk, Nick. That's where you come in. I don't need their damned money. I could contact the FDA but all I'd get is more words."

"OK. So what do you want to do?"

She took a deep breath.

"Whatever is necessary." She put spaces between the words and repeated with grim determination: "Whatever is necessary, Nick. To pay those bastards back."

Chapter 13
Backsliding

"S o ... tell me more about Miriam."

My position was difficult. Hard to respond. Hard to breathe. I shrugged as best I could. "There's not a lot to tell. Wait a sec ... let me move ... just a ..."

I raised my face from the pillow and loosened my arms and tugged the pillow down until it cushioned my neck and chest and my head flopped free. But now my head pitched forward, a more uncomfortable position. So I snagged it up a little and let my chin balance on the edge. I tested it to be sure it held and it did. That left my face free and I could speak.

Valerie straddled me at the waist. I felt her calves on my flanks as she pressed again on my back. I couldn't breathe for a minute as she readjusted. Once she was settled, she began moving her hands again in slow circles. I relaxed.

"They met by chance in Tel Aviv. They happened to be at some cafe and started talking and talked some more and walked down to Jaffa, then back to the Dan Tel Aviv for lunch. The rest was a typical meet cute story. They seemed suited to each other in a lot of ways. I know Nat loved her. I know she loved him too, but what that means is up to a couple. Right? It meant at the least that Miriam could live with a spy and not mind the craziness and he could be as free as a marriage might allow. It isn't easy, linking up with a spy. They talked it out before they hitched but that's not the same as living it."

Valerie laughed. "Is that a warning or an observation?"

I smiled at the wrinkled sheet only inches from my face. 'Wait—there!" I said.

"There?"

"A little to the left—yes! Right—there."

She gave attention to the tension spot. She could relieve the pain for the moment but not its source which meant I'd feel it again soon. I didn't know why it kept coming back.

I relaxed again as best I could. I could smell her sleepy scent on the sheet. I could see a few of her hairs.

"God I love the way you smell," I said.

"I smell with my nose, like everyone," she laughed. She was moving to ease the stiffness all over, using her fingers and then pressing hard with the heels of her hands. "But you never answered my question. Was that a warning?"

"No," I said. "Because I'm not a spy now. I'm a former spy. I'm a whistle blower now. That's not a living, but it's who I am. For now, at any rate. You know that."

"You were in that life for a lot of years. You have to miss it some. Right?"

I wrote a quick sketch in my mind of a plausible denial but I let it dissolve and tried my new strategy, telling the simple truth. When it worked, it was so refreshing. It felt like drinking cold water on a hot day.

"Yes," I said. "Sometimes I miss everything and wish I was still in the game. I was good at what I did and I believed in what I did for a long time. But I know that if you talk yourself into thinking torture is a great thing to do, you've gone to the dark side. It becomes part of you and you invent justifications and lie to yourself until you don't question what you're doing. You recruit yourself, in a way, to be an unthinking agent for the agency. Torture stays in the playbook. You get good at picking people who don't mind doing it and move from there to people who enjoy it. You have a pretty good pool of recruits, believe me, once they know they get official cover, and pretty soon—"

Valerie shivered. "I don't need to know that," she said. "I don't want to know it."

I squirmed into a position that let me turn and she adjusted to my pivot. She was still on me, knees back. She settled on my waist, looking down into my eyes. I saw the fear in her eyes that so many feel these days, knowing what we do, what we have become. The way the world works.

Part of me wanted to tell her everything. Most of me knew that wasn't a good idea.

"Tell me then, lady. What would you like to know?"

She moved down just a little but enough. She felt me respond and debated whether to continue. It felt good having her there, moving a little, letting her call the shots.

We looked at each other without words and something else happened, a moment of profound openness—a surge of love, a flow of shared emotion, I don't know—that dissolved our anxieties. There was suddenly no distance between us. For the moment, we lost ourselves and were present to each other in mutual surrender. When I grasped what was happening, when I observed myself having that experience, it killed it, turning it into a memory. I glimpsed it for a moment before I became "myself" again, like glimpsing the person instead of the animal in *Ladyhawke* during transitions.

"Miriam knew he might die on a mission, but she lived as if he wouldn't. All spy spouses do, they have to. You push it way to the back of your mind. She never dreamed he'd be futzing with a TV and static electricity would kill him. It didn't have to happen. No wonder she hates the people who did it. His murderers, she thinks. All for a little money, you know."

"I understand," Val said. She slid off and lay down at my side. My arm went around her bare shoulders and I held her close. I could feel her breathing on my neck. I could feel the beating of her heart.

"Don't go back, Nick. Talking things over with Miriam might weaken your resolve to let go of the old life. It already is, isn't it? The two of you are planning something, aren't you?"

"Val, you ought to be doing remote viewing, honestly. Nothing is hidden from you, is it?"

"I'll fill out an application."

She was kidding but I wasn't. I had heard that the best remote viewers had stunning results. Her intuitive knowledge bordered on the psychic. She felt my emotions shift or tilt the minute that they did. Her intuition linked the loops and she was almost always right.

"So what does she want from you, Nick? She might have just wanted to talk, but it feels like there's more."

"Yes, there was more." I tried to deflect her gaze, except it wasn't from her eyes, it was from inside her mind to mine. Valerie was locked on.

"OK, listen," I said. "Miriam wants us to join forces against the Syntactic CEO. She knows the regulators blow smoke. I don't know if they're bought off or just incompetent, but it doesn't matter. No one will do a damn thing. All the victims have are civil suits. Syntactic pays millions to families, never admits to anything, and with thirty billion bucks a year, they can buy whoever they need to buy. So if there's going to be a meaningful payback, it has to come from vigilantes, a whistle blower maybe, right? That's what Miriam thought. Someone who knows what it takes to stand up to the bigs."

"But what would that look like? I mean, what's the end-game? Get some press and hope there's repercussions? Or burst in on a C-level meeting with an AK-47 and massacre the bunch?"

I shrugged. "I don't know exactly. I know, sure, she'd like to kill the son-of-a-bitch. She said as much. I treated it as a joke."

"Can you control what she does? Are you confident of that?"

"Some. I mean, people get emotional when someone kills their spouse. When you start on a mission, you know what you hope to accomplish, but it's open-ended. You know the general direction, but it comes together on the way. You have to be flexible. That's how I have to be with this. It doesn't mean anything goes. If I got involved in something crazy like murdering a CEO, I'd be in jail for a long time."

Valerie pulled back and raised her face to look into mine. She struggled against the sheets to sit upright and leaned against the headboard and drew her knees up and took a position opposed to a come-on.

"You call it a mission. You're all in, aren't you? I mean, you said yes, you would help her, and once you started talking over options, it made it real, made it yours. You're thinking about it a lot, I can tell. You look off at nothing and your brain is humming away. You're not just thinking, Nick, you're planning. So what do *you* intend? You, not her."

"I haven't thought it through. I want to see my friend avenged and help his widow, but keep it within bounds. I'll consult my posse at the bar. They might know the best way to do it. "

"You're trying to arrange the pieces on the board, aren't you? See a few moves ahead?"

"Yes. I guess that's true."

"You miss the excitement. I know you do. You don't mind this a bit. You would love to be back in the game, like you said."

"Yes. I admit it, sure. To a degree. I do miss the life, I want that high again. Valerie, you can't know the power of the drug, once you're in the inner circle. You can't know the power of knowing, knowing what others don't know and using it. The pleasure of the hunt, the exhilaration of the chase. Planning an operation, practicing and practicing, and at last getting onto the field of battle. Winning is the only thing. When they don't know they lost, it's even better. We do want to prevail. It's in our DNA."

As Penny had seen clearly. The look in her eyes when she rose from the table, knowing that she could never win, because I played by different rules. She knew that no matter how much I told her, I would never surrender the high ground. I would hold myself back in significant ways. I would never tell her more than some of the truth.

I would never let her get inside.

"And you're thinking how to pull this off on your own, without an agency behind you?"

"Like I said, I'm thinking it through."

"Backsliding, they call it, Nick. You're like an addict. No, I take that back. You are an addict. Nat's death is an excuse. Drunks drink to celebrate, drunks drink to console themselves. There's always a reason but it's never the reason. Drinking is the reason. I lived with that once, Nick, I won't live with it again. Miriam's the pusher. The drug is getting even, as if he's Miles Archer and you're Sam Spade. You believe those stories, Nick. Fiction permeates your thinking.

Those stories are your bible. You mythologize your life to make it shine with radiance, and you mythologize Nat's death, but Jesus, Nick, this isn't a movie, it isn't a book. You laugh at people who quote the bible but you quote Raymond Chandler and Dashiell Hammett. Down these mean streets a whistle blower has to go, as if you're a knight, whatever he said. Like Don Quixote reading about chivalry and believing it. Hammett and Chandler and Hemingway were drunks. They are not ideal guides, not for real life. Pulp fiction, film noir, are not good guides. Think about what you're doing!"

"It was a mistake to watch *The Maltese Falcon* with you." I smiled, but she was not ready to lighten up.

"And if those people at Syntactic have no qualms about killing so many people, if they can just write it off, they'll have no qualms about hurting you—or us—in other ways. They can't get implants into everyone, but they have options—don't they? You've made that clear. You said they come after spouses too."

"I said that about recruitment, Val. Increasing the pressure to make a person come to us. Not about this."

This was not the conversation I intended when I asked for a massage.

"But they might try to hurt you. Or me."

"Don't get ahead of yourself, Val. Right now I'm thinking things through. Nothing's happened yet. I doubt it'll get like that. I'm just helping out a friend." My self-justification ran right off a cliff into reassuring words, wishful thinking, throwing the truth under the bus. "I'll make sure you're safe. You matter more than anything, Val, including my own life."

She looked at me edgewise. "Is there more to this, Nick? Is it really just a caper? It has nothing to do with Miriam, right? Who just happens to be rich, and beautiful, and vulnerable, and needy—-trigger trigger trigger trigger, if I know you at all. And closer to your age so you don't have to, what did he say in *Peggy Sue Got Married*, explain who the Big Bopper is?"

"I wouldn't say beautiful ... she's attractive, I guess, in a middle-age way."

Valerie's laugh sounded like a snort. She swung her legs over the side of the bed, centered herself for a second, then stood up. She strode off toward the bathroom. I waited in the bed, the sheets covering my lower body, sitting up. We had shared such a nice moment during the massage. Well, so much for that. She dressed and went off into another room, doing one thing or another, what there is to do if one has nothing else to do, and when it became clear that she wasn't coming back I got out of bed and dressed.

Chapter 14
The Back Room at the Barbican

"Oh Danny Boy, the pipes the pipes are calling ..."

"Oh, please! Cut the bullshit, will you?"

Dan refused to sanction the whole hierarchy thing, himself at the top, but we knew why: he felt so damned guilty about holding back for so long (we know what that'a like, don't we, crew?) that he felt our praise as pain. Nevertheless, he was the dean of us well-intended dreamers, because because because because because, because of the wonderful thing he did. He blew the whistle at the highest level and he did it the right way. He sacrificed his livelihood, his distinguished career, and he almost went to jail for a long long time. Dan showed the world that the president was a crook. Other revelations followed, one after the other, of crookedness and crookedness squared, the whole corrupt enterprise. So when Dan told the truth, got the papers published, did his best to rinse the blood from his hands, the power people tried to destroy him. They have only one play in their playbook, punish and retaliate, so that's what they did. They broke a dozen laws along the way and tried him first in the press, then in a courtroom. But the judge ended the trial and Dan had a new career. He gave speeches, making beau coup bucks, telling the world what he did and why and he wrote a best seller.

It was easy for "blowers" to celebrate that triumph. But when we sobered up, we knew better. The war went on with more than a million dead, all needless deaths. His bravery did not make a blip in the real world except as a narrative we could use to console ourselves. We all had PTSD from the war, the whole damned country, but veterans had it worse. Nightmares plagued our long nights, suicides increased, and we ached inside.

So the President was a crook. So he tried to co-opt the CIA and FBI and Justice to do his bidding. Did he go to jail? Of course not. Jail is for stick-up men—and whistle blowers, right? Viet Nam was ... a mistake. We called it a mistake. Not a domino tipping on the way to toppling, only a civil war in a small country fighting for independence.

Lots of us know we're wrong when it's too late, after the money machine has gobbled up its last dollar. A whistle blower many years back, General Smedley Butler, titled a rant full of rage, *War is a Racket*, after World War One. You can find his book in the stacks, a neglected footnote to a bloody history, covered with dust.

My decision to reveal the normalization of torture accomplished little too, but we want to believe there is some akashic or etheric or cosmic record that records that a human life is an ultimate value. Our actions have soul force, moral power, we all say. A cynic might say that's compensatory thinking. We understand that position. We don't press our case.

Still, we have to believe it matters. Don't you see, that's all we have. That plank on which we try to stand is like a board floating in a stormy sea. We pitch and yaw, trying not to fall. We have to believe that doing the right thing is essential to the universe, not a rationalization. We have to believe. An active conscience demands that we go all in. There is no "half slave half free" about it.

That's why the back room at the Barbican was important. Our meetings sustained us. We held each other up, we kept one another believing. Of course it isn't easy, maintaining our positions. That's why we repeat the same bromides over and over again. Churches repeat the same things Sunday after Sunday like an alarm clock that has to go off again and again. If we learned the first time, we wouldn't need to do that. We have to be trued up again and again. But we knew that when we were done stamping our feet, all red-faced and out of breath, the world on its enameled tracks would hurtle on, indifferent to our witness.

All we own is ourselves. They take everything else, but they can't take that.

Dan's action was a Very Big Deal, and he's our leader when we meet in the back room, have drinks, discuss whatever is happening, and angle for ways to get back into a purposeful life. Those who are broke don't ask for help, but we do what we can. For some, suicide recurs as an option, and we do our best to prevent it. The brutal impact of what they do to us is difficult to grasp. Divorces plague our number—BJ and Steve were typical—and maybe me too, in a way. Penny left. I am plagued by the way her face looked when she rose from the table and disappeared into the snow. Nothing but wet snow pelting the window with icy pellets and people passing, collars up and heads down in the bitter wind, indifferent to my grief. I sat at the table and watched the winter suffocate the world, alone and abandoned.

Until I found Valerie. I honestly think that Valerie saved my life.

A few find good jobs and another spouse. Wigand did. But they're the minority. Most families break, and once we have told the truth, we have no choice but to continue to bear witness. Telling the truth becomes our vocation. No wonder they want us to go away. Our presence in the world is a rebuke. But it's a hard road to travel, basing our lives on a sometime thing.

It never took long for Dan to slip into a mea culpa mini-rant. The poor guy felt so guilty, he even promoted a poster at DOD that said, "Don't do what I did! Don't wait!" He was always saying things like, "Do what I wish I had done, years before I acted." We understood, we all wished we had spoken up before we did. But let's be honest: Dan like the rest of us loved the work. He loved the privileges. I loved what I got to do and who I got to do it with. But I wasn't burdened like Dan was, because my contribution was much less. Dan did a big reveal equal to the weight of the guilt that plagued him forever. He had been a good soldier, a company man, for so long.

He had to pivot from the security world where everything is gray. He redefined the world in black and white. He read Gandhi and Martin Luther King. He integrated their thinking into his. He forged an identity for his new career—lucrative speaking, something most can't do—repeating the same history, the same insights, the same stories, for audiences paying big bucks to share a sense of vindication, righteousness, and above all, the illusion that we won *some*thing. He was willing to play the role of a saint. The adulation and applause buoyed him. I didn't have that opportunity: My memoir found its way into a few hands but royalties were few and far between. The average reader of a blog is one, the person who wrote it. Publishers prefer predictable pap that fits the niches of reader and writer alike.

I'll concede his sainthood, his martyrdom, his need to airbrush the complex realities of polity and politics. We cut him some slack. When we engaged with Dan, we avoided mention of Snowden. Dan had convinced himself that Snowden did as he had. I believe deep down he knew that was disingenuous. Snowden put lives at risk and Dan knew it. A data dump is not an act of careful discrimination. But you won't hear us criticize others at our meetings. You'll only hear how right we are.

So the game was crooked, sure, but the only game in town. Where else could we go? Was there another Troy for us to burn?

My decision to avenge Nat had mixed motivations. I admit it. As I told Val, I did miss my old life. If I couldn't serve my country, I decided, I would serve the higher good. I'd serve Nat, and Miriam, whose grief affected me deeply, and a universe built on some kind of principle, instead of factions waging wars that never stopped. I had to angle my life toward a new direction that was hard to define.

I remember one fateful Wednesday night (fateful for me, just another night for most) in the back room at the Barbican. A soft autumn rain could be heard on the windows. The windows were black except for the drops that reflected the streetlight like iridescent insects. When we tried to peer outside, all we could see were the reflections of our own faces and reflections of people behind us, a quasi-community gathering itself for a night of mutual admiration. Our camaraderie was seductive, bursts of hilarity happening now and then and bolstering morale. The drinks kept coming. Valerie knew what everybody drank and her tips from our "club" paid the rent for a month. She worked the crowd like a pro. We agreed to stay professional: I ordered, she brought. We exchanged glances now and then. Once in a great while she would lean to reach a glass and whisper in my ear, who was saying what on the other side of the room. Before the janitor emptied the baskets of paper waste, she rifled through it for scribbled notes. A diligent acolyte, my gal Val. The more I knew about my pals, the easier it was to build new relationships.

My new friends sometimes felt like real friends but we couldn't make up for decades during which we had never known each other. There was no shared history. Older people don't find friends easily. Once your self is mature, your previously porous boundaries stiffen like arthritic joints. You 're more contained, more detached. Reruns of *Friends* make you nostalgic, remembering when you were open to friendships like that, decades earlier. "The best friends I had were when I was twelve," Gordie said in *Stand By Me*, a line that brings a tear to my eye.

We populated the back room with high spirits and laughter and insights into the foibles of the world. It really was a glorious time. There was Dan with his feet up on a chair and his white hair and his gravelly voice that sounded like he was under water. Ping him and he'll reward you with paragraph after paragraph of his current political thinking. Ask him about the seventies and they'll come alive as if fifty years had not passed. The nuclear crowd picked his brain too, his domain of expertise. He would do a one-man Dan show as if he were channeling himself at the drop of a hat.

If I had a camera, I would pan around the room. There in a far corner was Serpico, back from Europe and looking his age, not talking to anyone, which I would do, I guess, if colleagues had pushed me up front to take a bullet in the face. Colleen was often there, still living down the abuse she endured at the Bureau. Had she been heeded, she would have saved a lot of lives. But she lived in the middle of the country, and what good thing had ever come out of the Twin Cities Field Office?

I recall an intimate talk one night with Sherron Watkins. She took a lot of heat for sending a memo about fraud to people inside Enron. She waited months before making it known to the world. She was still a little shaky. She said you can't understand how lonely it is when you take a stand and power people do everything they can to bring you down. She extolled her lawyers for keeping her free, and she gives talks and wrote a book. "It never makes up for what you lost," she said with a quivering lip, "never being able to work again in your chosen profession. I was a damned good accountant," she said, her near-tears turning to anger at the bastards at the top. 'I'll never forgive them, what they did.'"

The desire for revenge sustains us for a good while.

Sherron's story touched me. I leaned from my chair to give her an awkward hug. Valerie brought her a third drink. She thanked Val intensely, more than bringing a drink deserved.

I don't mean that Val was not deserving of thanks. She was great in there, sensitive to mood and nuance and need, and she took good care of her charges at the bar. It was natural for her, but also resulted in better tips. Until I found something steady—until I found something period—her tips sustained us, just. I meant that Sherron's emotions were not resolved, that the trauma of her ordeal was the source of her intensity.

I think Val will read this. If it's on Kindle, she'll search for mentions of her name. I don't want to make mistakes.

Dan was a moving target for the groupies who sought his counsel. His concerns about nuclear weaponry, wars, policies that were off the rails, everything insane by any rational standard, made him a natural for nuclear blowers. He struggled a bit to lift himself from the chair but once he was up, he was good to go and ambled with amiability to the chair reserved for the chief of their loose circle. Their questions often drew long thoughtful responses. He was still a good thinker, as enraged about our policies as he had been about the war, but he could have used a good editor.

Their patron saint was Silkwood, of course, as much a martyr as Joan of Arc, and justifiably so. After they tortured her with needless scrubbing, having planted plutonium on her body and in her home (for which her bereaved family received 1.38 million, without admission of blame), after they tried to shut her up. Kerr-McGee had her killed. When corporations order a hit, they use pros. They are not amateurs. They will have exhausted legal and illegal ways to shut someone down until their only option is a kill. I learned in my work that having someone killed was reasonably easy. The target is recast as deserving of death, transformed from a human being into an object (inside Kerr-McGee, they called Silkwood "a goddamned lesbian cunt.") She told the Atomic Energy

Commission about her concerns and was on her way to a meeting with a reporter with revelatory documents that disappeared after the crash when her car was maneuvered into an abutment. All that was left was a movie that implied the truth, contested by the company.

Thoughts and prayers. Grief and rage.

The purpose of movies like that is to make people leave the theater feeling as if the long arc of history does bend toward justice. As if the Second Coming is right around the corner.

The nuclear blowers were quite a bunch. Joy Adams was fired for supporting allegations about safety at Savannah River. Howard Nunn won his case against Duke which fired him for telling the truth about their station at Catawba. Joe Macktel paid a steeper price—Halliburton Brown and Root was his enemy, and he did win a settlement but seven years in court voided the whole thing because he had violated an NDA. I imagine you can guess what those seven years were like.

Joy hung out with Linda Mitchell quite a bit. Linda had worked at Palo Alto, at a generating station, and blew the whistle on Arizona Public Service. There were lots of safety concerns, and they responded with harassment. But her lawsuit was upheld. She was wounded but alive.

Like Colleen, George Galagtis wound up on *Time*. He was outraged when Millstone 1 Nuclear Power Plant used unsafe practices for refueling reactors and when he went to the NRC he learned they knew about it for years. After he told his story, they retaliated, naturally, but the IG agreed with George. They closed the plant for good a couple of years later.

Another who paid a steep price was Ron Goldstein. It was painful to watch him, with a visible tic and a leg that was always shaking. After he filed a complaint, he was fired. He sued because he thought he was protected but the courts said, no, private programs aren't covered. So he lost his case—but the law was amended to prevent retaliation in the future in cases like his. Which did him a lot of good, right? But you know who helped him stay sane? Marvin Hobby, who informed on Georgia Power and was taken off his job. A decision against the company brought George four million bucks (minus lawyer's fees, of course). He used a lot of it, bless his heart, to help his co-conspirators.

Enough already, right? I could go on and on but I bet you're tired of hearing about one after another, punished with a fine or a manageable settlement while the blower is ground to powder. There are many more stories, but that's enough. The pattern is always the same: someone tells the truth, the response is brutal, and little changes.

I wanted to talk that night to blowers who had been involved with device makers like the people who killed Nat. They had their own pod, several tables full, and that's where I went.

I remember Valerie, in the doorway, watching. I felt her eyes follow me, I felt her apprehension. I knew how well she conected the dots and guessed what was coming next. She knew I needed help in crafting a plan and to keep Miriam sane. She didn't really think it was worth the risk, taking on Syntactic, but backed my need to do it. She has backed me all the way.

Beatrice. Dulcinea. Valerie Patchett.

When I moved into Val's apartment, her friend Sally asked. "Are you sure you know what you're getting into?"

I never asked Val what she said.

Chapter 15
Do No Harm

"**M**y name is Nick Cerk, and I am a whistle blower," I said to general laughter. Then I added more soberly, "I need your help."

They waited politely, their silence an invitation.

"Shoot," Pete Buxtun said. "What's going on?"

"I have an issue with Syntactic—any of you know that company?"

A chorus of affirmations echoed in our corner.

I needed advice on what to do and how to prevent Miriam from going off the rails. The CEO was the target, but how far were we prepared to go? I had done the research and had hundreds of pages of data. Open source intelligence these days is a treasure trove, especially if you know how to hack Google. I talked to a whistleblower who had worked at Syntactic and an employee who quit in disgust when they they took the direct labor manufacturing employees off the floor for two hours to teach them, not about safety, but only about cash flow.

"OK, listen, this is what they say about deaths from their devices: 'Syntactic takes this very seriously and, over the past five years, we have worked closely with the FDA and engaged external experts to resolve the issues noted in warning letters. The FDA is aware of the steps Syntactic has taken to address the underlying concerns.'"

Pete laughed. "Let's deconstruct the bullshit. 'We have worked closely' means we had warm bodies in a room, talking and gesturing, coming and going, back and forth, meeting after meeting. Some sat at tables with papers before them and some had open cases, implying a lot of work. 'We hired experts' doesn't say a word about what the experts said or what got fixed. Which is, as it happens, nothing at all. Then they shift to the FDA, using familiar weasel words, saying the FDA was well aware of what they did—which means, hey, it's not on us. 'Addressing concerns' means they talked and talked but never fixed a thing until they couldn't ignore it any more, because so many people died. ... but why pick Syntactic, Nick? There's plenty of others doing the same things. Some are even worse."

It helped to know the posse had my back. They were a good collection, and I should remind you how we got there, coming from different places, different points in time, through portals in the narrative structure. When we have a meeting, the portals allow us to assemble a group from every place and time. We gather like kids in a high school cafeteria in tiers and ranks and by common interests. We meet in a single conversation. It makes sense to us, because we find ourselves in one place, talking with one another.

Call it "magical realism."

That night, everyone in my corner had tackled medical issues—pharmaceuticals, medical devices, all kinds of fraud.

"It's personal, Pete. That's why. My partner and best friend from agency days had an implant from Syntactic. It was intended to save his life but it killed him instead. The same device killed thousands of others too."

"How many implants we talking about?"

Pete liked facts like the ones he gave the world about the

Tuskegee syphilis plot. He documents everything.

"A lot. Nat's widow was contacted about a class action suit. She called around and talked to other families. You want to hear a story or two?"

Pete reclined as best he could on the wood-back chair and sipped his drink. "Sure," he said. "Tell us a story."

"I'll try not to put you to sleep," I said.

Dave Franklin snored loudly at a cartoon level and everybody laughed. Then they settled down.

"Jim Finney was young, a father, a husband, dying of heart failure when they gave him the device. His wife, Lina, said he seemed to be doing better. He didn't know that months before his implant, the FDA put the company on notice for not properly monitoring or repairing defects like faulty batteries and short circuits caused by static electricity, that had killed patients. The agency issued a warning letter demanding fixes in fifteen days, but neither the FDA nor Syntactic did a thing. One afternoon, Jim's kids heard an alarm and found their dad on the floor. They called 911, but when the EMT got there, he was already cold. He died two days later.

"The Finneys filed a wrongful death suit and the company settled, not admitting blame, of course. Yes, the FDA had sent warnings but didn't follow up even after the device kept failing inspections. The FDA says it counts on device makers to voluntarily fix problems. Syntactic didn't. They put that thing into 19,000 patients, and after a year, there were more than 3,000 deaths. The FDA never issued penalties even though Syntactic issued fifteen recalls. Lina said, if we'd known any of that, we never would have accepted their offer.

"The FDA says it met with the company more than 100 times. It initiated formal reviews. They had meetings for two years and nothing got fixed. Finally they stopped selling the device, after the deaths threatened their reputation.

"One patient bled out internally and died after surgery because a tube attached to the pump tore open. Another's heart tissue was charred after a short-circuit sent high voltage surging through the pump."

"The good old FDA," Pete said. A murmur of anger rose from the others too. "They're supposed to be the adult in the room. They're responsible for making sure that risky devices are safe and effective. They can seize products, order injunctions, issue fines, but they hardly ever do."

"They didn't penalize the company, even with 15 major recalls, more than any other high-risk device in their database. Meanwhile, patients were in the dark. A year after Finney died, Syntactic recalled 18,000 potentially faulty batteries. Lina found the notice online with her husband's battery serial numbers on the list. The company never told her."

"So they sued?"

"Sure. And some filed a class action suit alleging deception. Six anonymous former employees of Syntactic said the details mirror the scandal at Theranos. One of them said, 'Nothing worked right— alarms, touch screens, nothing. But nothing was done.'"

"What happened with the lawsuits?"

Syntactic settled, $55 million. No liability or fault. They got what they wanted. When the device was approved as 'destination therapy' for anyone, an executive said, 'We're beyond excited. It's a real game changer in that market.' In other words, ka-ching. And the FDA put it into their fast-track approval process for high-risk devices."

"And all that was public?"

"Yes. All out in the open. Miriam talked to a woman named

Nancy Bismuth who found a news story about the recall notice sent to medical providers two months before her device failed. The notice said there was a problem with pump restarts that could cause heart attacks. Nineteen patients had been seriously injured by then and two had died. 'Syntactic said they notified patients,' Nancy said. 'Who did they contact? No one told me.'

"You want more?"

No one said yes but no one said no. The perverse pleasure of righteous rage drove my narrative forward.

"OK, Lettie McCain. She's 33 and one of 14,000 patients still relying on that device. She got the pump after being diagnosed with heart failure. She needed an emergency procedure to clear out blood clots in her device, then developed a bad infection. Doctors said she needed surgery to replace the pump. But her new pump had problems right away. The suction alarms, which alert the patient when the pump is trying to pull in more blood than is available in the heart, sounded multiple times a day for hours at a time. Her team solved it by turning off the alarm. Then she learned that a patient had died because a belt had ripped, yanking on the cable that connected the controller to the pump. She replaced her belt but it frayed and had to be replaced in six weeks.

"'Are they just going to let it run its course until none of us are left?' she said.

"Syntactic charges $80,000 for each device. In one year it brought in $276 million. That's a hell of an incentive. When the FDA kept telling them to fix the problem. Syntactic said, and I quote, 'we have robust systems in place to monitor the safety of all products.' What they monitored was market share. 'The cardiac rhythm management business reached the highest level of market share in a decade,' they crowed. That one took in 400 million."

"Were there issues with other devices?'

"Heart implants, insulin pumps, you name it. They had to get out of the insulin pump business entirely. 'We take responsibility,' Murphy said. 'We'll get this right. We're increasing accountability and accelerating plans to enhance patient safety. Safety is our top priority.' The stock went up six points and the same day, they issued a Class 1 recall for cranial software."

"Reminds me of an article in the *Onion*: 'Customers are our second most important priority.'"

"They can't generate new products fast enough. They had over 180 product approvals in the last year. 'We're moving in the right direction,' the CEO says, 'driving a culture that embraces bold action, competing to win and moving with speed.' Then they play *We Are the Champions* and hoot and holler and dance in a circle. Hell, when they had doctors in there, the ones they pay big bucks to push products that aren't approved or effective, they said, 'Hey! we hit a billion last year! Who's in for a second billion?' The doctors cheered like fanboys at a rally."

I stopped, A few of the guys got up and went to the restroom to escape the stories. I was triggering PTSD.

I waited for people to return and lost myself in my own dark thoughts.

"Nick? Are you OK?"

I blinked. My inquisitor's face came into focus, He was looking at me with concern.

"Sure. Why?"

"I asked you three times, so what do you want? You made the sale, we get it, but what do you want from us?"

"Oh. Thanks. " I steadied myself. "Thanks, David."

David was a superstar. He went ballistic when Pfizer/Parke Davis pushed a drug for epilepsy that it knew didn't work. He exposed a massive conspiracy among doctors, big pharma, marketers and sales reps to "consult" for high fees and push bogus claims. "Respectable" journals published studies that had little merit. The medical profession was rendered so cynically unfit for human consumption that anyone with integrity was embarrassed. As a result of his revelations, false claims were made a legal basis for criminal violations.

P/PD paid seven billion dollars in settlements and fines. They must have deep pockets. When a whistle blower disclosed how Pfizer sold Bextra, they paid out two billion more in fines and settlements.

"David," I asked, "can we do with Syntactic what you did with Pfizer?"

"No," he said simply, "The medical device highways are littered with collateral damage. They drive through the debris. 'It's the nature of the industry,' they say."

I blinked. "What can we do, then? You took it all the way. Can't we do the same?"

"Nick, by your own acount, there's judgements against Syntactic up the kazoo. You described the low-hanging fruit. It simply doesn't matter." He leaned forward seriously. "Listen to me, please: Their deeds are not hidden. That's the point. You can't blow the whistle Nick,when everybody knows. Those settlements and fines are a cost of doing business. That's just what's so."

I sank back into my chair. On one level, I knew he was right. There have been years of allegations of fraud against Syntactic. The Taxpayers Against Fraud gave them their own page in a Hall of Shame. Syntactic paid over $150 million to resolve settlements for false claims about products. They bribed physicians to push pacemakers, lied to Medicare about procedures, and promoted unapproved procedures for all kinds of things. They set aside hundreds of millions for litigation and carried on without changing their ways.

And everybody knows.

"Nick, money talks and bullshit walks. You know that."

"Yes, but there is much more. They have a bone graft product for lumbar degenerative disc disorder implanted in the spine. It was never approved. A patient got 4 million dollars when it made his pain worse, not better, And there's—"

"Nick, stop."

"David! Doesn't their hypocrisy gripe your ass? Have you seen their web site? Videos of people thanking them for saving their lives."

"I know, Nick, I get it. But Nick, I'm not getting through to you." He paused to let his silence compel me to focus. "Nick, the lawsuits and payoffs are public. Everybody knows. There's no whistle to blow. "

I didn't want to hear it.

"You want my advice?" he continued. "Say the serenity prayer. Say it until it says itself in your sleep. You of all people should know, Nick: We live in a broken world. Have we stopped torture because you told people we torture?" A rhetorical question, that. "You did what you could. Now let it go."

He was speaking truth to powerlessness. I felt deflated, defeated. My revelations were bombs bursting in mid-air, shrapnel going nowhere. Fireworks on the nightly news, oohs and aahs, wisps of smoke, then everyone goes home.

And as it sank in, I felt even worse: If I wasn't a whistle blower, who was I? If I couldn't find identity and purpose in that role ...

what *could* I do?

David rose and turned me gently to face him, holding my shoulders in his hands. His face was all compassion and concern. He could feel me trembling with helplessness and rage.

"Nick, tend your garden. You learned the value of human life. You were lucky. Lots of people never do. Live out of that experience, Nick. If you can't, you'll drive yourself crazy. Leave the rest to God. Remember the Bible. 'Vengeance is mine, saith the Lord, I will repay.'"

That made me even angrier. "You want me to wait for that to happen?"

David smiled. "Then pick another story, Nick. Remember Judith? After she snuck in and got the bad guy drunk and cut off his head, the men said, 'Yay! God delivered us!' Know what she said?"

"What?

"God, my ass."

It was up to me and Miriam, then, to get to his tent and cut off his head. So to speak.

Val had been listening. My intense emotions affected everyone nearby and she came up behind me and put her arms around me from behind. She let her chin rest on my shoulder and I turned and held her so tightly. She held me as if her heart would break. Maybe she was afraid of what might happen next. Maybe she was afraid of the way the world worked. Maybe she wondered, what *had* she gotten herself into?

My life felt like loss after loss. Friends, family, my former life— all lost. Innocence lost. Now this one last opportunity ... lost.

As losses accumulate, grief casts a shadow across our paths. Our eyes tear up and we can't see clearly. A veil drifts over us like a cold mist. We conceal our pain. We make up arbitrary goals and chase them as if they matter. If we're lucky, they distract us for a time. I should have known. I should have seen the truth before David had to spell it out.

"I love you so much," Valerie whispered. David was polite enough to pretend he didn't hear. He squeezed my arm and went off to talk with someone else.

David was right. Our small contribution—our lifetime of effort—is all we can offer. Get out of bed, do what we can, and surrender the rest.

Arjuna on the field of battle. Ready yourself and enter the fray. The din and clamor of battle drowns out the silence of life and death. Seek no end but engagement, pursue no other goal. Remember what that shaman said:

"We are built to live in space that is gateless, unbounded, free.

Chapter 16
Threesome

"I t's very beautiful," Val said, as if she had never before seen such opulence and splendor.

In fact, she hadn't. I often forgot how limited her experience, compared to my globe-trotting. I had slept in shacks and palaces; I was desensitized to squalor and luxury alike. I didn't give it much thought but had assumed she absorbed by osmosis where I had been, what I had done, what I had seen. As if my experience was hers. (I know, I know, not good boundaries.) She hadn't, of course. She had moved from Des Moines to Chicago and taken trips around the Midwest. She had been to the North Shore of Lake Superior and the Indiana dunes. She had been to the driftless area and the badlands. She had been to Deadwood and seen the grave of Calamity Jane. She spent weekends at Starved Rock. From Detroit she went into Canada and spent an afternoon, about two hours too much, she said. She loved the Midwest and didn't understand why it wasn't enough for anyone. Stretches of pristine prairie filled her with delight.

So she was struck by the luxury, the little she could see from the doorway toward the living room.

Miriam had met us at the door, preferring the personal touch to letting one of the servants show us in. We weren't in some Philip Marlowe novel, where butlers and chauffeurs moved through the pages, giving the hero meaningful looks. We were stuck in reality, hoping to plan a strategy for dealing with Syntactic. Miriam stepped back to let us come in, wearing a white pantsuit with a golden patterned scarf around her neck. Her auburn hair, recently trimmed by Waldo at Chez Marie, shone in the sunlight. The old fashioned flared cuffs of her white trousers were just high enough to reveal bare ankles and red-tipped toes in three-inch heels, a concession to comfort compared to the four and five-inchers the fetish purveyors had foisted on women and gotten away with somehow (a form of hobbling that Miriam embraced, loving the way the heels made her sway). Her presence was bold, the sunlight from behind us lighting her up like a torch. Valerie felt it too. I felt her shrink from the older woman's confidence, Miriam in the ascendant.

"When she opened the door, it was like that symphony when the cymbals crash and the drums begin beating, the tympani I mean. She certainly—I don't know ..." she trailed off, leaving the rest unsaid. I leaned to kiss her awkwardly as we were walking down the street, my hand on her arm slowing her but neither of us stopping, a reassuring gesture that had the opposite effect. When you try to protest, it's hard not to to do it a little too much. "I love you, babe," I said. "You have nothing to worry about, Val."

She knew there was a wide world beyond the doors of the Barbican and that the rich, as they said, were different. But she hadn't expected to visit one of their magic castles quite so soon. Miriam had asked if she would like to come to lunch, sensing perhaps that our time together planning our revenge might leave Val feeling out of it. I thought she was just being considerate, and I was surprised when Val said yes. "You expose me to places I've never been," she said, part of her attraction to me, I think. I told her exciting stories of my former adventures, some of them true. I was still trying to sell her on myself. The difference in ages was never far from my mind. Younger well-built macho-men drank at the Barbican and I counted on Vals' aversion to alcoholics, based on prior relationships, to keep them at arms length. I couldn't grasp that she liked the totality of who I was, not just the stories. She told me later, in fact, that my obvious attempts to impress her got in the way. "You don't need to do that," she said. "Just be yourself." I wouldn't have been able to hear that, then, early in the relationship. My self-esteem had taken a beating and I wasn't very objective. I thought stories were all I had. Besides, "being myself" was a work-in-progress.

And ... while I still performed well enough, I was genuinely shocked that I didn't want to, quite as much. I had never not wanted to before. I was always locked and loaded and ready and randy and eager to oblige. Not only with Val, but with others, random trysts like chilled white wine on hot summer nights. Suddenly (or gradually, but it felt like suddenly) I was content to do things that had nothing to do with sex at all. I would realize only later that I hadn't even thought of it for hours at a time. That was new. It had always been just under the surface, bobbing up and down. I thought when it lessened I might be getting sick, but I googled the symptoms and learned I was just getting older.

I knew that happened to others. Old people were everywhere. I had to go around them on walks and on the highway. I just hadn't grasped that it would happen to *me*, long before I thought it might, at eighty or ninety, not in mid-life.

I should have read the book.

"It's very breezy," Miriam said, "so I asked Felipe to serve lunch upstairs in the solarium. The sun's high enough so we won't be blinded if we sit there, unless the glare off the water is too bright. If it is, we can tint that window to dim it. I can do it automatically."

"Like *Bladerunner*," I said.

Miriam and Valerie let the comment pass. It meant nothing to them. In my activated memory, the scene played out, Rachel saying, "Very," when Deckard said the owl must be expensive. I saw Rachel walk across the room to do the Voight-Kampff. Then the scene whitened in my mind.

Miriam suggested we leave our shoes at the door and led us through the vestibule to the spiraling stairs layered with thick white carpeting. It looked as clean as the day it was installed. We wound up and around, looking down across the long living room, then followed her down a hallway past a sitting room but not as far as the bedroom suites to doors that opened onto the solarium. The double glass doors did not make a sound and we followed her into the brightness. The long wrap-around glass-fronted room made the view of the lake look like an impressionist painting. The whitecaps were crisp, breaking onto the narrowing strip of beach, then splashing back into the turbulent water. We had to squint in the blinding light.

"Beautiful," Val said again.

"Yes," I said, "but eat a fish a week from that pond, you risk your life."

"Like getting an implant from Syntactic," added Miriam, bringing the conversation down to earth. It landed with a thud and stayed there, putting a damper on small talk.

Valerie missed the grief in Miriam's voice. She was locked into the spell of the place. She looked out on the sun-brightened expanse to the horizon, a thin blue line. A tanker headed south, barely visible in the glare. Sailboats closer to shore tacked in the stiff wind.

"Just gorgeous," Val said.

Miriam smiled. "It's nice at first, but you get used to it. It gets like a picture on the wall. You don't even see it anymore."

I knew what Val was thinking—*what a first world problem.*

A glass table was set for three. Flowered napkins fluffed just right in their wooden rings. Mats that looked like linen. Silverware, waiting for plates. Glasses waiting for the pour.

The scent of cooking, sensuous, from the kitchen below.

"If you want more than water, we can tell Felipe to fix drinks."

Both of us passed. I wanted to be clear for the conversation.

Valerie watched gulls wheeling, trying to hear them through the glass. Imagining their cries, I imagined. They wheeled and soared, their acrobatics muted. Miriam watched her watching them, her face devoid of tells. Miriam took composure to a higher level. Just what Nat needed, I thought. He didn't like women displaying their inner lives. They might trigger something he remembered, and he didn't want that. He wanted to be insulated, isolated from himself.

"You remind me of Nick Adams in *Big Two-hearted River*," I told him once. "Barely keeping it at bay. The blackbird not whistling, but just after."

"We do what we need to do," he said. "I never read that story. Is it any good? The blackbird thing sounds like a poem."

"Yes, it is, and the story is one of his best. Executed perfectly."

"The way," Nat said, "I exercise my art and craft."

I did not know a single spy who lacked grandiosity.

Val turned away from the seascape and smiled. "I don't think I'd get used to the view that fast. But I know what you mean. There's a painting at the Barbican that was entrancing when I first went to work there. A woman in gold. Her sitting for it was supposed to kill an affair the woman had with the painter; her husband told her to do it. I wouldn't think that would work, myself. I would think, the more he looked at her, the more he saw, the more he would want to put down his brush and rip her clothes off. Anyway, I used to look at it a lot, but now it's just something on the wall."

"Yes," Miriam said. "Exactly."

We stood for a moment in silence.

"Well, shall we sit?" said Miriam, turning toward the table. I deftly drew back two chairs at once and nestled both women close to the table, then sat myself. An old habit, not suggesting helplessness, just being nice.

Felipe rose soundlessly on back stairs with a tray well-balanced with plates with hot melts, gooey cheese on fresh veggies and sliced turkey, a dollop of aioli on sourdough toast, slices of fruit on the side, and a pitcher of ice water. He set it all down with the practice of years, plate by plate, then poured from the pitcher without spilling a drop.

"Thanks," Val said. "I know from experience, that takes practice."

Felipe's lips smiled silently.

We unfurled our napkins and ate. Miriam played the host.

"Valerie, tell me about yourself. How did you and Nick meet?"

Valerie wiped a piece of clinging cheese from the corner of her mouth. It turned into a tiny elastic string which she rolled into an even tinier ball and popped into her mouth.

"We met where I work, the Barbican. It's a restaurant, a bar, and a fantasyland for noir effects—at least the owner thinks so. It does have atmosphere, though. Nick started coming to meet other whistle blowers, people who tried to save the world. The back room at the Barbican is a whistle blower haven. They need a place to hang I guess, and they do drink a lot, and they need to support one another. Some are waiting for trial now. Some are waiting for sentencing. Some were just released. A few became millionaires. I thought what Nick did took guts. I still do. So we started talking one day and well, we kept on talking, and one day he moved in and now we're living together. It just happened, the way things happen to happen."

Miriam said. "I met Nat in a similar way, but we were in Israel. It didn't take long for me to figure out his work. Holes in his narrative, you know. But that didn't tell me what exactly he did. His particular assignments. Being a spy is not one thing. The bottom line, I believe, is getting information, stealing secrets. It doesn't matter how, does it, Nick?"

"No," I said. "It doesn't. Agents are best but they take time to cultivate. Sometimes a black bag job is quicker, and these days, hacking, anything that works. We're into every system in the world, and unfortunately, so are they."

"Nat said relationships were key. People had to think you're a friend, or at least, not a threat. You read Nick's memoir, I imagine?"

"I have not," Val said. "He wants me to wait."

Miriam looked at me. "Oh? I would have thought—"

I gave Miriam the look.

"All in due time," I said.

Miriam smiled. "Nick, for heaven's sake, don't you think it's time?"

I stared stupidly.

Valerie laughed. "You don't have to be coy. I know about Penny."

I did a double take. I had kept her away from the memoir precisely to keep that part of my life locked down.

Valerie smiled, not with a gotcha vibe but to let me know it was old news.

"Nick talks in his sleep. He wakes up sometimes murmuring, 'Penny. Penny. Penny' under his breath. Then he catches himself and stops. I don't need the details. Miriam, look, I've been around, I have my own rabbit holes. Don't we all? Besides, I can't compete with a ghost. I know that. But it's Nick who's haunted, not me"

Miriam nodded. "You're very wise."

"What other choice is there? Life's too short to waste time on things you can't change. I care about us now, not in the past."

You see what she's like? Why I think she's a pretty good companion?

"OK," Val said. "Enough about that. Why don't you two get down to business? I can stay or wander around, whatever works."

"Stay," Miriam and I said at the same time. I added, "I want you to be part of this, Val. No need for secrets." In fact, I wanted her as a second check on Miriam.

When Felipe had taken the dishes, Miriam suggested we go to the sitting room down the hall. It was more comfortable, with deep plush chairs and objects of art on tables, each of which must have cost the same as a 2BR house in a third-ring suburb, and paintings on the wall. There were a number of signed Chagall lithographs. I went from one to another, thinking of Nat. They all depicted Jerusalem. I am sure they were his picks. I flashed on walking those silent streets waiting for civil war after an Israeli has slaughtered worshippers in a mosque. No one else was on the streets. The tension was palpable, dense with foreboding. Nat and I were foolish to leave a safe place and take a walk. But we wanted to see what was going down. As it turned out, it was less dangerous than installing a new Samsung TV when you had a Syntactic implant.

We had hurried back from the West Bank. Shutters falling on closing shops, stones raining on our cars. An oppressive pall over ancient streets. More dead. More grief. More intense hatred.

Val seemed to be at ease. I could tell she felt more at home. I loved the way she read the environment and curved herself into it, fitting in like a cat on a lap.

As she adapted to me and my quirks.

"I don't want a civil war," Miriam said, meaning with Syntactic, not in the mideast. "We want to be swift, and clean, and ever so sweet."

Val looked at me but didn't say a word. Her eyes, however, said, What *are* you getting into?

"We'd better define what we mean," I said. "There shouldn't be any confusion."

Miriam crossed her legs and sat back in the deep chair. One high heel slipped down and dangled from her toe. She bounced it in rhythm as she talked.

"I don't want the worker bees who just follow orders. They do what they're told. The executives. though, don't do a damn thing to prevent deaths. It's the CEO I want. Jim Murphy. He's the one who determines the culture and its values, and he makes the most money—the most blood money, Nick. He should pay for Nat's death."

"That can mean a lot of things, pay for Nat's death, What are you thinking, Miriam?"

She looked at Val who sat on the edge of her chair like a moviegoer waiting for a slasher to jump out of the bushes. "Are you OK, being here, Valerie? Because I won't continue if you're not."

Valerie nodded.

"That's how it happens," Val said later, "isn't it, Nick? You're on the edge of a conversation, and if you don't get up and leave, you're an accessory after the fact or some damn thing, aren't you?"

"Yes," I said. "Yes, you are."

"I watched *Orange is the New Black*. I didn't like what I saw."

"It's a lot worse inside than what they showed. You don't want to find out. But don't worry, Miriam is sane. You'll be fine."

Back to our planning.

"Miriam," I said, "what are you thinking?"

She looked at me and said without a twitch, "I want him to suffer. It won't bring Nat back, but maybe some other corporate killer will think twice before doing the same thing. I want him humiliated, Nick. I want the world to know.""

"Suffer how?" Valerie said.

Miriam said, turning toward her. "Do you ever read the Bible?"

"No," Val said. "I know some of the stories, I guess. Why?"

"I want to cut off his head. Like Judith did. Metaphorically of course."

Judith again. What the hell?

"Miriam? What exactly do you have in mind?"

"Nick, you know the games you played. There are lots of dirty tricks. Nat said when someone's in the way, you have to do what's necessary, right?" She didn't wait for my reply. "I want him to think twice, at least. About what he does."

She was more than reserved. She was ice cold.

"But you'll leave the Glock at home?"

Miriam sighed. "Yes, Nick. I don't want to kill the son-of-a-bitch, just humiliate him in public. I do, actually, want to kill him, but I won't. Will you help? "

Valerie rose and crossed the room to a window that looked out on a garden. The fading flowers and blowing leaves were as beautiful as the lake, but she couldn't see beauty any more. She didn't say, "How beautiful." She turned back around and our eyes met. She didn't say a word. She didn't need to. The twisted plot— whatever Miriam planned—had knotted itself in her heart and head, and nothing sane or ordinary, nothing easy to think about, could find its way out of that thicket. She imagined Miriam actually cutting off his head. But heard her say she wouldn't be so stupid.

"Expose him. In public. That's the plan?"

"Yes. Somebody has to say, stop."

Miriam had inched forward, sliding her foot into her shoe, her knees together, leaning into her pitch. Her intensity was disarming. She wore an expression that wasn't an expression. This was the single-minded woman Nat described, right there in the flesh.

"Miriam? Be specific. What do you have in mind?"

Chapter 17
Plan B, Part One

"That's exactly how it happens," Val said, "isn't it, Nick? You're on the edge of a conversation, and if you don't get up and leave, you're an accessory after the fact or some damn thing, aren't you?"

"Yes," I said. "Yes, you are."

"I watched *Orange is the New Black*. I didn't like what I saw."

"It's a lot worse than what they showed. You don't want to find out."

"I certainly don't. Am I in this now? Because I was there?"

"In a way. But not if we both deny that you were in the room. That's easy. I wouldn't worry. We can say you went to watch the gulls or wander about the house, looking at how the one percent live. In any case, she promised she wouldn't put us at risk. No gun," I laughed.

"That's a relief. Miriam—I don't know ..." she trailed off, leaving the rest unsaid. I leaned to kiss her awkwardly as we were walking down the street, my hand on her arm slowing her but neither of us stopping, a reassuring gesture that had the opposite effect. When you try to protest, it's hard not to to do it a little too much. "I love you, babe," I said. "You have nothing to worry about, Val."

"I'm not worried, Nick." She thought for a moment. Then said, "No. I'm not worried."

We had parked blocks away and decided to walk in the twilight while it was still warm. There was a small neighborhood park a few blocks distant from which we could watch the sun sink below the trees. We did that, sitting in silence on a bench, the edge of the disc reddening before it disappeared. Then we reversed course, taking a long way home. Three and four-story apartments and parked cars were all there was to see, and fading mums and asters in patches in front of buildings, and a lot of dry leaves. We savored twilights which seemed to open portals to other dimensions, revealing a universe somehow connected to our small city neighborhood, a world in a grain of sand.

I think we felt as much like a couple as we could. We had knitted together as the darkness knitted the world into a mass of shadows, an indistinct latticework of branches, shaken by the wind, and walkups that faded into the dusk. Window lights brightened as neighbors turned on lights in a random pattern, neighbors whose names we would never know. A silhouette of someone on the second floor taking off their jacket. A couple hugging before they closed the drapes. No one on the walk but us.

We were alone, together.

Val was a gift I had not expected to get. Had you asked me to list the attributes I might want in a mate, they wouldn't have been Valerie's. That's how little I knew myself. I was still raw, very exposed, nowhere near healed. The trauma of blowing the whistle, a long interrogation, meeting with lawyers and fears of prison, had left me pounded, kneaded, cooked. Valerie slipped into my life right through my defenses. The restaurant—Tom Kat Thai—where we went for dinner that first night became an iconic destination to which we returned to remember and renew that moment of unexpected grace. Val always ordered Pad See Yew and I always had some soup.

The restaurant closed a year later, replaced by Tony's Subs.

Valerie was not-me, her life was not-my-life in so many ways. She left Iowa for the big city and the city taught her what it was. It tutored her, step by step, in a seminar in reality, who people are, what they do. Her adventures were sometimes negative but she learned to learn, the most important life lesson. She dreamed of having a family still. When she spoke of having a child, I blanched but didn't run. I stayed in the relationship, letting it develop.

There was no room for a family in my plans. When you work for an agency, you can't have bonds based on honesty and love. You lie to your children from the time they're born. We were encouraged to marry inside the circus so mutual understanding could help us stay the course, but those incestuous bonds distorted us even more. You just don't know how normal people live. You observe people the way a biologist studies a different order of life, as I thought of the childhood Val described in a two-story wood-frame house with a closed-in porch where on summer nights the family played board games. A drive over to Forest for a "nutty sundae" (three scoops of vanilla in a plastic boat with nuts and hot fudge), learning to swim at Ashworth Pool in Greenwood Park and a walk along the Raccoon, were as alien to me as Mons Olympus.

Val was a normal person, more or less. The twists and turns in her past were the kinds that a lot of people experience. Here a hurdle, there a pit. She emerged from the Barbican cafe like one of the clay people in a Flash Gordon serial. One day she was invisible and the next she was in my arms. She urged me to give the everyday world a fair opportunity. I wasn't ready to retire, but she read advice from articles about how to do it aloud over breakfast—try new things, get creative, see what works. I did my best, but when you're special, being "normal" is not a trivial endeavor.

Planning a vengeful attack on a CEO was not "normal." I thought

I knew what Miriam intended, but maybe not. Miriam's anger had frightened Val, and me too to a lesser extent. I wanted to keep the focus on doing right by Nat, but not at our expense. We came first.

"Well, I am a little worried," Val said. "Aren't you?"

"She was talking out of anger, Val. I think she'll go with the sensible plan. "

"She won't talk you into killing him? Is that what you mean? This won't be a predictable script from film noir? I've seen those movies spool at the Barbican in the video room, over and over again. You're sure a beautiful blonde won't turn you into a killer? I know the lines by heart. 'He's going to die and the only reason is, we want him dead.' 'Sometimes you just wish him dead.' That sort of thing is not going to happen?"

I laughed, hoping it sounded sincere. "Film noir is fun but not our story, Val. I'm not falling into a trap. Besides, she isn't a blonde."

She kept gnawing that bone."But she is attractive. Wouldn't you say? Do you like that held-back held-inside sort of wealthy well-tended North Shore Nancy tight-ass type?"

I laughed again. "I like Miriam, but no, she's not my type." I looked at her face in the faint light of a streetlight under which we passed. "You're my type, Val. Remember what you said that first night?"

"Of course. You were tumbling into my life. I had already picked you out. 'I must be your type,' I said—I was trolling, you know. I wanted to know if we only had one night. You said the right thing: "I like *you*,' you said, 'not a type.'"

"That was true. By the time we finished dinner, I was yours. I hadn't meant it to happen, but like you said, things do happen to happen."

Her voice softened. "It's deeper, now, isn't it? I mean, this is getting real, isn't it? Whatever it is?"

"Yes. I gave up my lease. I moved in. I took over a closet. I burned my boats. But sometimes I'm afraid you'll get tired of an old has-been lounging around."

"You're not a has-been, Nick. You're changing directions. You're testing ideas and seeing where they lead. It's not your past adventures that I love or even your heroics. Don't you know that by now? It's your spirit, Nick. It's like you said. It's *you*."

I put my arm around her as we walked. It didn't remove my anxiety but it sure made it less. "The end of time" is a long view we can't really grasp. I imagined her in middle age and me in my seventies, her energy high. mine low. I imagined her dancing with younger men while I was detaching more and more.

The light from the sky was gone. The shadows-and-shapes of the city street replaced it. The breeze after sundown was cooler, too. We were side by side in a world that for the moment seemed hospitable. I forgot what I knew of the world, accepting Valerie's calmer if equally distorted point of view. Our hands found each other's and clasped tightly, like teenagers in love, which in a way we always are, when we fall in love, regardless of age. I made us keep walking instead of going straight home to our apartment— ours, I kept repeating, not hers. Ours. I wanted to take the long way home—the longest imaginable way—and never get to the end of our seemingly enchanted walk.

But then there was that other thing. There always is some other thing.

"So what did you decide? Seriously."

"Miriam travels in some of the same circles as the CEO. She's doesn't think he even knows he killed someone he knew. Nat's name was on a long list and he knew Miriam by her real name,

Lloyd, not Herman. She wants to confront him in front of his peers. She wants me to escort her to a party at their country club. She wants to trap him and make everyone listen, pretend she's offering a toast, then bring him down."

"But not shoot him."

"No."

"So what does she want from you?"

"She wants me to learn what I can about his life. She wants me to background the bastard so she can have the facts and hopefully some dirt. Throw the dirt in his eyes before she starts in. Distract him with things he thinks he hid by blurting them out in public. She wants me to be there for support."

"As if his peers don't know his history. His stockholders know it, you can bet. His peers will feel bad for him, if she attacks him like that. They'll be angry at Miriam for embarrassing one of their own. Members of 'our crowd' are always forgiven. 'Oh, that's just Joe, yeah, he has a temper,' letting him off the hook for murdering some inconsequential human being."

"We still have to do what we can. Remember what I said? If we don't, then they win."

Valerie made a dismissive noise. "Isn't that what your friend said right before he shot himself? The agency acknowledged a decade later that they did everything he said, when it didn't matter, after he was dead. They paid that South American guy to deny what he told your friend. It was a set-up, you said."

I felt the old familiar pain. "Yes," I said. "That's what they did."

"So who won, Nick?"

"That's my line," I said, trying to make it a joke. It was no joke, though. The moral victory my friend had tried to claim was a phantom. Only if there was life after death, real life, not some vague shades flitting about the ether, and we knew ourselves and others by name, and we remembered each other and what we had been and done, and people were people, not drops of consciousness in a vast ocean. Only if moral law was stitched into the fabric of the universe might there be justice. The odds for that, based on the data, were not good.

"Indulge me, Val. I need to believe a few lies. 'The lies that enable us to live,' Bill Webb called them. 'My stock in trade.'"

Bill Webb was an unexpected gift.

We always met in his study in late afternoon. He seldom referred to the bible, but he did say matter-of-factly once, "Mark was the only Gospel writer who told the truth: a grief-stricken family and friends weeping after their leader is killed, and then—nothing. That was the end of the story. Revisionists added 'alternative facts' later, appearances and mistaken identities, a real mixed bag, using them to claim he was still alive. Or alive again. Something."

"Which do you believe?" I said. "The bitter story Mark told? or the revision?"

Bill shrugged. "Damned if I know," he said, and we laughed at his joke.

I remembered how Bill looked, his red wine in hand, his smile dismissing his troubled faith. Val felt me thinking of something else and lapsed into silence. The wider silence of the night revealed itself as a backdrop. The sound of our feet through the dry leaves marked time like a ticking clock.

We trod a familiar path around the block and turned back at the corner; the breeze picked up and it felt a little chilly, my hand on her bare shoulder, shivering as I held her close, our hips brushing as we walked, unconsciously aligning, and we headed home at last.

❖ ❖ ❖

"How much did you know? About him, I mean?" I asked Bob D., who had blown the whistle on Syntactic for fraudulent marketing of devices for off-label uses.

"About the guy personally? Not much. I stayed with what I knew."

"OK, so how did they respond?"

Bob shrugged. "Honestly, the blowback wasn't bad. Because the division I worked for was a small player, it's like no one noticed. I left sales for recruiting and was never asked about it. The one negative was, I tried to apply to neuromodulation companies—cool start-ups—but they never returned my calls because of my whistleblower status. Believe it or not, Syntactic ended up hiring my new company. I guess they never put two and two together. The invoices went to the company, not Bob D., so maybe they never caught on.

"I don't think they thought it was worth their attention. The settlement was small relative to the amount of fraud I witnessed. Six hundred thou was a pittance to them. They made a lot more than they spent to pay me off. They used dozens of doctors all across the country but not one of them would speak up. Without their help, my case was weakened. I'm glad I did it, don't get me wrong, the fraud was harming patients, they knew they should never sell those things for unapproved purposes—but the suit and settlement talks took a whole decade. It was exhausting—that's their strategy, legal you down. There were tons of meetings with lawyers and endless documents to review." He looked off into his memories. "I'm glad I did it, but I don't know that I'd do it again."

I waited. Then I said:

"Anyway, do you know *anything* about him personally?"

"Mister Cash Flow. That's what they call him. We had tons of meetings at the company and that's all we ever discussed. That and quarterly profits. He did some goody-goody stuff to enhance his reputation, and PR puffed him up to heroic proportions with hype. He was canned by his former employer and was bitter about that, but there was nothing to exploit. His ego made him angry, but egotism is not a crime.... let's see, what else do I know ... he played lacrosse at his prep school—he was good, apparently—and went to Penn State and played there too. There were stories, sure, that he jumped on a girl at a party, just like Gorsuch, but no one could prove it. He got drunk a lot at the prep school and did drugs, but nothing out of the usual. At State, he knew about the predators, everybody did, but never said a word. So he was part of a cover-up, but so were lots of others.

"They did save lives, some—but he never says how many they might have saved had they done it right. The FDA just cranks out words, and anyway, Nick, they don't do the recall, the company does. And others are even worse, You know that. So there's evil in the world. So its goes. Thweeet."

"But we have to fight it, Bob. Yes?"

He shrugged and downed the rest of his drink, swallowing his answer with a little bit of ice.

We called it opposition research, digging up everything we could, and I spent time looking into the life story of the CEO, but Bob D. was right. Nothing would stick. Tales followed him and then trailed off. He was greedy and arrogant, he lied a lot, but that wasn't unusual. That's what shareholders loved.

I dug into his phone calls, his texts, his tweets, his public remarks. I paid a janitor to take documents from the trash. I presented myself as an insurance adjuster and questioned people from his past. I even paid interns to put together shredded papers. I google-hacked his history but the son-of-a-bitch had swept his past clean.

I told Miriam how little I found. Their misdeeds were out in the open. Everyone knew and no one cared.

"I'm not surprised. Are you?"

"Not really. So let's go ahead with Plan B. OK?"

"I have Nat's gun. He showed me how to use it." She sighed. " But I don't have the guts. I wish I did."

"Plan B, Miriam. Stick with Plan B."

"You will come with me, yes? The dinner at the Club is next week. An annual celebration, a fall festival, another excuse to celebrate ourselves and drink. He'll be there I'm sure. You can be my plus one."

"What club is that again?" As if I didn't know.

"The Great Lakes Country Club."

I thought of Nat in the parking lot. I thought of our conversations far into the night. You can't replace a friend like that.

I owed him a memorial.

"OK," I said. "Do I need to wear a tux?'

Chapter 18
Twilight and Wine

I needed a break from these heavy thoughts. I needed a break from how seriously I took myself. The world seems to have managed quite nicely before I was born as it will again after I'm dead. I needed comic relief. There was no better place to find it than our search for a church, a secular quest to meet a few people.

St. Sisyphus, as I said before, put forward a faux-Gothic face behind an electric sign that said, "All are welcome! Seriously! Everyone is welcome! Everyone!" as if that might entice a non-believer from a bicycle as they zoomed past on a Sunday morning and passed ten more churches in the next ten minutes. The first time we attended, that portly bearded prelate, Johnny BG, led the show. The second time the rector, Bill Webb, anchored the procession.

The ushers welcomed us with decorum, unlike an Evangelical church we had passed where greeters were on the lawn, waving and shouting with big grins, beckoning all who drove past. I doubt that worked, but it made them feel as if they gave their all, like Mormons dipping and dunking to add new members who happened to be dead or Witnesses going door to door until they had handed out their Watchtower quota. Those Evangelicals were like big dogs that jumped up, paws on our chests, licking our faces while we winced. Members of St. Sis would have been embarrassed by such a display, or any display of emotion, in fact, instead of dutiful compliance with long established norms. They shushed and said "Be still!" to kids brought in for communion, training them to be silent so when they grew up they would enter a church and be silent without even thinking.

The organist played a quiet-down-now-and-get ready sort of thing and when it ended, there was rustle of anticipation. It was show time. The tension built until the organist pounded out the entrance hymn with gusto, and after the first verse, when everyone had found the hymnal instead of the Bible or the Prayer Book, then found the right hymn, mistaking the hymn number for a page number which meant a lot of leafing back and forth, then and only then did the choir begin their triumphal march down the aisle to the front led by a verger, as she was called, a woman in her eighties with a cross held high. I looked back, then nudged Val gently with my elbow and she knew without turning what I was seeing and wanting her to see, too. She saw Johnny swaying along and sighed. The portly prelate was in full strut. He preceded Bill who looked like the essence of propriety, sober, solemn, and in pretty good shape for a middle-aged man.

The procession parted at the sanctuary and everybody went to their appointed spots. The choir director insisted on singing all the verses of the hymns, and we came at last to the seventh and final verse. Everyone was out of breath. Then the rector headed into the prayers. We had stood to sing and stayed standing until he was done, then we would be told to sit until the next hymn, then we would be told to stand and stay standing, then we would be told to sit, and that went on for an hour. The only respite was that one could kneel too if one could and so chose, here and there. One faced front except when instructed to turn and shake a stranger's hand and say, "Peace." That passed for fellowship. All this instruction and movement lulled the complacent to be like little children, although I doubt that's what was meant by those words, once upon a time. So I was standing, then sitting, then standing again, then sitting again, until Bill said some common-sense words and we realized we could listen to the man without wincing.

Thus endeth the comic relief.

My relationship with Bill got real. I called for an appointment. I never thought I would do that, but he seemed sane and capable of listening. I learn how I feel by talking things out, so I thought he might help. If it didn't work, nothing lost but time. And there was no one else to ask.

I called him Bill and he called me Nick. Because of my background, approach, and demeanor, and because I wasn't a member, he could talk to me pretty openly. He talked about how weary he was after years of tending others. He talked about how clergy behaved behind the curtain, as he put it, when they could step out of their roles.

He had recently been on a retreat, for example, and the leader had held a session for what they called baby bishops. He told Bill how sad it was, seeing newly elected bishops all excited and full of enthusiasm and then, a year later, come back beaten down, drinking too much or gaining forty pounds or sleeping with an assistant.

It became clear that Bill was nearing the end of his ability to cope, trying to dilute his growing unhappiness. He was looking for ways to stay in a career he no longer wanted. So as much as I wanted someone to listen, so did he, and we got to a point where we both talked, taking turns.

Did I use whistle blowing as a way to escape a career I no longer wanted? Was that my version of a wrong-way affair?

I never thought of that before.

"I laughed at your notion of food and sex, but you may be onto something, Nick." He said he had counseled a woman recently whose husband was the priest of a nearby church while she was the secretary of a church downtown. Hers was what they called "high church" which meant long dramatic liturgies, doctrinal rigidity, chanting instead of speaking whenever they could work it in, lots of colorful costumes, ancient names like verger and sub-deacon for bit players, clouds of smoke from vigorous swings of a thurible, and a mid-sized congregation of mostly gay men who went to Sunday brunch at the rectory to make political decisions. The previous bishop was gay and lived with his partner hiddenly for decades; they took separate flights to island hotels and never appeared in public holding hands; they were a couple as long as Penny and I, and everybody knew it, but that was the way it had to be, back then.

The most recent bishop wasn't gay, but he liked to fuck women, at least one, his attractive lay assistant, Denise Porter. She carried on for six months, then made him an offer he couldn't refuse: if he resigned and paid a settlement she would not press charges and wouldn't tell. He did pay and he did resign, claiming a medical condition. "My arthritis prevents the fulfillment of my duties," said his sad letter to the diocese which, taking him at his word, threw a big bash to say goodbye. His long-suffering spouse continued to play the good wife although everyone had seen his photo on the refrigerator under which she wrote, "Children, this is your father." Denise apparently did tell, one at least, because Bill knew it and so did anyone who cared.

The secretary said the men would stop in and chat, but she often felt like there was a hidden smirk behind their smiles and didn't know why. Then one told her: her husband was grazing in that pasture, going from one to another. He had told her he was bi but claimed he never acted out (the word "celibate" was often used instead of "oversexed") and she had chosen not to know what she long suspected. She confronted him and he said that yes, he had been having sex with all those men and enjoying every minute. They were a hell of a lot better and infinitely more creative, he said, than what I was stuck with here at home. She filed for divorce and he said fine, I'm good with that, but if she ratted him out, she wouldn't get alimony. Her well-being depended on him getting a job in another state. She was angry, of course, but knew he was right, so she brought her helpless rage to Bill. All he could do was listen, tsk-tsk, and when he saw her spouse, act as if he didn't know a thing. Her husband did secure a job in Dallas where the living was easy and cotton was high.

"That kind of crap is not unusual," Bill said, At the retreat, because he had a reputation for keeping his mouth closed, a number of fellow clergy took walks with him around the grounds and bled off their anxieties. Confessors apparently need to confess too, especially when they fear being found out and fired.

One young priest laughed as he said, "The truth is, Bill, I love to fuck girls and the parish is loaded with great-looking girls."

Uh-huh, Bill said.

Bill went on and on—about a veteran priest who didn't understand why Bill thought sleeping with dozens of women in his parish ("they adore me," he said with a smile, "and most of them are single") wasn't a good idea; about one who loved going to strip clubs, watching the dancers and masturbating in place, buying a lap dance when he could afford it; about one who wore pantyhose under his clerical garb, signaling his transvestism when his alb fluttered in the wind. There were a couple of plain vanilla married men who slept with just one woman from the parish, other than their wives, run-of-the-mill affairs. There were gay clergy who made the rounds of tenors in the choir. There were tenors who slept with the organist.

One poor guy was in tears when he learned his wife was sleeping with a priest from the next parish. Therapy for everyone, then everyone moved to other places in a game of musical chairs. The worst he heard was a guy who was arrested when one of the young boys he'd been molesting told his parents and the parents called the police. The priest's unhappy memories were centered on the sirens he heard with their frightening doppler wail, meaning jail time for him. He felt no remorse, Bill said, and said the boys enjoyed it. He sat there, Bill repeated, shaking his head, and told us they enjoyed it.

He unloaded stories until I was exhausted. I became the sacrificial goat's sacrificial goat.

I wasn't surprised by anything he said. He described the human condition. The church, however, had to pretend that clergy weren't human. That made everything worse. Bill thought a twelve step program for everyone, clergy and lay alike, would allow a process of mutual redemption, but "fat fucking chance of that. That would destroy the system which depends on projections. Being real wouldn't cut it."

"I understand," I said. "You're describing some of the reasons it was easy to recruit agents. Most chose to work with us lest their antics become public knowledge. Marriages, careers, we didn't care, you can keep all that, just do as we ask. Remember the scene in *All The President's Men*? I don't care that you were in Sally's apartment, I just want to know what you said in Sally's apartment. Journalism, politics, same, the same. You too, in a way, but when you hear their confessions, you try to help. It's a power trip, sure, but you do try to help. Isn't that right?"

"It is," he said.

"Well, not us. We did it to control."

I told Val when Bill started to confide in me. I said I sometimes had to work to get in my own stories. She didn't act surprised. She understood more than I had thought. After we had been together for a while, she told me more about her past. I told her more about mine. Our deal was, keep the past in the past and stay faithful now. Not even monogamish.

"Of course," she said. "I mean, we have a deal. Right?"

"Right," I said. "And compared to things I did, sex was the least of it." Then I said without thinking, God knows why, "We were way way too long in those goddamn rooms—"

"Stop. I don't want to know what happened in those rooms."

I stopped. I bit off the memory and felt its acrid taste in my brain. I slid into the darkness of my history. It felt like falling into the mud. I was always walking around the edge and that time I slipped. Valerie felt my sudden fear, felt me drop into the pit. She saw the past come alive in my eyes as if it was happening now. I pushed hard to escape the prison of my memories, but the harder I pushed, the more intense they became. My face betrayed my helplessness and terror.

Valerie moved close and took my face in her hands.

"Nick, Nick, oh, Nick," she said. "Darling, I love you so much, I know what it did to you"—darling was a first; she never called me that before; and she didn't know what it did to me, because no one could—"Trust me, darling, I understand. You're safe with me. Please please know that you're safe with me. You'll always be safe with me. "

She held my face firmly in her hands until I more or less returned. Quaking inside, but stabilizing, coming back. I could see her face, not what I had been seeing. I anchored in the present. Then she held me close.

She knew more than Penny ... and she stayed.

Valerie stayed.

All I could think to say was "thank you, Valerie," as she held me until I was free of myself.

Thank you. I began saying "thank you" from some deep place as soon as I awakened. It was an unconscious shift I didn't understand. Thank you for what? I was grateful for Valerie, of course, that the first thing I saw was her. But more than that, I was grateful for being alive, having options, having the freedom to make choices. When her eyes opened and she smiled, glad to see me too, I felt grateful for ... everything.

That was a new way of being in the world, a state of being, I believe, elicited by my young love and her endless forbearance, and one more reason why, despite her lapses, lacks and irritating traits, I loved that woman so damned much.

I found a friend in Bill Webb, more or less. You may not think that's relevant to the story, but you'll see that it is in *Mobius Out of Time*. That's why I am taking time to layer him into the narrative. Sitting in his study in the late afternoon, in the silence between sentences, insights rose in my mind like messages in a Magic Eight Ball. I told myself the truth, more and more. At a certain age, a man has nothing to lose by telling the truth. Who cares, really, what others think? I was ripening. I was—dare I say it—maturing.

We referred to the parish as St. Sisyphus. Bill calls Sisyphus the patron saint of clergy. Sisyphus, you recall, pushed the boulder up the hill again and again, day after day. Then he stood at the top and watched it roll down, his face impassive, like clergy, like a spy. Then, after a pause, Sisyphus walked down the steep slope to the bottom, took a deep breath, looked up at the hill, and pushed the boulder up again.

"That's parish life," Bill said with a laugh. "Like Sisyphus, I imagine myself happy."

His humor was defensive.

Because I encountered Bill at the end of his term, the timing was right for what we both needed. He had punched all his tickets and was being offered the best parishes—the most prestigious, the largest congregations, the best salary packages. One offer included a million dollar house on the ocean in Maui. Another dangled a five-story Back Bay townhouse but, he said, you had to live in a museum. Funny, he said, how you started out intending to do good and wound up doing really well.

It was ironic, he said, to be offered positions he once thought he would want and for which he had made his career moves like a climber toward the top of the wall, when the mere thought of them now left him empty. His authentic passion for ministry had issued, he believed, from internalizing the archetypal energy of a "priest." It was like dealing himself the right Tarot card at the right time. People invested him with the power to be their priest by treating him as a priest and that enabled him to be one. I got the sense that, like my time in intelligence work, he deeply loved everything about it—until he didn't. That archetypal energy diminished when he passed the age at which his father died. You can unpack that as you like, he said with a wry smile, but it's obvious, isn't it? We don't know why we're doing things until we stop doing them. One day he woke up and the energy was gone and he wasn't a shaman anymore, he was a plain human being. But he hung on in the role long past the time he should have left. He thought he might recover what he lost, but it didn't happen. He could act out with one of the beauties in his parish to get himself removed or take the high road out of the profession. That's what it had become, a profession, not a calling. It didn't make him happy any more. No one who is happy has to imagine themselves happy. I could see all that and more, but Bill had taught me that a good counselor chooses when to use what he sees for the benefit of the client. Don't just blurt it out to show how perceptive you are. So I nodded, making empathetic noises, as he often did, as I had in my former work, and shelved sharing my insights until an appropriate time.

To imagining ourselves happy, then, I say, and we raise and clink glasses and sip some really good wine. We didn't drink communion wine, we used his private stash. Then we sit for a moment in silence. The afternoon light fades until we can barely see each other. Only then does he get up and turn on a lamp. We are in his warm office, the deepening blue of twilight through the tall windows looking out on the quiet street. A hush descends. I feel hopeful in the moment but I don't know why. Maybe it's the wine. Whatever the source, I feel that things can work out. My anxiety lessens. The moment brims with a sense that there is more for me to do.

I said, "Bill, something has to change. Being a whistle blower, hanging with others who did similar things, that's not a way of life. There comes a time when you know it doesn't work any more."

We whistle blowers were like football stars reliving the catch that saved the game, a *Goodbye, Columbus* sort of thing. I was growing tired of the sound of my own voice in that back room and of their voices too. I had to trial-and-error my way to a new path, a path that had heart.

"Faith can help a human deal with all kinds of pain," Bill said, "but it has a trap door that can open any time. You know what it is?"

I shook my head.

"Faith wants to promise certainty but can't. You don't know that, not really, when you push in all your chips. You don't say 'I think' or 'I believe,' you say 'I know.' But you don't know, because no one can. If we're honest with ourselves, we know that we live with an unsolvable mystery. That's why we settle for hope. That certainty you hear from those who pretend to have it is desperation. not faith, a need for control that turns so easily into contempt for everyone else."

I said uh-huh, uh-huh, and when it was my turn, I returned to my own narrative. I said I felt like something was coming but didn't know what. Tony singing the *West Side Story* song. I talked about Valerie and how much I needed her but I knew she couldn't resolve my challenges for me. No one can. If someone says they can, they make you their slave. If you meet the Buddha on the road, kill him.

Bill's faith in his Christian myths was like a balloon that had escaped a child's grip. He felt it slip away. and remembered how it felt to hold the string as he watched the tiny speck shrink into the glare of the sky.

The myths of the intelligence world were based on similar fictions. Our system was equally fragile, sustained by a refusal to look at the lunch we were eating, the naked lunch on the end of the fork. We too had to believe or it wouldn't work. Once you had clearances, you stopped talking to people who lacked them as some Christians dismissed statements by unbelievers as irrelevant. But people without clearances and agnostics and atheists make up the world. They're the water in which we swim and we ignore them to our peril.

"Water again." A universal solvent. A metaphor that worked for Robert Towne too.

I liked sitting in that office in the late afternoon. Bill and I always sat in the same chairs with a table between. He saw behind me his many books on shelves and I saw his desk across the room and tall windows along the wall. It was sometimes a struggle to get my words in. The important thing was thinking them whether I said them or not. Our conversation enabled me to become more conscious. I had to find my own way. Maybe a counselor is always a catalyst for that. Somehow our dialogue enabled me to make headway.

Meeting in late afternoon was ideal. The setting sun turned the shades of his windows liquid gold. Bill would set two glasses on the desk, fill them with wine from a crystal decanter on a sideboard and hand me one, then we went to opposing chairs with the table between "for therapeutic distance." We sipped our wine as the sun's glare diminished. Bill let go of his clergy persona and I did my best to forgot I had been a spy. We practiced being plain people.

That memory recurs, again and again, as a safe place, a warm snug cubby.

"So here I am, Nick" he said, "in the middle of a dark wood with no Virgil as a guide. I need to leave the role. I need a new path."

"Me too," I said. "Me too."

He paused and I said, "Bill, I'm going to dinner with Nat's widow Miriam. She wants to confront the man who killed her husband. I have to make sure she hasn't any weapons in her purse. I don't want to get roped into some film noir scenario."

"You think she might try to kill him?"

"I don't, but I'd rather be safe than sorry. She wants to expose him for what he is in front of his peers. She'll slap the shit out of him, a la Will Smith."

"Will that be enough?"

"It will for me. What else can we do? The world goes on. Our better angels fight the good fight but all victories are pyrrhic. I want to help Miriam, I have to honor the memory of my friend, but then I have to move on."

"I see," he said.

And that's where we left it.

I finished my wine, set the glass on the table, and rose. Bill rose too and walked me to the door. He started to speak, but realized too, I think, there was nothing more to say.

We embraced briefly in a dignified man-hug. Thanks, I said. Thank you, he responded.   Then I made my way through the maze of hallways past the empty chapel to the front door and drove home.

Chapter 19
Plan B, Part Two

I had never been to the Great Lakes Country Club. I knew it by reputation as an enclave for elites. I learned in my work that sources of fortunes are many and never an indicator of quality or success. Money indicates the presence of money, a lot of it from ill-gotten gains. That's not prejudice, just observation. "Behind every great fortune is a crime."

All groups use gossip to define themselves. The members of the country club were no exception. They used one another for mutual validation and to know what to think like mirrors reflecting one another. They protected their boundaries by keeping interlopers out. They hid from self-doubt with illusions of entitlement. That's a high price to pay for fool's gold and the pleasure of eating meals and playing golf with the same people week in and week out, long after one has grown weary of their platitudes. But leaving the group is unthinkable. The group provides identity and the nineteenth hole is salvation.

Those uncharitable thoughts were on my mind as Miriam's chauffeur Roman brought her Maybach up the long curving drive to the clubhouse. Trees were on both sides of the road, shedding leaves in the autumn breeze. The curves in the road made it seem like a longer drive to the welcoming lights of the clubhouse under the darkening skies. Trees and traps and fairways faded into the dusk. It felt like we were getting home just before dark and the hearth would be crackling with fire. Leaves blew across the beams of the headlights and onto the practice green. One last cart with a driver and a passenger came up the path and handed over the cart to Fred, an attendant who had been with the club for eighteen years, who would clean the irons and stow the bag.The sound of their cleats on the concrete walk as they made their way to the locker room said hurry hurry late for drinks late for drinks.

Roman hurried around to open Miriam's door. I slid across the scat to exit through the same door, waving off his intention to scoot around to the other door. "I'm pretty spry."

"Of course you are," he dutifully said.

Roman was eastern European and very very big. Nat hired him as protection for when he was gone for weeks at a time. I don't know if he knew how to use a sap, but with his size, he probably didn't need it.

Miriam had told me I did not need to wear a tux, just a nice suit. I wore the best one I had but everyone else was in a tux. Miriam said she was sorry, she had not paid attention to the invitation. She should have double checked.

"Ignore them," she said, meaning the disapproving looks, "you look lovely." She turned and adjusted the shoulders of my jacket with a couple of pats and jiggles. "Thank you for coming."

"Wouldn't miss it for the world," I said, and she sort of smiled. She held her clutch-purse tightly and I took it to offer my arm and feel for a weapon. It was too small for the Glock. I couldn't detect a bulge.

Someone ahead of us stepped aside to open the door for Miriam and I let her go through. She did look good in tans and browns with rust-colored accessories and her face in the indoor light so smooth and wrinkle-free. We looked like a couple arriving for dinner, one attractive, the other in an old suit.

When we entered the building, the crowd noise from the bar adjacent to the dining room was a muffled din. There must have been a dozen people at the bar, jostling for position. Two bartenders did what they could to keep up with the crush. A number of people chatted, old acquaintances, old friends. There was warm camaraderie, indistinct conversation, clubhouse affection, some display of ego. As we moved toward the bar, a number of them greeted Miriam. No one mentioned Nat or asked how she was handling her grief and may not even have known. I imagine Nat's absences, long and frequent, had accustomed members to expect her to come alone. I knew for a fact that Nat went with her as seldom as possible because he was so bored there.

We confided to each other, Nat and I, that one of the amusing aspects of our work was how different it was to be a particular someone compared with pretending to be a particular someone. If you were a prosperous businessman flush with a new contract, say, with the Navy for making underwear, it might make you rich but not a great conversationalist. That person was likely quite boring. But if you pretend to be that person, acting for a purpose in your work, the added dimension brightened the experience. Instead of wearing a two-thousand-dollar suit because you did, you wore it as a costume, which made it an extension of your craft. Your focus shifted to doing the role right, remembering the details you scattered on the path like bread crumbs, keeping an eye out for birds. One mode was boring, the other was challenging. The game of life taken neat never lived up to the Great Game that made our work zesty. Just being yourself was like losing your taste buds. You could still chew, but it wasn't very enjoyable.

"I'll have the Monkey Shoulder Blend, please," I said, "neat." That was a treat I seldom had. The bartender delivered a swift perfect pour. Miriam had been spirited away by conversation and was waiting for her drink, engaging in small talk with a guy I had seen on the news, reassuring investors when their stocks went down. I joined her and she introduced me and I said how much I valued his expertise, which of course made him beam. Then another came up and I shook his hand, we faked smiles for a moment, then joined the crowd with our drinks, edging toward the dining room. Final touches were being added to the tables. Through the open door we watched someone come from the kitchen far across the room and look over the scene, then slip back into the kitchen.

We killed time circulating among the members. The buzz of their conversations filled the room. There was laughter now and then and the unmistakeable loudness of someone speaking importantly over the noise or who swept his arms in a way that made people give him the room he was due. I was content to tag along quietly beside my date, playing my role as an escort.

Dinner was announced by a double chime and the herd pressed through three double doors into the main dining room. By habit I looked to see how we could leave, should a crisis ensue. There were paths through the tables that led to the three doors and fire exits in the back of the room. I mapped them all in my head.

"We're at Table Nine," Miriam said. "Over there." She pointed with her face. I followed her toward the table where others were setting down drinks and pourers were asking "red or white?" as people sat, filling glasses deftly and with care. It took a bit for people to sit but soon enough we all did, and Miriam said to me in a whisper, "He's at Table Four. Do you see him?"

I looked and sure enough, there he was. He was sitting with his wife and three other couples. The way they engaged with one another said they belonged in a way I never would, even if they let me in, which they wouldn't, of course.

A few years back, Nat would not have been allowed to join the club because he was a Jew. Once they modified the rules, he could piggyback on Miriam. The members honored the change and never said to his face what they said to one another. They dismissed what they thought was his vain effort to become respectable by piggybacking on a Protestant.

I studied Murphy carefully. He wore his tux well, I could tell he worked out and was well-toned. His face was flushed with his first drinks and perhaps, I imagined, with the knowledge that Syntactic had revenue of thirty billion dollars and everybody knew it.

A familiar tinkle of spoon on glass signaled for silence. The murmur continued. Tinkle again, more loudly. Finally the crowd hushed. There is always one conversation that continues until they realize that everyone is waiting for them to stop.

The President of the club was at a dais with a mic. He adjusted the neck of the podium mic but it didn't seem to work so he took up a handheld mic. When he started to speak, feedback shrilly shrieked through huge speakers and he turned with a disturbed look and said to a hapless tech, can't you fix the goddamned thing? That was picked up by the mic, of course, and everyone laughed. The tech scrambled to fix it and next time his voice was normally loud. The Prez welcomed them all to the annual autumn celebration kicking off the winter season and wished everyone well. He described the meal with pleasure: where they had managed to find the best kobe beef, the names of the greens in the salad, then dessert, a freshly made ganache. He discussed the wines being served at great length and concluded, after applause for the rare vintage, "And now I would like to offer a toast." That's when Miriam stood and called, "Paul? Oh Paul? May I propose a toast before you do the official formalities?"

He looked to where her voice had seemed to come from and his eyes landed.

"Ah! Miriam! There you are. How nice to see you, dear. Yes, yes, of course, will you do us the honors, please?"

Miriam left her drink on the table and walked through two tables until she stood next to Murphy at Table Four. She stood a bit back of him while a tech ran the handheld mic from the dais to her hand. He flicked the switch and tapped it twice, the sound resounding through the room, then gave it to Miriam with a smile. Murphy turned a little in his chair, the better to see her behind him at an angle. Miriam lifted the mic to her lips.

She said, "Testing," once, and it worked fine. Then she turned with her back to the Murphy party and said slowly and with care:

"I want to acknowledge the achievements of one of our members. He has been on my mind a lot these weeks." She turned toward Murphy and asked him to stand. He looked surprised, but not surprised that someone might want to honor him, and he stood, pushing back his chair as he edged out into the space where Miriam was waiting.

"James, or Jimmy to many of you, is at the helm of a very successful company called Syntactic. Their annual revenues are nearly thirty billion dollars. They sell more implants, appliances, devices, call them what you will, than their competitors combined. They continuously innovate and push out new products at a remarkable pace. Nearly two hundred new devices were pushed into the marketplace just last year.

"But they do more than put new devices into the heads and hearts of innocent people. So much more. They put their products into people who expect them to work miracles, keep them alive or make them healthy again. At the least, they expect them to work. But ..." She turned and spoke into the face of the honoree, "sometimes they don't quite work as promised, and when that happens, do you know what the company does? Nothing. They do not do a damned thing. Do they, James? They string along the authorities, the so-called regulators, and buy time and sell more defective products and when those time bombs go off, they kill people by the thousands."

It was starting to dawn on some guests that this was not an ordinary toast. Murphy didn't know what to do. He couldn't grab the mic or wrestle her to the floor. He sort of swallowed, sort of stared, as Miriam plowed on.

"My husband Nat Herman received a heart implant from this man. Nat's heart was not moving blood as it should. The implant was intended to fix that problem. The company knew that something as common as static electricity might short circuit the device, but that didn't stop them from putting it into thousands of people. Nat was setting up a new television when static electricity leaped to his implant and he dropped dead on the spot. I found his body wedged between a sofa and the TV. He joined the thousands of others who had been killed by that device, killed by this son-of-a-bitch and all his co-conspirators. James Murphy, you knew it, the FDA knew, it, everybody knew it, and no one did a goddamned thing.

"My husband Nat Herman, I am telling you, you bastard," she was not addressing the crowd any more but Murphy to his face, so some missed her conclusion and had to ask for it afterward, "my husband is dead because of your greed and you should be dead too, you piece of shit. But I can't do what the courts should have done. I can't put you in jail. All I can do is tell the world that you have killed thousands of innocent people who believed your false claims and bought your faulty products and you knew they were faulty and you are guilty of fraud a thousand times over, yet you stand there like the king of the world instead of the scum of the earth that you are."

With that she raised the mic and brought it down on Murphy's head. It cut him enough to leave a thin bleed and as he winced and backed away, she hit him again in the face. I think she hit the bridge of the nose so there was more blood than injury, but it looked pretty bad. Then her arm went chop chop chop, hitting him over the head with the mic which made a loud sound with every impact. The mic was working quite well.

I know for a fact that she had intended only to hit him in the face with her hand. She planned to bitch slap the bastard then backhand him if she could. She could not have known that a weapon would be delivered to her like God arming David with a sling and a stone. I told the suburban police when they came around she had never intended to use a sap.

No one wanted a public scandal or even a report of the event. The local paper didn't cover it and the club directors intervened to be sure it was not featured by local media. So the wider audience Miriam might have achieved did not materialize, to her disappointment.

Still, everyone at the dinner heard what she said. The thing was, they were not surprised; they knew the stories about Syntactic and many owned the stock, because practices like theirs ensured returns that would beat any industry average.

By the time Miriam had finished, Murphy ducking and backing off and turning away from her blows, others from neighboring tables came to his rescue. Someone grabbed the mic from Miriam's hands and someone else grabbed her from behind and walked her away while others attended to the wounded CEO who now had a bloody napkin at his face.

And where was I while this was taking place? I had risen quietly with my cell phone when she started her speech and quietly moved through the tables toward her and made a little video. I had to stop when the hubbub started and I shouldered others out of the way, saying, "I'll take her, thank you," freeing her arms from the grasp of a gorilla, saying, "Come on, asshole, you don't want a law suit, do you?" which he didn't so he let go and I hurried Miriam toward the door. Diners all around us were on their feet, some asking, what did she say? what just happened? with others answering or shrugging or reaching for a crisp carrot from a relish tray. All in all, the place went nuts.

I got her through the door into the chilly evening, Chauffeurs were standing around, and Roman leapt to his feet and said, "Should I get the car?"

"Yes," I said. "We have to leave early."

He ran off in the dark and the Maybach arrived in minutes, the chauffeur leaping out to escort his boss into the car. I slid in and we shot off into the night.

All I could see was Miriam's well-composed face in the lights of oncoming cars once we were on the main road. Neither of us said a word. She breathed deeply and steadily, staring straight ahead until we arrived at her home, a short ride from the club, where we left the Maybach and I walked her to the front door.

I followed her inside. She turned on the light in the vestibule and I saw a few streaks of blood on her dress but the same composure as always. She didn't cry, but her expression included satisfaction now as well as anger and grief.

"Well, Nick, we did it, didn't we? Plan B worked—oh damn!" she said. "I should have taken a video."

I held out my cell phone. "I'll send you the clip. I'm sure it'll go viral."

"Oh, that's wonderful! Thank you so much!"

She eased forward into my arms and we held each other for a long time. I held her with mixed emotions until she stepped back. I knew any thought of charges would be quashed. I knew she would watch the event on youtube and vimeo and tiktok and instagram and everywhere else she could put it. I knew I had done what I could for my friend Nat.

"Thank you, Nick."

"Are you all right, here, alone? Do you need—"

"Oh no, I'm fine. Thank you for offering. I'm used to being alone." She lowered her eyes."You knew how it is, being married to a spy. I liked being married to Nat and it worked out for both of us. We both had what we needed. Nat wasn't here much, and when he was, he was so locked up inside himself. Yes, he shared some things with me, but as a rule he would talk a bit and then just stop. He would go off into himself and ... you know he loved astronomy?"

"I did. He talked about it some."

"There's a big telescope in the shed that he used on cloudless nights. He built walls to block the light. He said it's called a Dobsonian and he loved it. He described galaxies and nebulae and planets. I wasn't as interested but what he showed me was so beautiful. It's not a dark sky at all, it's filled with colors. Nat would stay out for hours and lose himself in the stars. I was usually asleep when he came in.

"So I appreciate it, Nick, but I'm used to being alone. At a certain age, we all have losses, don't we? Grief never goes away. You know that. Don't you?"

I looked at her and tried to not feel what I felt. "I do know that," I said. My chest tightened and my breathing grew shallow."Nat was my closest friend."

Everything else that occurred to me to say sounded trite. So I didn't say anything more. Miriam walked me to the door, kissed me on the cheek, and closed the door behind me as I left.

Then I was alone, walking to my Prius down the driveway in the dark. I paused to look up at the stars that Nat had loved to wander in his dreams. It put things into perspective, he used to say. But the sky was full of clouds and no stars were visible. I waited for the clouds to part but they never did and I grew chilly and gave up.

I got into the car and drove home through quiet streets. The traffic was light at that hour. I took a long slow route back to our apartment. When I arrived at our neighborhood, it felt like I was home. There wasn't a street—there wasn't a building—that wasn't connected to some new memory in my mind. There I was having dinner with Valerie. There I was in the pocket park watching the sun go down, waiting for the next stage of my life.

When I finally came in, Valerie was just home from work and I told her everything about my dinner with Miriam.

Chapter 20
An Unexpected Event (or Two)

I asked a colleague to relate the tale of my breakdown in *Mobius: A Memoir*, and I asked Val to do her best on this episode as well. She did pretty good, speaking in her own idiom, but I did rewrite a bit so parts may sound like me. I respect her style, but as you know, the editor has the last word.

Val wrote:

He never had trouble with stairs before.

We lived on the second floor, and Nick often carried the groceries, two big bulging bags, one in each arm, up the stairs at his usual clip. He always moved quickly, and sometimes I had to slow him down so he didn't zoom ahead on a walk. *We* are taking a walk, I had to say, not me following you. He couldn't help it, though; he did everything fast, walking talking thinking whatever—his brain was always on and I could tell when he was thinking as he slept. I could feel the humming in his brain. He often told himself to solve a problem while he slept and when he woke up, he often had the answer.

I guess we all come into life with our motors set. People were always telling Nick to slow down and he had to resist telling them to speed up.

Sometimes he was so much into his thoughts that I told him I needed a balloon filled with beans on a stick to bang him on the head and bring him back to earth. (He told me about that from some literary work in which air-headed philosophers needed to be banged on the noggin to have a conversation with normal folks down here—humplings, as he called them, which is not a polite term at all).

Nick was proud of having coined two new words—humpling and megapounder. I would not have been so proud, myself. How about making up a word, I suggested, for the joy you feel when you fall in love with the right person? He said he would give it some thought. I could tell from his expression, though, that he got it; he knew he had done just that.

The word for which he searched was "Valerie," duh.

Nick had to suffer folks who didn't think as fast or see as much as quickly as he did. He couldn't help it, he said when he grew impatient at Slowy Slowertons. It must be lonely, I said, wanting people to get what you say right away but instead they stare at you like dopes. It can be annoying, he confessed. I prefer an exchange at parity.

His impatience began to lessen when he realized that other ways of thinking were as valid as his. He explored the mindsets of others in his prior work like a spelunker lowering himself into the darkness of a Plato-cave, as he called it, where most people spent their lives. He understood people really well when he did his work but I don't think he respected them. When you spend your life outwitting people who don't even know they're in a game, it can't help but create an attitude. In his work, Nick said, he never considered anyone an end in themselves; they were always a means to an end. He collected people to use and if he gave them something in return, it was based on estimating their value to him now or in the future. I told him I couldn't believe he lived like that all the time, and he said, well, not every minute, but damn near. He justified himself by saying the work required that, and anyway, most people do it, they just don't know they do it or do it with much awareness.

He was thinking of Penny when he said that. He told himself that he and Penny used each other equally. He wasn't specific, he just said she knew what she was doing. He can't get why Penny never returned. I didn't know the nature of their relationship, not at first, only that he couldn't seem to quit her. Not in his head, I mean. I had to let him work it through the best way he could. Once that box of letters came and he told me the whole story, I was taken aback. I was, in fact, shocked. How can spies live like that? How can anyone live like that?

More easily than you think, he said. Most people never have to face the fact that under the right circumstances, they're capable of anything.

That was part of a *Chinatown* quote. Nick was always quoting movies. Men do that more. Fictional people are more real to them than people they know. He never took people at face value, he was always analyzing what they said and why, but he believed works of fiction. That's funny, right? Believing in lies more than real things? Fiction, he liked to say, is the only way a spy can tell the truth. When you don't have religion—and he didn't, not in the traditional sense— you still need some mythical narrative that helps make sense of the world. Nick said he got it from the agencies and also from books— from literature, by which he meant the classics, the "canon," not the entertainment kind, what he called shovelware with more than a touch of disdain—and from good films. A lot of his favorite films were made in the 70s. I wasn't even born then.

The canon he mentions is no longer relevant. Mostly old, mostly dead, mostly white males, writing often offensive things about women, blacks, gays, Jews, you name it. Books too heavy and big to hold up in bed with a light clipped on. He says anything more than 300 pages is rejected out of hand. Most people these days can't even parse a complex paragraph. Fads and fashions drive what's in and out through revolving doors, and don't get banged in the ass if you move too slowly. Mention the word "influencer" and watch his face twitch.

I don't know how much I would have liked him, had I met him when he was a spy instead of at the Barbican. Post-traumatic Nick was in my opinion a much better Nick to be around. He wouldn't have been interested in me before, anyway, I'm sure. I wouldn't have been a way to get information or connect to someone useful, or anything, really, of value. He might have wanted me for sex, but the way he was, what I am saying, is, I wouldn't have wanted him. If I wanted sex, it wasn't hard to get. I needed to like the people I went to bed with, and when Nick and I fell into each others' lives, I more than liked him, I had grown to almost love him before we even knew each other. The things he said at the Barbican were wonderful, I thought. The way he treated people, in a gentler way, after they beat him up. The guts it took to tell the world about torture and pay such a heavy price. I loved the person I sensed he was or could be or wanted to become, even if he hadn't gotten there yet.

All he needed was the right woman, I believed, with her hand on the rudder of his life.

The things that made him a good spy—empathy, being easy to talk to, easy to like, easy to believe—certainly were attractive traits. When he made the pivot into the world of humplings, those qualities emerged in a purer form. He learned to relate to people as they thought of themselves, as they presented themselves, and for the first time, he let himself like them, just plain enjoy them, even when they were shallow or slow or even pretty dumb. He learned to look for something good. He was like a child who had eaten only two things—macaroni and cheese and ramen—and suddenly started to eat everything. Once he realized how he had walled himself off from relationships with people and realized that people were all around, it was like a smorgasbord, a buffet. He stuffed himself with real people. He talked to people in lines at the store, he chatted with receptionists, he even talked to strangers waiting for a light to change.

So anyway, I noticed when he began to have trouble with stairs and slowed noticeably at the first landing and came up the rest of the steps at a slower pace. He went ahead to unlock the door and stood inside the door to catch his breath. He was breathing very heavily. He didn't move with his usual quickness. An alarm went off in my head as I watched him sit for a bit before he had even taken off his coat.

"Are you OK?" I said.

He looked puzzled "Sure," he said. "Why wouldn't I be?"

"You got so out of breath. That's not like you, Nick."

He shrugged. "I should probably drop a few pounds. I haven't been on a scale for a while."

Not one to put things off, he removed his coat and went to the bathroom to get on the scale. I heard it ringing as he put it on the tile so he could get a truer read. I heard a clunk as he put it back. He reappeared, puzzled still.

"Actually, I lost a few pounds. So that isn't it." He looked for a better reason, non-concerning ones, of course. "I didn't get much sleep last night. Maybe I was just tired."

"Maybe," I said, but I decided to keep a closer watch. I had to be at the Barbican to start my shift at three. "Call me if you don't feel right, OK?"

He shrugged.

"I mean it, Nick."

"Sure, Val. of course. Okay."

He decided to go for a jog and didn't tell me it was a test. He worked out enough to stay in shape but he got pretty winded right away. He hadn't gone a block before he had to stop and catch his breath, and he hadn't been jogging fast. He told me that later, when I was with him in the ER, waiting for Doctor Jamolski.

The next day he woke up feeling tired. As a rule he bounded out of bed, unless we were under the sheets with the blankets pulled up over our heads. Something wasn't right, but all I could do was tell him what I thought. I said he should see his doctor.

"I'll call him," he said, and he did. He made an appointment to see him the following week. I was distracted with work in the meantime so I waited to hear what the doctor said, concerned but not super worried.

The Barbican was going through changes. I knew I wouldn't stay. The owner sold it to one of the young bond salesmen from a nearby office tower who bought it for a hobby, I think, because he had a lot of good times over the years. Those guys were awash in money and looked for things to do with it. Like Michael Jordan betting thousands on which raindrop would go down a window first. Pretty sick, right? Those younger guys didn't know what film noir was. They didn't understand the time in which the films were made, the source of the darkness. They believed in *belle epochs*. They thought they would never end. Nick told me all about film noir, he thought the best ones were genius level, but above all, he resonated with the viewpoint, the darkness, the despair. He said people thought his dark vision was cynical. I'm cynical? he said with a laugh. Valerie, I'm a realist.

The Barbican was something special. Maybe we all feel that way about the places where we work for a long time. Our team is always better than their team, that sort of thing, which I understand happens when we choose up sides; it's innate, Nick says. I was there for seven years when I met Nick, tending bar, waiting tables, and keeping the customers happy. I have a knack for raising the heartbeat enough to keep them buzzing but not cross any lines, and if they try, which some do, naturally, I know how to whip them back into shape. Nick saw that and trusted me to manage the guys who got too drunk to know what they were doing. Fact is, I enjoyed playing the game, and they enjoyed it too, I think. After a while I had so many "protectors" among the regulars I could count on my brawny brawlers to step up if I needed help. I was deft at turning aside the worst of them without getting nasty. I know I was because they came back.

Jake didn't tolerate crap either. He wanted the place to be fun but not crazy. It had a blend of clientele—traders in markets of different kinds as well as the least and the last and the lost, as Nick put it. Jake had saturated the place with film noir themes, nice little touches I thought. He ran old movies and one TV was always tuned to TCM. When some expert on the genre was on, they turned up the sound and people actually listened and learned. There were posters too from the old movies and glossy photos of the stars. Everything was in black and white and justice was never done. Some poor sap, leading with his dick, always went down. Jake set up a few bright lights to cast stark shadows here and there, doing his best to echo stairways, nightfall, gloomy rain-soaked city streets. They had film nights and trivia nights and a karaoke night for a while. But all things do end, as Nick is always quoting, and when Jake had his second stroke, he called it a day.

The new owner changed everything. No more film noir. More karaoke. a section of three tables behind a screen devoted to what he called "fine dining" after seven, with tablecloths and silver instead of plastic. You didn't have to be a weatherman, as the man said, to know which way the wind was blowing. The clientele changed. I didn't enjoy it much any more, and my relationship with Nick changed things too. I held more in reserve for him that had been scattered like pieces of bread before a flock of hungry birds. It became clear to me that leaving was not an if but a when. I just didn't belong there any more.

"I have time off coming," I said. "Want me to come with you to see the doc?"

"Why?"

I shrugged. "They say it helps to have someone along to listen. Sometimes news blindsides a guy and they can't hear it."

Nick thought for a moment. I thought he would take the macho way, but he didn't. "I think I'm just tired," he said, "but that makes sense. Sure. The appointment's at two. Let's grab a bite at Willy's before."

So that's what we tried to do. Willy's didn't take reservations and lunch hour during the week could be crowded. Sure enough, it was, and we would have to wait an hour for a table, so that didn't work. We were standing inside the door discussing where to go next when Nick got real woozy. I saw his eyes were not quite focused and he put a hand on the wall and held on. He looked for a free chair and fell into it, and I realized he was passing out and I got scared. Someone waiting to be seated leaned in when I cried out and he looked at Nick and said, call 911. Before we did, Nick came back to himself and I had to tell him what happened, "Jesus!" was all he said. "Let's get to the doctor's."

I managed to flag a taxi and Nick walked unsteadily, holding my arm. The hospital wasn't far and the doctor's office was in an adjacent tower. Nick started to fail again as we walked in and they rushed him straight to the ER. They did what they do, they listened and looked and ran tests and it became clear what was happening.

"Good thing you were on your way," the doc said. "This could have been bad. It's bad, but we can handle it. Listen," he said, leaning close to Nick was was sitting on the edge of the bed, "you have a problem with your heart. Bradycardia we call it. That's why you got so tired, that's why you fainted. You need a pacemaker, Nick, to get the heartbeat regular, and my advice is, do it now. Don't wait. Let's get it done."

"What? Wait a minute. What if—?

"Get a second opinion if you want, but be real. This condition hits more men after sixty and you're not quite there yet, but it can happen at any age—obviously. You need a pacemaker, Nick, and you'll be fine. I recommend the smallest one, it's called a mini, you won't even know it's there. But your heart will know. It'll tick to a healthy rhythm again."

"For how long?"

"The average pacemaker lasts a decade, but that's a statistical average. They can go much longer. Valerie," he looked at me, standing there silently. "Tell him."

"Do it, Nick," I said. "Just do it."

My voice softened his resistance.

"A mini, you say?"

"Yes. It's from Syntactic. They own the pacemaker field. They made the first ones. You've heard of Syntactic, I imagine."

Nick looked away.

"Yes," he said.

"Let's do it, OK? Let me be sure there's a room. It's a local. It's just a little slit."

So that's what was done. Soon a Syntactic pacemaker was sending its lifesaving juice into Nick's heart and he felt a little better right away and a few weeks later felt much more like himself. He hated how well it worked. He hated that it came from Syntactic. They told him to avoid strong currents which could send the gadget into a tizzy. "Use cellphones on speaker phone. Watch out for a infections, swelling, bruising or bleeding, blood clots or a collapsed lung." The doctor smiled at me. "You keep watch, Val. If there's a thick foul-smelling discharge from the incision, tell us right away."

"I think I would notice," Nick said.

"Don't lift anything heavy, OK? You may not be able to lift weights."

"For how long?"

"Oh," the doctor laughed, "forever. You have to live with this. Look, you're a lucky man. If you hadn't been nearby, you might have died. You need to appreciate that."

Nick was not ready to appreciate anything. "I'll save appreciation for another day," he said. "Right now it is so fucking ironic."

"Ironic?" the doctor said. "How so?"

"I'll tell you another time," Nick said.

So we didn't expect that, did we? Who does? We're fine until we're not. Nick had been healthy and thought he would stay trim and fit until he was a hundred. He did not intend to join the great majority for another few decades.

Meanwhile, as Nick recovered, he looked for work. He wanted to contribute. It bothered him more than it bothered me that I carried the freight. We were prudent, we lived within our means, but as the Barbican changed hands, I began looking for work, too, and harboring thoughts of having a child. We were into a new phase. We needed to think differently.

Nick was more patient than I expected. He even slowed down a bit and did as he was told. He wasn't the old Nick, and you know what? That was just fine with me.

❖ ❖ ❖

And then ... one fine autumn day he received an email to "Nick Cerk." He had opened an account in his "real" name and wondered who, besides scammers and spammers and marketers, would bother to write. The games he played with names were crazy, to me at least, since I never lived in a context of cover and deception. It was really self-deception, since if a spy used fake IDs for a long time, he would wake up one day and realize he had no idea who he really was. An occupational hazard, Nick said. For a while I thought "Divor" was his name—that's what he had said—but I learned it was one more made-up name.

"You told me a whole bunch of names," I said. "Are any of them really yours?"

"Yes and no. They were all me, at the time. But if you mean, is that what my mother called me, no."

"So what's your real name?" We had been living together for some time. It was absurd that I didn't know who he was.

"Let's stay with Nick Cerk," he said. "It's good enough."

Later, of course, he told me what his name was, his real name at birth. He showed me his birth certificate. He was born in a hospital on Wellington on the near north side. I checked and I got documents that backed up what he said. It was a pretty common name and not very exciting so we stayed with Nick Cerk. He thought of himself as Nick Cerk. That's how I think of him, still. His "real" name sounds fake. He hadn't used it for years.

So Nick Cerk was the name on his email and cell phone account and Signal and proton-mail and a Linked In Account and Facebook and Instagram and TikTok. He was having fun with all those since he hadn't been able to use them when he worked. The email came from "Russell Lagopus," a made-up name for sure, he thought, a spammer, a bot, a prankster from the agency. But something made him view it in a preview pane and not delete it.

"Hello. I am looking for Nick Cerk," it said, "who used to be friends with a woman name Penelope Delphine, who he would have known as Penny. Several Nick Cerks show up in my searches. Are you the Nick Cerk I am seeking?"

The phrasing sounded a bit foreignish, so it might have been malware or spam. He wrote back, "I believe I am. I did know a woman named Penny and we were friends for many years. We met when we were students. Tell me more."

After he sent a reply, he checked his account at least once an hour. "What?" I finally asked, the second day he did it, his urgency obvious.

He told me it was about Penny. I asked if he was ready to tell me more about her. He said he was, but let's see what this is about.

Most people expect a response to an email at once. They often grow testy when someone waits a day or two. That was Nick, irritated and testy, living back in the past and besides, still adapting to having a pacemaker and ticked off at who made it.

A reply came after three days.

"It sounds as if you are the one. If you are, I will need an address for sending some letters Penny saved. I have not read them but can do so if you need verification of identity or such. I must tell you unfortunate news, however. Penny expired recently from a rare form of leukemia. I have lived with Penny for two years. We thought she was doing well when it reared up again and she was dead in three days. There was no funeral. I scattered her ashes as she wanted in the lake on a beautiful day near a cafe that Penny once said was where dreams went to die. I asked her what that meant and she never replied and never mentioned it again. In any case, are you willing to send an address so I can send this box of letters that she kept?"

Nick was stunned. A cluster of emotions warred with one

another—shock, grief, excitement, fear, the most obvious ones. He stared at the message for a long long time. At last he read it aloud. "Is it real, do you think? It sounds real. But I would never give my address to someone I don't know."

He wrote back, "Read one of the letters and give me an idea what it says. That will tell we what I need to know."

Again he had to wait several days. When the reply came, it said, "I read two letters. They describe springtime on a campus in Missouri and discuss a class in English you were teaching. You talked about the students, how frustrating they were, and suggested a time you might be free to return to the city to see her. Does that sound like you?"

Nick began to sob. Deep wracking sobs tore from his gut as he grasped what had happened—that Penny had died, and that she saved the letters he had written over all those years.

When his sobbing subsided, he looked at me. I was waiting patiently at our little dining room table where a three hundred piece jigsaw puzzle was halfway solved if that, and his eyes were red and his breathing was long and drawn out.

"I'll suggest a place to meet," he said, and that's what he did. He suggested the coffee-and-pastry shop near the park where the ashes had been scattered and where, as it happened, he said later, they had their final meeting. He went at the appointed time and a middle-aged man with an accent waited just inside the door. "I do not drink coffee or eat sugar," he said with pride, then he gave a box to Nick on top of which had been lettered, "Penny's memories" and inside which were all the letters he had sent over all the years they had stayed friends, all of which she had saved, "all of which she saved," he repeated, showing me the box and the letters stuffed into it, and greeting cards, and a few picture post cards of the fake places where he told her he was living, his cover so complete, his deception so elegant all those years.

He fingered the treasure of letters and disappeared to read them all. He was back in the past with his Penny, his lover, his friend, the focus of his many lies.

It took a while before he was able to return to the present. As he read through the letters, all designed to mask his true work and whereabouts and of course his true identity, it brought back not only the excellence of his fictional narratives but the places he had really been, when he wrote those letters. Long-term memories from their first meetings, long exchanges about events they genuinely shared when together, plans for the next meeting and the next and the next, gossip about their lives and lovers and friends, hers allegedly actual and his demonstrably false, a record of a relationship that ended when he told the simple truth she couldn't hear.

I did the only thing I could. "I can't compete with a ghost," I said. "Take the time you need to work it through, do what you have to do. I'm here. When you're ready, come home."

One of my finest moments, if I say so myself. I was right. He read all the letters, one by one, then shredded them all. It was an act of demolition designed to free him from his grief and his unrequited honesty, and it sort of did that, I believe.

When he was ready, he told me about Penny. He told me bits of her bio that suggested who she was, which was plenty for me, having no need to know the dead woman more than that. He told me how he had generated a complete story of who he never was, "the man who never was," he laughed, invoking the story of the dead body planted during World War 2 for the Germans to find. "I never said it that way, the man who never was. But that was my whole life, Val. I was a man who didn't exist. Now you can read my memoir and see who I was in relationship to Penny. Please, read it, OK?"

"Ok," I said. "It's time, isn't it?"

"It is," he said. "I want you to know who I was, who I am."

I read *Mobius: A Memoir* in two days. I couldn't put it down. I realized why a reviewer said, at the end you know you don't know anything about the man at all, because you realize that none of us know anything about anything. That review opened my eyes to the depths my man had layered into the most truth he could tell, the least untruthful things, congruent with his loyalties, congruent with the NDA he had signed that would put him in jail if he divulged anything without modification or gave a real name. Nick protected his friends long after they ceased to be his friends. He hated who he had become in that life, but he honored who he was.

And on the Sunday night of the weekend I had spent reading his story, he told me more. For the first time, I didn't say stop, I don't want to know that. I had to steel myself to listen but I owed him that, listening to the horror he had witnessed, the horror he had done, the pain he inflicted on people for a long time before he saw in that woman's eyes the humanity of everyone he tortured, everyone who died in those horrible places. It had taken longer than it should have, I had to think, for him to grasp what he had done, but you can't judge what it takes for someone else, it takes what it takes, and for Nick it took beating people and confining people in impossible positions for weeks, cold and naked in dank rooms, stinking in their shit and piss, their hands bound behind them, filthy rags stuffed into their mouths, unable to move or even scream except inside their heads, an agony impossible to imagine, freezing them and heating them, keeping them naked, giving them shocks and burns, beating them with clubs and pipes, breaking their bones, whipping them with wire, and all because some of them might know someone who might have done us harm, while many did not and died for their lack of knowledge. Nick spent two hours telling me what they did, what he had done, and when he finished he sobbed and sobbed and I held him in my arms until he was empty of the grief, if only for the moment, because the toll it took would never end, the nightmares that awakened him and me, too, of course, his terrified screams in the night as he dreamed of others doing to him what he had done to them, that would be part of him forever, and part of the American nightmare we can not confess to any priest, lest we blow our cover and destroy the vast fictional narrative we cleverly invented to tell ourselves who we aren't.

Chapter 21
Intimations of (Im)mortality

"**H**e wanted to be seen. He wanted to be known. He wanted to be understood."

That's how Valerie described me to her friend, Simone, after I told her what we had done.

Scratch that. After I told her what I had done.

She had seen me feeling down but never quite like that. She held me in her arms until I settled down. I told her I was fine, which is what I say no matter what. I needed time to gather myself together again. She wisely left me to myself, knowing I'd ask if I needed her to be there.

I didn't. I needed to let my self confrontation rock itself to sleep.

After such knowledge, what forgiveness? More than a line in a poem. Fear, anxiety, and shame: fear of the future, anxiety in the present, shame about the past. If only exorcism worked.

The events of my past were like time bombs and exploded when least expected. Shrapnel wounds were everywhere. I had deeply feared disclosure of what I did. Unresolved, unconfessed, unrevealed to another, I was tormented, haunted; but once I confronted my actions, I could include them as part of myself, integrate them into my whole being. We are all revolving yin/yang symbols, darkness and light, one and then the other, a pinwheel spinning faster and faster throughout our lives until they blur into a gray. Once I acknowledged what I did, my isolation lessened. I felt more included in the human race, not because I was special or smarter than others, as I had thought, but because I was not the worst imaginable human being. I was just another person who succumbed to a delusional commitment to a structure that seemed to provide purpose and identity and led me to do, as Roy said, questionable things ... until I found a way to break bread with my better self. The illusion of an isolated self no longer had a stranglehold on my self-conception. My grief eased, my self-loathing diminished. The fears, self-doubts, and insecurities that had powered my arrogance lessened.

A nightmare that had plagued me found me running through dark alleys in downtown Chicago. The walls of buildings hemmed me in on all sides, latticed with shadows of fire escapes. I was always pursued by some bad actor and could hear his footsteps coming close. I always woke up screaming—until, after that catharsis, I dreamed that instead of running, I turned and waited. The pursuer burst out of the alley and stopped cold. He stared at me uncomprehending, looking *WTF?* I was supposed to be running in fear, not waiting to embrace him. But embrace him I did, stepping forward, opening my arms—and I woke up, not with a scream, but free.

I never had that dream again.

And the biggest thing of all, thanks to Valerie ... I learned that I could love and be loved. I hadn't known either was possible. Penny never gave me that, nor could. Nor did I know I needed it. In retrospect Penny was a companion. Valerie was a means to redemption.

A few days later, after Valerie had returned from work and we were in the living room, I felt she wanted me to talk more about it. She hadn't brought it up, leaving me to choose the time, but I felt her expectation. I was about to respond to her unspoken invitation when her cell phone rang and she went to the kitchen to talk.

I heard her talking to her friend Simone, who had worked with her once, before Val went to the Barbican. They worked in a call center using branching answers on a chart to reply to questions about products that apparently were not easy to assemble. Customers asked for explanations of instructions written in pidgin English but the call center workers were just as lost. They could escalate to supervisors but if they did that too often, they were fired, so they tried to guess what was meant. Some customers laughed along with their mutual attempts to decipher the words or understand the twisted syntax and some—about two thirds—ranted and raved with rage. Front line employees always take the heat.

They sat in neighboring cubicles with about eighty others and were always on line. Simone had helped Val move out of a difficult situation—she wasn't in danger, she didn't think, but because you never knew what a guy might do, they thought it best to sneak out on a weekend when he was off fishing—and Simone fronted her rent for two months, the kind of thing one never forgets. She never heard from the guy again.

I wasn't trying to listen to her call, but when you're raw and vulnerable, and someone is describing you, and you're in the next room and they're on a cell phone twenty feet away but could have gone into the bedroom or out into the hallway had they wanted the call to be private, it's difficult not to be very very still and listen with intense focus, because how you are perceived is important when you're not sure how to perceive yourself. The point of view of someone who loves you matters and you want to know what it is. They can describe you better than you can describe yourself.

Valerie was right. After years of hiding behind lies, I wanted to be seen, I wanted to be known, I wanted to be understood. After my breakdown, I had turned inside out and what had been hidden was exposed. The combination of whistle blowing and the episode with my heart and having to get a Syntactic device of all things, left me wide open. I was way over sensitive. A poke could feel like an ice pick. My defenses weakened and grieving for Penny weakened me even more. I was overwhelmed by the horror of it all, and I told Val everything. I told her more than she told you in the last chapter. How much do you need to know? If you need more details, email me. Tell me who you are and why you want to know. I don't traffic in torture porn. I traffic in the truth.

Or read *The Heart of Darkness*. It isn't long.

As I tried to go to sleep at night, I imagined I heard the *tick tick tick* of the pacemaker or my less-than-perfect heart, when in fact of course I could hear neither. The mini from Syntactic seemed to be working, none of the side effects I feared had taken place, and other than following a few new rules like, let Valerie carry the groceries, I had no reason to think my death was imminent, no more than it had been, when every day is a crap shoot and any day, any time, anyone might die.

I wasn't feeling weak or fainting anymore but I needed to rest and gave myself permission. I found myself sitting and thinking a lot, which was rare for a man with a mission like myself.

The fact of mortality permeated my thinking. I had been healthy all my life so it came as a shock that I would one day, all too soon perhaps, join the great majority. We are built well but not to last was a great line in a movie but not so much in life. All the work I had done, the impact I had hoped to have as a spy and then a blower, my whole life's work, would flicker like a firefly and wink out and fall like a cinder into the black river and be carried out to sea. I said I wanted to be all used up but that, I discovered, wasn't the same as *being* all used up. I know that sounds foolish, that I was surprised by the obvious, that people die, that I would die, but denial is a trickster, a great magician, making the obvious disappear. They tell us the unconscious can't believe in its own extinction. I buy that. I can't imagine not being, and I can't imagine not being *me*. The threat of extinction was no longer abstract; it was existential. I quoted Updike's lines, that temporality is not invalidating, but it sure seems to come close. I don't know how he felt about that, lying dying, cancer eating him alive, yet affirming life still by writing some of his best stories.

The *Mobius Trilogy*? That's *My Father's Tears*, my way. An affirmation of life.

It's not that I fear death. When I fainted, it was like death in a way, and I have seen a lot of people die. One moment they're animated, warm, and breathing, and the next they're like paper mache. A desiccated corpse is a statement all its own. You can't argue with a dry papery hand that doesn't squeeze back. You can sit at the bedside for a time but sooner or later you have to get up and go home alone. You have to walk back to the hotel, as it were, in the rain. You can call death a journey all you want, but you go nowhere fast. You can stand at a grave and ask the silence for an answer but the silence becomes the question. Then it becomes a deafening wind and you fill up your life with noise to block it out.

My arrogance diminished (it never disappears, let's be honest, shall we?). I thought I had a good grasp of the bigger picture but the phase change through which I went exposed that fallacy.

I listened to the silence. I sat in a chair that had become mine when Val agreed to give it up, moving to the love seat as her new perch, and I watched the gray sky and falling leaves and the grass turn greenless. Bare branches with only a few clinging leaves fluttering in the wind was my view from our drafty apartment. The sky was often cloudy but featureless, opaque. I tried to scry, I wanted an omen that foretold something meaningful and real.

People turn to horoscopes and crystal balls when anxiety compels a need to know. Some open bibles and turn around twice and let their finger land on a passage (when it doesn't make sense, they do it again). Anxiety had driven me, a need to know machine, all my life. No prognostication fooled me into thinking I was a precog. Sitting and waiting filled my days.

"Who was that?" I said when Val came back into the living room, although I knew.

"Simone," Val said. "She wanted to know how you were doing."

"What did you say? How am I doing?"

She stood in the doorway and looked across the living room. She didn't look excessively concerned; she looked as if she had to choose her words with care. "I said you're doing exactly as one would expect you to be doing, after going through all that."

"Did you tell her everything?"

"No, Nick," she said with a sigh. "You can trust me to do the right thing. I told her about your heart. The pacemaker thing. That it's making you a little wobbly. I protect you, Nick."

"I'm embarrassed by how emotional I got. I didn't expect that to happen. I broke, I broke open. But I think I'm coming back. You be the judge. Am I?" I looked at her closely."Valerie, can you live with me, knowing who I am?"

She thought for a long time, long enough to do justice to the importance of the question. "Yes," she said at last. "Of course. I have so far." She thought a little more. "Nick, I think in some ways I've always known who you were. I'm not naive. I know what humans do. I won't be glib. What you did was horrific. I get that." She shook her head. "But in a way, we're all complicit, aren't we? If we don't speak up, we're all shirking our duty, aren't we?"

"I guess we are."

"You think I'd talk about all that with Simone? As if it was gossip? I dare not think, much less speak, those words to anyone, including myself. Give me some credit, will you? If I need to talk to someone about you, I'll tell you. You were traumatized, Nick. Telling me the truth was the right thing to do. It helps when someone who loves you listens. I read that just yesterday in *Ask Marilyn*. A doctor who listens with care can heal a person more than drugs. Just because I don't talk about everything like you do, it doesn't mean I don't understand."

"Val, do you remember how Jodie Foster in *Contact* said, *'I had no idea?'* Remember that scene? She was seeing the universe. She said those words so beautifully."

"Which is relevant how?"

"I feel like that right now. When I grasp what you do for me— who you are willing to be for me— it feels like that. Wonder, I guess. It's unbelievable, really. It's certainly undeserved. I never knew what real love was like."

"Didn't your mother love you, however twisted it might have been?"

I smiled. "Joyce said, 'There are only two forms of love in the world, the love of a mother for her child and the love of a man for his lies.' I know one of them, at least."

Valerie laughed. "You always quote a movie or a book. You know what I'd like you to do? We have a month-anniversary soon. Here's what I want for a present: Instead of citing books or movies or other made-up stuff, cite something from your own history. Make yourself or me or something we've done a point of reference, not what someone else said. Can you do that?"

She didn't know what she was asking. I had invented so many narratives, all about me but none about me, except obliquely, on a meta-level. "It'll take practice. I can try."

She smiled and shook her head again. "Why do men need to quote other people all the time? Are you that insecure? Maybe you *are* little boys, like Mattie Walker said. You know, Nicky, I wasn't as interested in your stories as you thought. I was more interested in how you looked at me ... during dinner at the Tom Kat. Afterward. The way you looked when you touched me, after we made love. The way I see you look at me now, when you don't know I'm watching."

I laughed sort of stupidly. Laughter is easier than letting yourself feel deeply.

"Like a slow hand?"

"Oh God! You really can't help it, can you?"

We laughed together, and I relished the fulgent moment.

We really might make it, I thought. *We really might.*

Valerie came across the room and sat on my lap and drew my head closer for a soft kiss. It was not erotic, just reassuring.

"We'll get through this too, you know. It's a lot at once. You want to find work, a direction in life, you have to get used to a pacemaker, you have to manage your PTSD, now that it's out in the open, and I'm looking for work, I'm leaving the Barbican which for years was kind of a home away, and we were talking about having a kid—"

I blinked.

"Or should I say, I was talking about a kid?"

"I'm nearly sixty, Val."

"You're in your mid-fifties, Nick. Low middle-age. The middle of middle age. People live to a hundred now. By the time you're a hundred, they'll live to a hundred and thirty-two. You've got a long way to go."

I drew her head down onto my chest. "*Tick tick tick* ... Can you hear it? Can you hear that thing?"

She listened. "Nope," she said. "Can't hear a thing. What do you think you hear?"

"Oh," I said, trying to smile, "just the mortality express coming down the track."

tick tick tick

tick tick tick

The next weeks were a time of slow recovery, slower than I expected, not only because of the implant but from the impact of everything. I looked for jobs on the internet. I applied for a few, just because, and no one responded. I struggled to define myself as a salable commodity.

I felt better physically. I no longer lifted weights but I did jog a little and take long walks. I was a good patient and did what they advised. I adapted to the fact that I would be a patient forever. Val did not seem to think it a big deal. She said she didn't think about it much. I sure did. I imagined myself in a nursing home while Val was still in middle-age. The options I imagined were all bad.

Val stayed at the Barbican while she looked for other work. It was renamed the Wild Rose, morphing into a wine bar and tapas sort of place, attracting more of a younger crowd from neighboring towers. The noirish accoutrements vanished one by one. They played different music that didn't sound like music to me. They catered to generations that had letters instead of names. I couldn't keep them straight. The latest was alpha, which didn't mean what it seemed to suggest. They weren't the beginning of anything. They were just what happened to come next.

The younger patrons saw Val as an older woman. I thought that was funny, that someone in her late thirties seemed like an old lady to them. Meanwhile she used the internet and submitted her resume here and there, for all that was worth if you didn't have an in, and she talked to friends about possibilities. She interviewed for one and they wanted her but she said no, she wouldn't take just anything. She wanted benefits and a better schedule than she had had for seven years. She felt stronger in herself, more confident. I did a few odd jobs on a temporary basis, knowing our plight wouldn't last forever—because, I knew, nothing does. I often did clerical work, embarrassed to mention it aloud.

Miriam went her own way. She traveled a lot and had a place in southern Spain and a condo on St.Thomas. The Great Lakes Country Club wanted to avoid a scandal and neither they nor the CEO pressed charges (she had committed assault, after all) in exchange for which she handed over the video. Syntactic let it slide into the memory hole and focused on what was important to them. Miriam walked along the sea in different climes and treated herself to a hedonistic life.

Two copies of the video are safely tucked away, encrypted, on two USB drives, one in a safe deposit box, the other in a secret place.

Because you never know.

My life settled into a more predictable pattern. But I had changed and wasn't sure how. I thought about things in a different light. I sat and thought about nothing instead of trying to figure it all out. My doctor called it meditation, which I guess it was. He wanted me to do things like use a mantra, count my breaths. He said sitting and thinking of nothing was doing something, in a way, and I didn't argue. I didn't have the energy to argue about irrelevancies. Sitting and watching my thoughts became a habit, and sometimes I hated to come out into the world of noise and distractions. It was pretty peaceful in there much of the time. Sometimes not, sometimes it was a nightmare, but hey, nothing is perfect.

As it turned out, I was practicing for what came next and didn't know it. Bill Webb said I was ripening, experiencing what he called another advent, a time of anticipation, knowing something was coming but not knowing what. "It's where the spiral of ongoing transformation ends and then begins again," he said. "A long season that you might have thought was permanent becomes transparent as it fades. Something is coming that you can't quite see. A change in the wind, said Mary Poppins, or was it Bert? Whoever. The helix turns and takes you up to the next level. The stages are predictable, but not the content of your trip. We have to find that for ourselves, we all do, every time. That's why symbols like advent, Christmas, all the six seasons, are useful as symbols, but we have to unpack them into our lives. If we knew what was coming, it would take out all the mystery, and we need mystery, don't we? Mystery is the seasoning, Nick. It keeps life spicy and alive."

Valerie saw more clearly than I did what was going on. She heard me complain when I came back from hanging with my posse, hearing all the same repetitive tropes. She must have been thinking about it for a good while, what to say and how to say it. I was sitting on the sofa reading *The Road Not Taken*, as it happened, when she bounced into the living room and let it all out.

"Listen to me," she said. I looked up.

"What?" I said.

"I mean it. Listen. Can you?"

"Sure," I said. I put down the book, a sign I wasn't taking a break merely but had turned my attention to Valerie.

"You whistle blowers," she said, "defend yourselves by adopting a posture of righteousness as a vocation or profession. You become permanently critical of the fuck-ups everybody makes, because humans are, I admit, a pretty fucked-up species. A kind of moral sickness seeps into our souls from the real world, is what you said. If we engage with real life instead of hiding, how can it not? How can our hands not get dirty, doing the work you did? Life is not a seminar room, is it? Where even the worst evils are discussed calmly?

"Am I remembering right, what you said, Mister Wizard?"

"Pretty much," I smiled. I had said that if we had the guts to do battle on a blood-soaked field, we came away with the stink all over ourselves and can never wash it out. Val brought it down to earth: "PTSD is a less poetic way of saying the same thing."

She wasn't finished. "Your friend Dan is the king of the mea culpas, permanently pickled in his guilt."

"Whipped with wire and stewed in brine, smarting in lingering pickle," I said.

"Whatever. Is that more Joyce?"

"No. Shakespeare."

"Shakespeare. OK, fine. Anyway, it's painful to listen to him, Nick. His self-flagellation alternates with waiting for more corruption so he can criticize all the evil people who do what he did for so many years. You guys are like hunters in a blind, knowing the deer will come. You're worse than journalists, I think, but not much. You do it to have an identity. Some of you were genuine heroes, I know that, but it fades from memory fast in a ten-minute news-cycle world. You have to keep repeating, I struck a blow on behalf of freedom; I'm important; hear me roar.

"Nick, there's more to life than that. You did what you could to turn away from the horror. Now you have to take a different path. Find a way to enjoy life, at least a little, and find meaning somewhere else. You're a meaning-seeking freak, addicted to adrenalin, you don't do trivial, you don't do shallow. You want to live on the edges all the time. Fine, you were a spy for twenty years. Most of that time you loved it. Now it's done. The whistle blower thing is done. You needed to do it, but you did it more for yourself than for society. Society swallows evil whole and digests it like an anaconda with a pig in its belly. Those are your words.

"This is what I think, Nick: in its own perverse way, whistle blowing was exciting, too, wasn't it? It got you high. You just changed drugs."

I demurred.

"Whatever it was, it's done. You need to tick to a different clock. That's just my opinion, of course. But if you ask, I would say it's time for your next birth. The second birth is your own creation—isn't that a quote from Jung? A guy you cite more than *Body Heat*, even?"

"Something like that. You're a quick study."

"Nick, I love you. I love you so fucking much. I want you to find a way to live a more human life. Isn't it time? Isn't it time to move on?"

I wished her earnest plea, the depth of her emotion, the obviousness of her deep love for who I was and who I could become, wasn't sexualized at once, but I'm built the way I'm built. I wanted to take her then and there on the living room floor, I wanted to fuck her brains out, I wanted to feel her buck and pitch like an airplane in a storm. I wanted my body to say what my brain couldn't think, what my mouth couldn't say, that I loved how much she cared and dared to say. She had had relationships where saying things like that would end the whole deal or get her punched out. Her courage was an aphrodisiac. She was willing to risk everything to make us somehow better, somehow more.

But ... I was older. Everyone is, but I really was. There was a better option than pouncing on my pretty. I rose from the sofa and we let our eyes express whatever there was to know in the moment.

Valerie knew. I knew. Both of us knew. The entity we had become knew too.

The neighborhood streets did not exactly brim with useful symbols, so this was all I had: the last leaves fell past the gray-light of the window. A child cried. A door slammed down the hall. A dog barked. An automobile revved its engine. A windowpane rattled in a gust of wind. Those were what I had to use to define an objective correlative that somehow suggested the meaning of the moment. The world poured out its heart with sights and sounds. The transitory images of transitory things froze in the instant into one candescent burst of inexplicable splendor.

I wish I could say it better. It was Advent, all right. The world was pregnant, ripening, and the moment moved me closer to the light that didn't exist in time but illuminated everything.

"Man," I said, "Joe! I haven't seen you here before. God, how long has it been?"

Joe Pantaglia was sitting at the bar. I had just arrived and the Barbican was quiet. Jake had already sold our happy place and it wasn't the same but some of us still hung on. Jake would work as long as the new owner needed, he was that kind of guy. I had been heading home but something made me turn back to the Barbican where Joe was waiting. Some would call it fate. I called it being thirsty.

Joe was an analyst at a think tank the agency sort of owned and sort of used. The relationships to corporates, non-profits, media, even mom-and-pop's was hidden behind a screen of shells and anonymous transactions. Joe had worked in the visible light for the think tank and in the dark for the agency. We hadn't been much in touch, but he was a good guy, and as far as I knew, he wasn't a hostile. I didn't think he would be pissed off by what I had done.

I'd find out by saying hello. So I said hello.

"Hello, Nick," he said back with a smile that looked genuine. "I had a meeting down the street and I wanted a quiet drink. I don't think I've been here before." He looked around. "I like the vibe."

"I'd better let you alone," I said. "It sounds like you need what my lady friend calls me-time."

"I didn't mean it that way. Sit down. What've you been up to? How long has it been? A year or two? More?"

"About a year and a half," I said. I slid up onto the stool beside. "I'm still looking for some kind of permanent situation. Are you still connecting dots?"

"On occasion, now and then, but in a new way: I shifted my focus." He looked around by habit, seeing Jake twenty feet away, no one else in earshot. Valerie wasn't at work yet and the tables were mostly empty. He lowered his voice anyway.

"You know about remote viewing, I imagine?"

"I've heard of it," I said. "I heard you couldn't always know you got a hit, you needed confirmation, but some hits were striking."

"They were, they are," he said. "And you always need confirmation for any kind of intelligence. You didn't know that I was being trained to do that, did you?"

"No. I thought the agencies phased it out when results were ambiguous. That's what Kit said."

"That's a cover story, Nick. It just went deeper underground. Talk to Hal about it, not Kit. We wanted the Other Guys to think it was a bust. But it wasn't. But at the same time, it isn't simple. Learning the protocols takes time. Not everyone can do it. If you have a gift, thanks to genetics, then the training works. You learn by practicing and get better. Every time it works, your ability to do it ramps up. If you don't have the genes, no amount of training can get you where you need to be. You can do it a little but not in a useful way."

"And you, I imagine, got results? Is that what you're saying?"

"Yes," he said. "Not every time, but enough." He looked around again and leaned in closer. It felt like the old days, when we made a decision to cross the line and talk out of school. "I am trying to think through what happens when I do it, Nick, what I was discovering. It wasn't so much the data points, the content, but the context in which they occurred. Like points of light in a dark sky, they redefine the space. They map the deeper structure of ... consciousness, I guess ... that much is apparent. Does that make sense? I wasn't just seeing a Russian boomer about to be launched from an inland facility, I was learning what it meant that I could. My field of perception changed. Spacetime on a new loom. Things were detected, yes, they were worthwhile to detect, but the most important thing was that they *could* be detected. I wasn't imagining what I experienced. The context became the content. It called into question—I know this sounds woo-woo—everything I thought about the universe itself, the entire cosmos, everything."

"That's all?" I smiled. "I'm waiting for *Twilight Zone* music. What are we talking about, Joe?"

"You think I'm making it up. But I'm not."

I waited.

"For one thing, I detected a presence, Nick. It was confirmed with sensors and other instruments, satellites, everything, pilots in the air. They come and go. Nobody knows where from. They manifest themselves in something like hyperspace."

We had all heard rumors that "the visitors," as a friend at NORAD called them, had been around for a long time. We knew they were real, we knew they'd been coming for decades at least, probably a lot longer, and we knew their technology and power wasn't anything we understood. They didn't attack, but the fact of their existence was a threat to our security. They engaged with us in a game of hide-and-peek. People ask why they don't communicate. But everybody knows what they are, in a superficial way. Showing yourself for decades here and there, now and then, according to no obvious pattern, is communicating. Intermittent reinforcement is always the best way. Now we know they're here. I told Joe that's all I knew. Nothing first hand. Nothing more.

"Well, there is more," he said. "There's a lot more." He turned back to his drink. "That's all I can say. Remote viewing gets results, and the universe is a goddamn stranger place than I thought."

What the hell does one say to all that?

"OK," I said. He sipped his drink, staring at the colored backlit bottles behind the bar. Jake was wiping down the bar but was still far away. "So you were meeting with someone. About this?"

He paused, then turned and said, "A few of us are partners in a new venture. You remember Sylvia Warner?"

"Sure."

"And Hal McCutcheon?"

"Sure, of course."

"They're involved. We want to create a remote viewing business, a private undertaking, Competitive intelligence in a way. Serve whatever clients come our way."

"Huh. That's fascinating, Joe."

He seemed to be looking at my shirt. His gaze was lower, at any rate. He wasn't looking into my eyes. "You don't have a steady job?"

"No," I said. "I'm looking."

"OK, so listen, Nick, I know why you did what you did. I'm not a blindly loyal guy, I have my commitments like everyone else but I'm not a slave of the agency. I think you were right to do it.

Somebody had to do it. We went way over the line. OK?"

"Sure," I said. "OK."

"OK. So you're a pretty intuitive guy. You knew when to break the rules. You might be useful. I'm just thinking aloud. Are you interested in learning more? Maybe helping out? We'd have to figure out how you fit, if you do—let's not get ahead of ourselves— but why not take a look?"

"You're serious?"

"I'm serious," he said. "If you sign an NDA, we can discuss it. Make up your own mind. I have to decide, too, is this nostalgia, wanting to be back on the same side with you again, or is meeting this way what we call synchronicity? As my girl friend Gillian says, did the universe want this to happen?"

I said. "Where do I sign?"

He finished his drink and slid off the stool. "Come with me over to the office. It's right down the street. We can talk more easily there."

You're a meaning-seeking freak, addicted to adrenalin, you don't do trivial, you don't do shallow. You want to live on the edges all the time.

"Let's go," I said.

And down the rainy street we walked, watching out for puddles, not discussing anything yet, looking like two old friends getting wetter and wetter.

"Say what" Val said. "A mind reader? A fortune teller? What?"

"No," I said. "Forget the crazy stuff. They developed good protocols for using clairvoyance, yes, that's what it is, seeing clearly with a part of your mind that's usually not noticed. It's pretty right-brain, and I'm a right-brain guy. Maybe nothing will come of it, but maybe something will. If it works, it works. If not, what have I lost?"

Valerie was on the loveseat, legs tucked under, shoes off. She folded her arms, a little defensive, I thought. A book lay open on her lap, a new novel from one of her favorites, a guy whose name was on at least a hundred books. The lamplight highlighted her hair, the side of her face, her hand holding the book.

"How well do you know him?"

"As well as you know anyone that you don't know, doing the work. We chatted now and then. He was a good analyst. He picked up patterns in the traffic, he put things together really well. I remember one time he connected a phone conversation with a guy going to some unusual place, a place he should not be going. The two nodes connecting, that was all Joe needed to know what was happening."

"But your point is, this guy is smart and you trust him?"

"Yes. He did some amazing shit, putting things together. I joked at the time that he must be psychic. I never thought that maybe he was."

Val slid the flap of the book jacket into her stopping place and closed the book and put it on the table. She smiled and shook her lovely head. "Why am I not surprised that this is the kind of thing that shows up in your life? Nothing normal or ordinary, ever. I will say this, Nick Cerk, or whoever you are" (we laughed because she knew my real name), "living with you is an adventure."

I just shrugged. "None of the jobs I saw were appealing. This sounds really interesting. What have I got to lose? It's worth exploring, don't you think?"

"Sure. See what it is."

I looked at her smile. That was the face I saw before I went to sleep and the face I saw when I woke up. She was often in my dreams, but after meeting with Joe, I dreamed of other things too, unusual things, that I tried to remember when I woke. I felt like my brain was working full time, night and day, helping me tease out the meaning of Joe's obscure words. I wanted to learn fast, but it didn't work that way. It required one slow step at a time.

Practical matters first. I met with Joe at the nondescript office— not a posh suite in one of the high rise towers but a second floor set of ordinary rooms in an older brick building off the main avenue. A few blocks west of State. There were three floors of offices, a chiropractor, an acupuncturist, insurance agents, an association headquarters, people like that. A directory in the vestibule with letters that pushed into the black backing was missing a letter "n." The bathroom in the hall needed help. I took it easy on the stairs, holding the railing, practicing my new habit of self-care.

"When you describe what happened to you, Nick, in that episode at the agency," Joe said, "it sounds you turned sort of inside out. That's what you'll have to do to learn the protocols, in a way, but more slowly and with discipline. You'll need to stay steady when the currents bounce you around. There's a lot of turbulence out there. In there. Wherever it is. The metaphors fall apart. Let's start with an NDA and then we can get to the real meat."

I signed the NDA and I listened to Joe, but I had to tell him to say things twice, because I couldn't grasp what I was hearing. My brain was trying to learn a different way of imagining the universe. I retained maybe twenty per cent of that first lesson. But it was a start, even if I felt like I was back in school and way behind.

"Just one foot after the other," Joe said. "A journey of a thousand miles and all that."

So my life was not quite over yet. I had to empty my cup, in the words of the Zen story, before I could fill it with new content. I had to trust the process, which began when I grasped how ignorant I was. I had to rearrange things I previously knew in a new schema. The relationships between them, which determine meaning, flexed like lines on a graph on a computer screen when the user changes variables. It didn't look the same at all. The inputs were recognizable but the outputs weren't, not yet. Not until I learned a new language. One with ideograms, not letters.

My Aunt Max told me how she watched a black-and-white TV when she was a kid. She loved Saturday morning serials which always left you hanging. A cliff-hanger she called it, the heroine dangling from a window, the hero about to be shot. This book, I promise you, will not end like that, because I am calmer now, more restrained in what I write. I have no intention of presenting information that frightens you. I manage my emotions so they don't slap-slap like water on a pier and make me slip and fall. I think of *Big Two-hearted River* and how it felt to a different Nick, Nick Adams, his feelings just under the surface. I am not fishing a river up in Michigan. I am fishing a river of words, but I am surrounded too by burned-out woods devoid of life. I am learning to handle ever so lightly the emotions that will lead me to say, I can only hope, "I have no idea," said the way Jodie said it and for the same reason.

I do want you to know that *Mobius Out of Time: The End of the Journey* will reveal how successful the agencies are at compartmenting knowledge, how totally out of the know we can be kept, even when we're working on a project, not just muggles but people with clearances like myself. What we knew fit into tiny compartments and we never knew what lay behind a thousand other doors. This time I was opening doors in an Advent calendar one by one, hoping to find the prize. I had thought I knew not only a lot about the world but how the world itself was built. How the epistemological or ontological space was constructed. I did not. The world around me was not what I had thought. I learned that endless forms most beautiful, creatures of beauty, complexity and strangeness, filled an expanding space that teemed with life. My dreams are alive with creatures with silvery wings hovering over oceans aglow with iridescent scales, with the heads of dragons, fire-breathing, and with gargoyles and angels, their glass skins the colors of amethysts, sapphires, and rubies, myriads of beings of a thousand shapes and hues streaming in the light of setting suns.

The universe itself, the ways things work, the "laws of nature," what we call "science," is the first condition. Everything that happens has to be congruent with the rules. From the "laws of science," constraining and enabling everything that evolves, it all flows, a cosmic cornucopia, a mystery, toward unpredictable ends. The universe itself is groping toward self-understanding. It apparently needs to allow every aperture that can evolve, to evolve, every means of looking in and looking out to add their eyes to the huge homunculus with more eyes than Argus. The great race of Yith.

We need new maps to find new cliffs. We need to risk vertigo, looking over, looking down. Then we need to step off.

When my second foot left the cliff, I was committed.

Learning to do remote viewing meant allowing subtle barely perceived traces of data or information to tease my brain so I could draw a target almost without thinking, my hand moving a pencil on a blank piece of paper on my lap. I could look later and see what I thought I saw. I had to save interpretation, analysis, after the "right brain" drew the drawing, I had to not think, I had to learn to not think. I felt suspended in deep consciousness like a diver at the right buoyancy in the ocean. There was neither up nor down, just hanging in suspension in the void.

I began to see the relationships between "things," and that "things" were nodes of information. Energy becomes mass we perceive as information. The universe writes the signatures of what we're here to read. We are like children spelling out words syllable by syllable. The excitement of learning that letters have meaningful sounds was repeated as I traced my fingers on codes in Braille, as it were. I loved learning new things.

Joe taught me a new model, building a little big bigger box than the one I had lived in all my life. In this box, miracles happen. That's just a name, of course, for manifesting acausal "things" by intention and design. A little bit bigger box is challenge enough. That vast configuration glows with its own inner light, bathing the world in pastel images. String theory ties itself in knots. Galaxies spin like whirligigs in spirals of cosmic dust. Spacetime doubles back on itself, effects precede causes, causality a casualty. It takes time to grasp patterns suggested by the data. It takes time to learn a new language. It takes time to grasp that precognition happens.

I will try to say what I saw. You try to see what I mean. Then you can see what I saw too. We have to try because reality and truth are what we are meant to pursue like astronomers chasing receding quasars.

I met the members of the team. I knew them before, but context does create content, the content of people's character, behavior, everything (think Germans before and after the war, for example) and they were different than I recalled. In the context of our work, I changed as well, and Valerie noticed. She sniffed out subtle shifts in my attitudes and actions and tried to understand their derivations. She needed to know more than I could tell her so I introduced her to the team and she liked the team and the team liked her. One thing led to another, and when she found she had the right stuff, she joined the game as a player, not just watching. Our relationship shifted into a different gear, a higher gear. We were willing to risk the leap from the cliff hand in hand.

I'll tell you about how and what and all that, and about Joe and Sylvia and Hal and the team, and Jelli and Brad, a big surprise, in

Mobius Out of Time, and I'll tell you how the meaning of "believing is seeing" came home to me. I'll try to do justice to Valerie's journey too, but she'll have more to say on her own. She'll tell her own stories. She got really good at that. She had less to unlearn, after all. I love that I learned so much from her. In a lot of ways, she was way way ahead of me. It was a relief to not always have to be the teacher.

You are my teachers, every single one of you. You are my brothers and sisters, my colleagues and co-conspirators. We are all jesters wearing conical hats with puff balls on top, dancing in harlequin garb. We are all the living creatures that exist, all civilizations, blazing with light for a moment before we disappear beyond the far horizon, beyond the reach of the speed of light. We fall like dominoes into the deep void beyond the end of the known and visible universe, beyond the edge of human sight and comprehension. But before we fall, we burn so very brightly. Before we lose the eyes with which we see.

Out of sight out of mind. Beyond the telling of the story. Beyond the momentary thought. Beyond the barely uttered words which wither with the ticking of the clock.

tick tick tick

tick tick tick

THE END